WAIT
FOR
ME

WAIT FOR ME

SARA SHEPARD

UNION
SQUARE
& CO.

NEW YORK

UNION
SQUARE
& CO.
NEW YORK

UNION SQUARE & CO. and the distinctive Union Square & Co. logo are trademarks of Sterling Publishing Co., Inc.

Union Square & Co., LLC, is a subsidiary of Sterling Publishing Co., Inc.

ISBN 978-1-4549-4577-2 (hardcover)
ISBN 978-1-4549-4579-6 (e-book)

Library of Congress Control Number: 2022015109

For information about custom editions, special sales, and premium purchases, please contact specialsales@unionsquareandco.com.

Printed in the United States of America

2 4 6 8 10 9 7 5 3 1

unionsquareandco.com

Cover design by Erin Fitzsimmons

Interior design by Marcie Lawrence

Cover image by Terry Bidgood / Trevillion Images

Cover and interior image (waves) by Karl Lundholm Images/Shutterstock.com

To Kevin and Julie

It's a killer day for a wedding.

The temperature is warm but not too warm. The sky, a brilliant, cloudless blue, sparkles off the waves. The seagulls' cries are musical, and the air is fragrant with salt and the sweet flowers that grow wild on the dunes. A helicopter, heading in from the city, glides over the water, bringing in guests who are too important to wait on the clogged highways. Maybe these are guests for this event. *Your* event.

You stand in the grand room that overlooks the beach. This room alone is bigger than any house you've ever lived in. It's the length of a bowling alley, with a marble fireplace and leather furniture so soft you question how it could have come from cowhide. You are sitting in a club chair like a queen. A makeup artist leans over you, putting the final touches on your lips and cheeks. When she's finished, she spins you around, and you look at yourself in the large antique mirror against the wall. What you see doesn't look like you anymore but like a pretty, perky princess about to be feted. You're going to be the toast of this seaside hamlet.

"Perfect," the makeup artist says, adding a final puff to your cheeks. She hums a few bars from a familiar song. In seconds, you realize why you know it: it's Kelly Clarkson's "Since U Been Gone." Not what you need today. That song makes you think of the not-so-distant past. When things were so . . . different.

The makeup artist comes into your field of view again. Her eyes dance up and down your figure, which is swathed in a lacy white dress. You think it makes you look like a doily, but it was your soon-to-be husband's grandmother's dress, and he likes to honor tradition.

Your soon-to-be husband. You feel a groundswell beneath you.

"Hun?"

The makeup artist's face is close to yours now, her perfectly shaped brows knit with concern. "You've lost all that beautiful color I just brushed on you," she says. "You all right?"

"I bet it's nerves!"

Someone new has burst into the room, and you turn. A woman walks in wearing a tight tweed suit that likely cost a fortune—and who wears tweed at this time of year? She smells like she's dumped the whole bottle of floral perfume on her pulse points. This is for sure one of your fiancé's aunts. You've met so many of them so far; all of them pluck and preen you like you're a prized animal in a fair. This one—Katherine? Matilda?—stands with her arms crossed and a know-it-all look on her face.

"I'd be nervous, too," she says. "You've got a lot to live up to, dear."

"Yeah, but she's ready." The makeup artist gives you a nudge. "Right?"

You feel their expectant stares. They're waiting for you to say something. So you muster a smile. You need to be ready. To say your betrothed is a good catch is an understatement. But you've got this.

You hope.

The aunt comes closer, looking at you worriedly. "You do look like you need a stiff drink, dear."

"She even old enough?" Another woman chuckles.

"I'll get you some wine," the makeup artist says, turning. "Don't worry. Every bride is nervous before the big moment."

The big moment. Your gaze slides to the patio door. "Maybe I'll just step outside? Feeling a little stuffy." You're out before they can even reply.

The sliding door leads into a small, open area that overlooks the water and provides a direct walkway down to the sand. Your heels click on the patio stones. You stare out at the waves, trying to find a rhythm to your breathing.

The tide is far out. A few towels still dot the beach; on them lie diehard sun worshippers reluctant to bid goodbye to the day. Down the shore are a battalion of pink cabanas; they belong to the exclusive beach club you've passed by your whole life but never had the privilege of stepping inside. Your fiancé is a member; soon enough, if you wish, you can be, too. It should be an exciting prospect.

But you know why it isn't.

To your right is the shiny new pier built just last year; it replaced the old, crumbling one that had been there for decades. You'd heard those on this side of town—the side with money—complained about the old pier, calling it an eyesore, so down it went. But you miss the old structure. So many of your memories are tied to it: standing far out on its planks, licking a perfect strawberry ice cream cone. Playing handheld video games on its steps with your friends from school. Sitting on one of its benches, as close as you could to him, that other boy, your heart throwing off sparks, your mind somersaulting with glee. If you stare hard enough at this new pier, you can almost see the old one superimposed on top of it like a ghost. You can almost see that beautiful boy coming toward you, too, smiling, stretching out his arms.

"There's my girl," you can almost hear him say. "You waited for me."

Stop thinking about him, you scold. *It's going to ruin you.*

You look over your shoulder. Your thoughts feel too naked, your desires too exposed. It's wrong to be thinking of the other boy now, and you know it. There's a reason he isn't here right now. Promises were broken. He forgot about you.

But you can't stop thinking of him. Against your better judgment, you reach into your clutch and pull out his picture. Your heart squeezes. You think of the clandestine phone call you made to his parents' house this morning. There you were, scrunched into that tiny back hall, your ears perked for intruders. You were using the cell phone your soon-to-be husband purchased for you—you'd never had one before. It felt wrong, using this new device to call *him*.

But you had to. You just wanted to know.

You're glad no one answered, though, and after you hung up, you figured out how to erase the number from the call log. You shouldn't toy with this new life. You definitely shouldn't go back on your word to your almost-husband.

You shrug your shoulders, tuck the photo back in your purse, and turn to go inside. It's time. Time to grow up. Time to let go. Time to forget your past and your winsome, blue-flame-hot first love. True, pure, timeless love, like what you had—it isn't realistic. This new path? It's a good one. A safe one. It will set you up for life.

But as you reach for the knob, you sense footsteps on the wooden walkway. You freeze just as a hand slithers around your waist. You're pulled backward, your feet lifting off the ground, your lungs suddenly crushed flat. You try to scream, but a hand presses over your mouth.

"Shh," a voice hisses in your ear. "You've been a bad girl."

And then you see nothing at all.

PART ONE

ONE

I wear many disguises. Minimalist ones, street-cool graffitied ones, and ones you'd find in a steamer trunk, carefully preserved. People might see my disguises as near copies of one another, just a tiny detail demarcating one from the next, but for me, each costume is a different Casey Rhodes for a different situation.

I'm studious, should-still-be-in-high-school Casey as I attend my fourth upperclassmen-level course of the day at New York University. I'm savvy, born-and-bred Brooklyner Casey who has no qualms about calling out the ogling pervert on the N train. And, since the most eligible nineteen-year-old guy in New York City has become my boyfriend, I've had to bust out a few new disguises. Cultured Casey, who's perfectly comfortable letting my boyfriend's doorman snag her a cab. Smug(ish) Uptown Casey who's trying not to wince in the slightly-too-small Prada heels she bought on consignment but look almost new.

I wear disguises because, for as long as I can remember, I've felt it easier to be a character than my true, vulnerable self.

Maybe everyone feels this way . . . at least a little. For me, the only way I can tamp down my anxiety of living in the world is to put myself behind a mask. It's gotten me through seventeen years. I must be doing something right.

Today, there's a new disguise I'm wearing as I'm heading toward the Metropolitan Opera where I'm meeting Marcus. This version of me is the most valuable in my costume collection—and the trickiest to pull off. This Casey disguise is the most confident and refined, one that screams, *I'm the Casey Who Deserves Things. I'm the Casey Who Belongs.* In this case, the disguise isn't just metaphorical, it's a literal one, too. I've got on a beautiful, silk, silver-colored gown with a halter neck and tall velvet heels, and I'm holding a small, beaded clutch purse. My dark hair is curled down my back. I spent hours on my makeup. What I am wearing on my body, at present, is probably worth more than the amount in my bank account. All of it is my armor.

"Gimme your location," my friend and roommate, Pippa, says breathlessly through the phone. She's called me for the play-by-play. "How close are you?"

"Columbus Circle." I sniff the air. "Ugh, that deli smells like sauerkraut. Hope the stink doesn't seep into my dress."

"Are you *walking*? On the actual *street*?" Pippa sounds like her head might explode. "Why didn't you get Marcus to send his driver?"

"I took the subway," I confess. "Just got off at Lincoln Center. I can see the fountain."

"Please tell me you're joking and didn't walk up actual subway stairs in that gown."

"It's not that big of a deal. I even scored a seat!" I try to laugh, but maybe this isn't funny—Pippa's the one who footed the bill for my gown. I left the tags on, though. Our hope is that once this night is over, she can return it to Saks for a full refund. I'm praying that the hem doesn't drag on the ground—I'm only five foot one, and technically I should have had the thing altered, but then I definitely wouldn't have been able to take it back.

Fine. I should have taken a cab at the very least. Except I don't ride in cars if I don't have to. Ever. It's kind of one of those things that's too hard to explain.

"So what's going on at the shop? What am I missing?" I ask Pippa as I wait at a light. (Admittedly, I do look a little unusual, clad in my fancy dress, amid all these people in their office wear.) Pippa and I became NYU college roommates this September. The second week of school, we both took a job at Pet Planet, an organic pet supply store not far from our dorm. We even wrangled it so that we work the same shifts most of the time. "Did that old lady who always wears Chanel suits come in with her Shiba Inu? Did we get a new shipment of snails? Someone was asking the other day . . ."

"Casey, we are *not* talking about the pet store," Pippa snaps. "Not with you heading to the biggest party of the season."

"No pressure!" I say lightly—though it comes off sounding kind of crazed. "Especially since I should be cramming for the Shakespeare exam. And art history. And advanced calculus." I think of my textbooks piled on my desk. It's kind of an overwhelming thought, though, so I push it out of my brain. "Actually, I have to go. I'm basically here."

"You are the luckiest girl alive, and I hate you. Tell me every detail when it's over, okay?" Pippa breaks into a high-pitched *ee* sound. "This is going to be amazing!"

"You just punctured my eardrum."

I hang up. My heart bangs against the dress's bodice as I catch sight of elegant people heading through the opera house's doors. And when I see Marcus—my boyfriend—waiting for me in front of the Met's famous fountain, my stomach starts to churn. I hold the hem of my gown. I pray I don't trip in my heels.

Marcus watches me coming toward him. "Hey, gorgeous," he says as I get close. "Wow."

"Wow yourself," I murmur, my voice a little off-pitch.

His body is backlit by the fountain's colorful lights. He's dressed in a black tuxedo with a matching cummerbund. Most guys at Marcus's age look like they're playing dress-up in a tux—all coat-hanger shoulders or pudgy frat-boy bodies in crooked bowties. But Marcus's white teeth gleam as brightly as the expensive Rolex watch he inherited from his grandfather. His black loafers are understated, but I was with him when he bought them. I had to control my reaction when I glanced at the discreet price tag, mentally compiling all the things that money could have paid for. *A used but decent late-model laptop. Two credit hours. Several doctor's appointment fees, paid for in cash because my father and Fran have decided to no longer include me on their health insurance plan.*

"Anyway," I say after Marcus looks me up and down. "Thanks for inviting me."

Marcus laughs. "You really think I would've asked someone else?" He touches my cheek. "You look amazing, Casey. You'll *be* amazing. You ready?"

I nod, but I can't speak. Am I ready? I've never been to anything like this before.

I feel guests' double takes as they pass. Likely, they're looking at Marcus because they recognize him. See, Marcus's family owns one of the largest entertainment conglomerates in the world, Coleman Media. Marcus's great-grandfather, Maurice Coleman, started it as a small publishing house at the turn of the twentieth century. After nurturing writers who went on to write classics and win Pulitzers and Nobels, Coleman Press grew and grew.

From there, Maurice Coleman bought up newspapers, magazines, television stations. He then passed the empire to Marcus's grandfather, who passed it Roland in the early 2000s. Apparently, there was a little hiccup with the business when his dad took it over—Marcus said the company nearly went under, but a business associate bailed him out with a generous loan. But now, more than two decades later, Roland has turned it into an enormous dynasty, not only with massive offices all over the world but a fleet of private planes, a town named after the family in Georgia, several movie studios under their control, and a prestigious literary award presented every year in some Scottish castle.

Pippa wasn't kidding about this being the coveted event of the holiday season: the Coleman Media holiday party invite list is basically a Who's Who of everyone interesting in New York City.

And Marcus. Despite not even working in the family business yet, Marcus has nearly a million followers on social media. The guy posts a brand of sneakers he's into, and suddenly those shoes are sold out everywhere. If he posts a picture of himself tanning shirtless near the Reservoir in Central Park? It breaks Instagram. He's friends with young filmmakers, fellow heirs to Fortune 500 companies, TikTokers and hip-hop artists alike. And now I'm tied to him, thanks to a chance meeting two months ago. It's no wonder the online gossips call me Cinderella. Everyone has posed the question: Why would Marcus Coleman go for a seventeen-year-old NYU scholarship student from an untrendy neighborhood in deep Brooklyn?

You don't think I'm asking myself that same thing?

Everyone's gaze slides from Marcus to me, and my spine straightens. I pray that my lipstick hasn't smudged, my nails haven't chipped, and that I don't smell like the sauerkraut that was wafting from that deli. But no eyes widen as I pass. There are no furrowed brows of confusion over why *I* am at such an important event on this It Guy's arm. Instead, I receive pleasant smiles and complacent nods. I might actually be meshing with this crowd, which feels like a small miracle. I almost want to text Pippa and tell her the good news.

But then my stomach clenches. This isn't even the first hurdle. This is nothing.

"You must be Casey!" a woman with ash-blond hair swept into a French twist croons as Marcus and I walk into the grand lobby. It's a splendor of red carpeting, crystal chandeliers, and sparkling Christmas ornaments on so many trees, banisters, tables, and columns that I feel that I've fallen into a snow globe.

The woman's cold fingers clasp mine. But her voice isn't cold at all. Neither are her eyes, which are welcoming and kind. "I'm so excited to meet you!" she says, looking me up and down.

"Casey, this is Miranda, my father's longtime assistant." Marcus leans down a bit to speak closer to my ear—I'm a good eight inches shorter than he is. He smells like the deep woods— like mossy, smoky secrets. "She basically runs Dad's life."

"Oh, well, I'm not sure that's true." Miranda ducks her head bashfully, though if Marcus's stories about Miranda are correct, she's like a pit bull with Roland Coleman's schedule and has a memory like a steel trap. But maybe she, too, wears a disguise— one of a quietly powerful woman who needs to file down her sharp edges to seem more feminine and nonthreatening.

"Runs my life too," Marcus says, pecking Miranda on the cheek. "In the best way possible."

I beam. So does Miranda. Marcus's real mother is estranged, but he's said that Miranda is the next best thing. I've been eager to meet her.

Miranda's gaze returns to me. "This your first time at the Met, Casey?"

"The Met? Oh, no." I shake my head. "I used to come here all the time."

One eyebrow arches. "How wonderful! You like opera?"

"Love it," I admit.

"Maybe we could all go together sometime," Miranda says. "I hear their production of *Carmen* coming up is going to be amazing."

"Uh, I'll have to take a pass on that one," Marcus groans. "Sorry, Case, but there's no way you're getting me to sit through four hours of people bellowing in Italian."

My laugh is silvery and sweet, but I feel a lonely pang. I am an opera fan, and that's not one of my disguises. In junior high—which wasn't that long ago—I came to Lincoln Center and waited outside the Met box office for that night's twenty-dollar standing room only tickets. I saw brilliant operas for twenty bucks—*Romeo and Juliet*, *Tosca*, *La Bohème*—often sung by the greatest tenors and sopranos and baritones in the world. Kids at school thought I was odd—if there was any reason to steal into the city, it was to go to a club or shoplift a shirt. Even seeing something on Broadway was more acceptable.

But then, kids thought I was odd anyway. I took senior-level classes as an eighth grader. That kind of sets you apart from your peers.

I loved the romance of the opera. I savored how the singers' emotions could seep into me even though I couldn't understand what they were saying. When I listen to an aria, I still close my eyes and swoon, wishing that someday I will feel that much passion for someone—the lust, the hate, the pain, all of it. It doesn't hurt that my mother loved opera, too. She used to hum bits of arias to me before bed. And we were listening to Pavarotti sing "E lucevan le stelle" the very last moments she was alive.

Those last moments haunt me. Just thinking about my mom fills me with a clenching, grasping sadness. But I cannot be sad tonight. I need to be at my best. So I push the thoughts from my brain.

"There's Dad," Marcus says, breaking me from my thoughts. He kisses Miranda again, and then clasps my hand and pulls me forward.

I see Roland Coleman, too. The man glows. He's every bit as striking as his son, but in a different kind of way—tall, broad chested, full head of dark hair. He's nursing a cocktail by the grand staircase and is deep in conversation with a squat man with pitted cheeks and a toadlike hunch. When Roland notices us, he pivots and smiles.

My stomach does a flip. *Do you even realize who you're rubbing elbows with?* I can hear Pippa exclaiming in that glass-shattering pitch she loves to use.

"This must be the famous Casey Rhodes," Roland says, his sharp gaze on me.

"Famous?" I say bashfully, ducking my head. "I don't know about that . . ."

"Famous to me," Marcus boasts.

I feel Roland appraising me like he's waiting for me to say something brilliant. I think of Marcus's ex-girlfriend, Caroline, a student with the School of American Ballet. Caroline's father is the US ambassador to Morocco, and her uncle created CarNow, a car service app that preceded Uber and made millions. It's hard not to compare myself to that.

But then, to my surprise, Roland gives a small nod and opens his arms to pull me in for a hug. I'm surprised as his strong arms curl around my back. "Wonderful to meet you. I've heard you're a very smart woman. Already a sophomore in college at seventeen?"

I pull back, my smile wobbly. "It's no big deal. And—thanks. And—great to meet you, too. I'm a huge admirer."

"You're leaning toward becoming a literature major, yes? Did you choose that because you like to read or because you like to write?"

"Write." As soon as I say it, though, I wonder if this is the wrong answer. This man is the CEO of a publishing company. "Though of course I love reading, too."

"Unlike someone." Roland shoots a pointed look at Marcus. "This one had to get a tutor just to get him through English back in high school. Broke my heart."

"Dad," Marcus whines, suddenly stiffening. "It was just for one course."

"Have you taken a single lit course in your college career?" Roland smiles at me sadly. "The son of a family enamored with words . . ."

"That's not true," Marcus protests. "I totally read!"

"What, Twitter? Sports analysis?"

A facial dance takes place between father and son. It makes me feel uneasy. Marcus prefaced me that he and his dad have a bit of a tempestuous relationship. And I realize—Marcus is nervous around him. Maybe as nervous as I am.

"Come on, Casey," Marcus says, taking my arm. "Let's get a drink."

"Nice to meet you," I say brightly to Marcus's dad. Roland Coleman gives me a sweet smile and wave.

We circulate. A lot of people we meet are members of Roland's vast empire, though I shake hands with people our age, too—other college students or early twentysomethings who are mostly children of the city's elite. Marcus holds my hand tightly the whole time. He seems proud of me. The unpleasantness with his father dissipates.

After a while, two young women approach—one is white, with ice-blond hair. The other one is Black with flawless skin and an afro. They are both ridiculously thin, and they're both looking at me with wolfish sneers.

"Hey, Marcus," the white girl croons in a fake-nice voice, fluttering her eyelashes. "It's been a while."

"Hi, Bronwyn," Marcus says cordially. He introduces her and then the other girl, Shay. Then he explains to me, "We all went to Deerfield together."

"With Caroline, too." Shay glances my way pointedly, seemingly gauging if I know who Marcus's ex is.

"Where'd you go to high school, Casey?" Bronwyn asks, narrowing her eyes. "I feel like I've seen you before."

"And are you still there?" Shay blurts, giggling. "She looks like jailbait, Marcus."

"Casey's at NYU," Marcus says. "A sophomore, same as us. And the rate she's going, she's probably going to graduate before us."

"Aw, NYU," Bronwyn says. "How fun!"

Fun?

Shay starts naming people from boarding school they all knew. Bronwyn laughs hysterically when Shay references a teacher they all had for advanced economics. She steps closer to Marcus, even touching his forearm. My heart starts to drop, but then Marcus jerks away, looks at her coldly, and takes my hand again.

"We gotta go," he tells the girls. "Good to see you."

Then he pulls me into the crowd. "God, they're so tiring. Still so stuck in high school. They run the alumni Reddit group and Deerfield's TikTok page. Like, who cares?"

I smile weakly. When I look back, Bronwyn is glaring at me. Shay is whispering in her ear. They're just jealous—that's what Pippa would say. I really hope she's right. I also hope I don't have a run-in with those two again.

Still, I try to smile brightly at every face I see. People seem delighted when we confirm I'm Marcus's new girlfriend. I slowly sip a glass from what I'm guessing is a very expensive bottle of champagne. I shake hands with famous people. I pose for pictures shot by a society photographer who promises they'll be posted tomorrow morning. More girls flirt with Marcus, but he barely seems to notice.

After another half hour of schmoozing, Marcus pulls me onto the dance floor. We swirl with other guests, and it really does feel like we're at a fairy tale ball. The Met's beautiful chandelier sparkles. The classical music swells. My dress glides, and I feel steady and graceful in my heels. And Marcus looks—well, he looks like a prince. As he holds me tightly and spins me expertly, I feel like a princess.

"You, Casey Jones, are a treasure," he whispers. He calls me Casey Jones after his favorite Grateful Dead song, which he'd had to play for me because I'd somehow never heard it before. "Are you having fun?"

"I am," I admit. "It's going way better than I thought."

"What did you expect?" He squeezes my hand. "It's just a party."

"What was that with your dad?" I glance at Roland, who is now standing by the bar, talking to a silver-haired man who I'm pretty sure is a senator. "Is everything okay?"

Marcus shrugs. "That's just the way he and I deal with each other. Has nothing to do with you." Darkness falls over him. He's told me, a little bit, all the ways he feels he's disappointed his dad—and all the ways his dad has disappointed him. "He loved you—but then, I knew he was going to love you."

I raise an eyebrow. "How did you know?" Roland seems pretty discerning.

There's a flicker of something unexpected across his face. Like he's been caught. But it's only there for a second. "I just did," he answers. "Because that's how it's supposed to be."

Then his hands cup the sides of my face, and he leans in to kiss me. I lean in, too. I can feel people smiling at us, though we're all alone in our bubble, arm's distance or more from anyone else. Suddenly, as his lips touch mine, I hear a voice.

You've been a bad girl.

I jolt backward, nearly bumping into a couple dancing behind us. I look at Marcus. "What did you say?" I blurt.

Marcus gives me a confused but flirtatious grin. "Sorry?"

I look around. Marcus had to have said it. No one else is near. And it was *in my ear*. Whispered. Nastily.

Involuntarily, I shiver with fear. This feels dangerous.

The music floats on. People are dancing, smiling, oblivious. I am standing feet away from Marcus, as though we've been blown apart. He looks at me like I've lost all sense of reality—and like he definitely has no idea what I'm talking about. I also notice Roland Coleman look over from his spot by the stairs. His gaze lingers on us a few seconds before he looks away.

I breathe out. I've got to get a grip. I am *not* going to screw this up. "Sorry. I'm a little . . . dizzy." I point to my temple. "I need to . . ."

I march off the dance floor, head down, my face going red. Marcus hurries behind me. "Let's sit." He guides me to a couch away from the crowd. "Here. Breathe. It's okay. It's really crowded out there."

I sink into the cushion, trying to calm my hammering heart. "Yeah. Sorry. God. I'm just—"

"It's okay." Marcus rubs my arm. "How 'bout I get you some water?"

"Yeah. Sure." I try to laugh. "I hardly ever drink . . ."

"No worries." Marcus stands. "Hang on. Be right back."

He steps back into the throng of dancers. Within moments, a waiter has appeared at his side. I watch, my head swimming, as Marcus's head bends in close, giving the man instructions.

I run my nails up and down my bare arms, trying to steady my breathing. What was that on the dance floor? What did he say to me? Why was he trying to pass it off like he hadn't said anything?

Marcus walks back to me and presents a tall glass with a flourish. "Here we are." Clear liquid bobs. Bubbles rise to the top.

"Thank you," I say, sipping. After I swallow a few gulps, I give him a brave smile. "It's helping."

"Good." Marcus laughs. "Guess it was the champagne. You're a lightweight."

"Guilty as charged."

I gulp down all the water. After a while, I feel better. I keep apologizing to Marcus, but really, I'm apologizing to myself, angry that I've let my Poised, Elegant Casey disguise slip. I'm supposed to be a princess tonight. Not . . . odd. Not jumpy.

I let Marcus pull me up. I walk on unsteady legs toward the dance floor again, and it goes okay. We glide. He smiles at me. I hear no more voices.

But I can't push the previous voice away. *You've been a bad girl.* And the tone, too: unfriendly. I look at my boyfriend again, and I feel that same fearful shiver again. Does something lurk beneath his shiny exterior?

I'm not sure I want to find out.

TWO

The following afternoon, Pippa and I sit on two twin mountains of dog food bags at the back of Pet Planet, our eyes on the door for customers. The only sounds in the store are the easy-listening station over the speakers and the subtle squeaks of a nearby hamster wheel. Pippa has procured us two pints of ice cream from the deli. I plunge my spoon into my rocky road with gusto while simultaneously staring at a series of Impressionist paintings in the hopes of memorizing the artists' names for my art history final. The boss and owner, Jeremy, doesn't like us eating anything with nuts on the job—he's very concerned about pet allergies. But Jeremy isn't here right now, so anything goes.

"So," Pippa says to me after she has a large lick of mocha almond fudge. "Are you going to tell me about your amazing Coleman Media party, or am I going to have to sic Buster on you?"

She glances at a cage nearby. Inside it sits a tarantula we've nicknamed Buster.

26

I muster a laugh as I flip a page. Seurat's *A Sunday Afternoon on the Island of La Grande Jatte* greets me. This one I know. It used to be one of my mother's favorites. "Sorry. It was . . . good."

Pippa sticks her spoon into the ice cream and frowns. "Casey, this ice cream is good. Getting a decent night's sleep is good. A party at Lincoln Center surrounded by celebrities should be *outstanding*."

I shrug and close the textbook. I have a feeling Marcus sensed something was off with me, too. Last night, before he put me in a cab, he looked at me again with concern. "You still feeling dizzy, or . . . ?" I assured him I'd had an amazing time, but I don't know if he bought it.

"No, it was outstanding," I tell Pippa. "I met some of my favorite authors. I drank from a bottle of champagne that probably costs more than my monthly dorm fees."

"And Marcus?"

"Marcus . . . was great. We danced like we were at the royal wedding."

Pippa leans back, making the top bag of dog food crinkle. "And yet you look like you've just been told you have six months to live."

"I'm just . . ." I swallow hard, fixing my gaze on a rack of chew toys instead of my friend. "Does it seem weird to you that Marcus is so into me?"

Pippa cocks her head.

"He's hot. He's ridiculously wealthy. Girls throw themselves at him—I saw it firsthand. This gorgeous blond girl named Bronwyn kept touching him . . . and some others, too." I shut my eyes. "Most guys I know aren't into . . . relationships. You know?" I think of the guys in our dorm. They either travel in packs, playing video games until the wee hours of the morning every night, or else they have a new conquest every weekend.

"Look, I'm as suspect of college guys as the next girl," Pippa says. "But why would Marcus invite you to his family's party if he didn't like you?"

"I know. I realize what I'm saying doesn't make sense."

"Do you not want Marcus as a boyfriend?"

"No, I do," I say.

Pippa raises a questioning eyebrow. "Are you sure? Because you just said that with a grimace on your face."

There are a lot of girls I know who just want to have fun right now. They want to date guys, or girls, or both—experiment and keep their options open. But I've never been like that. I've always craved security, the comfort of a solid, lasting relationship that builds over time. Someone to hang out with on a rainy day. Someone dependable to call. Someone to wake up next to, to talk about movies with, to plan a future with. It's probably because a stable relationship is something I lacked for some of my childhood.

"Are you attracted to Marcus?" Pippa presses.

I snort. "Of course not. Who would be into a guy with a symmetrical face and a swimmer's body who's traveled to every country imaginable and has hundreds of important people in their DMs?"

"Yeah, I'm not into enviable DMs, either." Pippa doesn't skip a beat. "So . . . do you love him?"

"Love?" I scoff. "I've only known him for a few months."

"So? Do you get weak-kneed when you see him? Do you have dreams about him? Do you feel . . . drawn to him? Like . . . electricity?"

"You sound like you're trapped in a really bad rom-com."

Pippa crosses her arms. "It's how I felt with James."

James was Pippa's high school boyfriend. They broke up once they left for different colleges, and she still regrets it.

"Yeah, but that's, like, puppy love," I say, licking my spoon. "No offense."

"Says the girl who hasn't been in love before," Pippa says haughtily.

I feel a wave of defensiveness. "It's not like I've been in that many relationships, sorry." Am I supposed to count my boyfriend, Teddy, from high school? Our relationship consisted of texting each other during study halls, meeting for pizza after school, and writing a graphic novel together, which never got past chapter three. Teddy was more like a close friend, especially because when we were in the same grade, I was almost two whole years younger. I think he saw me as his little sister.

And then, one day, Teddy called me in a panic, saying he'd taken a whole bottle of aspirin and was terrified. I rode with him to the hospital, our roles reversed—I was the caregiver, and he was the little boy. I waited while he had his stomach pumped. Afterward, he spent some time in the psychiatric unit. He was dealing with depression—though he'd hid it quite well. Later, his family moved away, but we kept in touch. Teddy eventually became a spokesperson for mental illness at his school, even starting a support group for kids going through the same stuff. I admired him for that. I loved Teddy for sure—though not love like that.

"Maybe you're not open to the idea of love, Casey," Pippa challenges. "Maybe you need to allow yourself to feel romance."

"And maybe you need to quit being an armchair psychologist," I quip back. But . . . could that be it? Maybe I'm afraid of the person I fall in love with leaving, just like my mom left me when I was eleven. Maybe that's why I wear all the disguises: if I don't show a significant other my true self, then I won't get hurt.

That's no way to live, though. Deep down, I'm dying to feel the kind of romantic love Pippa's talking about. The love from the operas. Finding that one person you can't live without. But that isn't real . . . is it?

"Is there some guy in your past you haven't told me about?" Pippa goads. "Some guy who's basically ruined you for all future love affairs?"

I cringe at the term *love affairs*. I swear Pippa was raised on afternoon soap operas.

"No," I insist. "There's no secret toxic boyfriend in my past. I would have told you."

I really do tell Pippa nearly everything—with her, my disguises aren't needed. I consider her my best friend even though we only met the first day of this term. My freshman year at NYU, I'd commuted, living with my father and my stepmother, Fran. But then, that situation imploded. Fran suggested—more like demanded—that I dorm in the city. Lots of kids my age went to boarding school, and this wasn't much different—that was her argument.

Most people would find moving out of their parents' house a step up—and I was happy to be rid of Fran. But I was also sad to leave my childhood bedroom. My room—the whole apartment—still reminded me deeply of my mother. Every doorway. Every window. Every crack in the wall. Even though Fran had removed a lot of my mom's knickknacks, I could still picture them sitting on the mantel. My room was the only one in the apartment that had gone virtually unchanged since the day of the car accident—for a long time, I even had the same Star Wars sheets, but then they became so threadbare I had to throw them out. I had a sinking feeling that once I moved out, Fran would change my room, too, ripping more memories of my mom away.

But I had no choice.

Fran helped me move. I didn't want her to, but I had a lot of luggage, and Fran had an SUV. She drove it from Brooklyn while I took the subway—there was no way in hell I was getting in a car with her. Fran always quietly rolled her eyes at my fear of cars, but she didn't question it. I resented that my father couldn't come along, but he was too unwell. He'd been diagnosed with throat cancer that summer, and the chemo had made him so weak.

I'd met Fran at the curb of my new dorm, where she was double-parked. We walked into the lobby of the converted Fifth Avenue hotel. Several upperclassmen sat at a long table, helping new people check in. Fran went up to one of them and spoke softly, angling her body away from mine. After a moment, an older, more official person walked over. They all spoke in low voices, glancing up at me every so often.

"No problem," the more official woman said after a while.

"No problem what?" I asked Fran when she returned to me.

Fran held up a room key triumphantly. "Got you a single."

"A single room?" I gawked. "I don't want to be alone!"

Fran's lips pursed, which brought forth a bunch of tiny wrinkles around her mouth that made her look a zillion years old. "You can concentrate on your schoolwork. Aren't you taking twenty credits this semester?"

"So?" In high school, I took an AP course load and some college courses on top of that. My freshman year of college, I'd made things easy for myself, only taking the normal number of classes, but I'd felt kind of bored. I needed a challenge.

"You'll get better sleep. Your resident advisor will be right next door." She pointed to one of the young women sitting at the check-in table. "Her name is Tanya. She said you absolutely can call on her day and night."

"But I want to make friends," I said. "That's harder when you have a room by yourself. People are already going to see me as a freak because I'm so young."

Fran pressed the pads of her fingers into my arm. Her eyes were as cold as her hands. "Casey. I don't think you're suited to living with other people. I think it's best if you were alone."

Over the years, Fran had gotten it into her head that I was *difficult*. This possibly was because I was difficult with her. But she made everything difficult for me, and I didn't want to live by her rules. Still, for some reason, I didn't argue with her that day.

Maybe that was because of how everyone was already staring—like I was the problem child, a bratty seventeen-year-old who probably wasn't mature enough to be here.

Begrudgingly, I followed her into the dorm's elevator. Fran made a big deal about unlocking the door to my single, and she crowed that the room would be all mine. But the single was tiny. It faced an airshaft full of mouse droppings. It was like living in someone's broom closet.

I whirled around and glared at Fran. "This sucks."

Fran sighed. "It's for your own good. It's also much cheaper, which I know is a concern."

My fingers loosened on my suitcases. Fran and I didn't talk about money much, but it was understood that I would be paying for all of the school fees that my scholarship didn't cover—the dorm being one of them. All of my dad's money, Fran explained, was going to his medical care. They couldn't spare the expense. Now, if I wanted to go to a state school, that would be different . . .

After Fran left, I sat on my small twin bed. Through the thin walls around me, I heard voices chattering gaily in rooms—roommates getting to know one another, comparing tastes in music and TV and Instagram follows. I didn't want to be alone. It felt cruel, what Fran had done. I started to do the rhythmic breathing I'd learned somewhere along the way. Eight counts in, six counts out . . . Sometimes it worked. That time, it didn't.

Back downstairs, the same girls were at the tables still checking people in. I went up to the same person Fran had spoken with—Tanya, the resident advisor. I told her that I didn't want a single after all.

Tanya cocked her head. "Seriously? Most people fight for those."

"Give it to someone else. I want a roommate."

The girl twisted her mouth, then looked down her list. "The thing is, everyone else is paired up . . ."

"I'm not," said a voice behind me in a Southern accent. I turned to see a girl with very curly dark brown hair, soft brown eyes, and an upturned nose. She was leaning on a giant plaid suitcase. Ear buds were slung around her neck, and the music still blared. Cardi B. I could tell the moment I set eyes on her that I liked her.

"I just found out my roommate decided to stay in the Philippines." She made a face. "I don't want to be alone either."

I turned back to the check-in girl, who looked torn. I couldn't understand why. "Look, that woman who spoke with you earlier is my stepmother," I insisted. "It's her job to piss me off. I'm the one paying my bills. I'll sign any paperwork."

"If you say so," Tanya the RA said, searching for the right keys.

The room Pippa and I share faced Fifth Avenue. It even had its own bathroom. That first day, Pippa was an open book—she'd already declared her psychology major with a minor in economics. She was either going to be a therapist, or she was going to work on Wall Street. She told me she'd slept with her boyfriend, James, in high school but felt a little pansexual these days. She told me that she still sometimes missed her ex-boyfriend, who might be the love of her life. And she told me that I was gorgeous, and did I realize?

34

"People say I look like my mother," I said quietly. It was what I always said when people commented on my looks.

Pippa's eyes grew wide. "Is she a model?"

I didn't have the heart to tell her right then my mom, Portia Rhodes—I'd always loved her name—was dead. I was afraid Pippa would regret asking me to room with her, like my tragedy was catching.

I was much more cautious about my personal life with Pippa than she was with me. I've always been withdrawn, biding my time before really getting into who I am with someone new. But Pippa had seemed okay with that. She put up with my moods; when I start to zone out, she always says, "You're going all Casey Spacey again." Never once has she indicated that I'm difficult, like Fran thinks.

I'm grateful I have Pippa. She fell into my life a lot like Marcus did—randomly but fortuitously. Though there's one big difference: I've never heard Pippa mutter something nasty to me under her breath.

A shiver darts up my spine.

Pippa was also with me the day I met Marcus. In early October, we went to a bar near NYU whose motto was "Every Day Is Mardi Gras!" They let in students with sketchy-looking fake IDs, even seventeen-year-olds. The place was dark and smelled like stale beer, but Pippa and I liked the pool tables. We were both pretty good—Pippa's family had a table growing up, and I picked up the game naturally, instantly understanding the importance of geometry when making a shot. My mind just works that way. My father tried to steer me toward engineering or math, and though I whizzed through all of my math courses, I don't love it like I love writing.

Halfway through our game, I noticed a guy watching us from the bar. He was quite a bit taller than I was, with a classically handsome face, a straight nose, prominent but not too prominent cheekbones, and expressive eyebrows. His hair was golden brown and wavy, the sort of hair Disney created for a Prince Charming. Unlike the other patrons in the bar, who wore ripped T-shirts, jogger pants, and ratty flip-flops, this guy had on jeans that looked expensive, a soft T-shirt that matched his blue eyes, and actual sneakers with laces. It was incongruous, kind of. Like he was a cardboard cutout, smooth and clean.

"Talk to him," Pippa said, nudging me. "He's gorgeous. And he looks kind of familiar."

Turns out I didn't have to make the first move. The guy walked over to me. He glanced at the pool table. "You're pretty good."

"Wanna play?" I told him. "What's your name?"

A muscle in his cheek flinched. His smile dimmed, but then he seemed to right himself. "Marcus."

Looking back on it, I wonder if he was surprised I didn't recognize him. Or maybe he was grateful to fly under the radar. I introduced myself, too.

"Buy you a drink, Casey?" he asked.

Pippa bowed out so Marcus and I could play alone. Marcus played confidently, taking a long time with his shot, smiling to himself when he sank a ball. As the game wore on, Pippa looked at Marcus more intensely—and her eyes started to widen. Back at our dorm, she told me she'd started to realize who he was from what she had seen on some gossip sites and was putting it all together.

I beat Marcus at pool—though just barely. "Where'd you learn to play like that?" I asked him.

"Harvard Club," he answered in a flippant voice. "My dad made me play growing up. You?"

"Oh, also Harvard Club," I teased, and then I felt self-conscious. I wasn't used to flirting. I wasn't sure I'd done it right.

"Really? Strange I never ran into you." He leaned on his cue. Then he blinked, understanding. "Oh, wait. You're messing with me."

I laughed, astonished that Marcus bought the lie. "I don't even know what the Harvard Club is."

So he was a rich city boy. It was only later, after three hours of sitting at the bar flirting, after he walked me back to the dorm and kissed me and asked for my number, I typed his name into Google: Marcus Coleman. As in the son of Roland Coleman. Columbia student. Man about town.

And. Well.

There was zero percent chance he'd call me, I figured. It was probably a total fluke that he was in a bar like that.

But then he did call—the next day. "We need a rematch," he said. "I keep thinking about those shots I got wrong."

On our second date, we went to Soho House, the private club he belonged to—a huge step up from the bar where we'd met. The décor was funky and beautiful, though when I took out my phone to take pictures, a waitress appeared from nowhere and practically ripped the thing from my hands. "No photographs," she snapped—like I was just supposed to know.

Marcus knew everyone in the place—beautiful girls, preppy guys, older dudes in suits. It was clear he was in his element, though at the end of the night, I felt drained. My head was growing foggy. It isn't that I'm antisocial, but I'd taken a quiz once about being introverted versus extroverted, and I'm definitely a person who gets recharged from staying in versus going out and talking to a million strangers.

"Let's get out of here," Marcus said when he noticed I was flagging.

On the street, a Mister Softee truck was parked at the curb. Marcus and I ordered the same thing—a double cone with dipped chocolate and nuts. We bonded over chasing down Mister Softee when we were kids, him on the Upper East Side, me in Bensonhurst. But as he put me in a cab and asked if he could see me again, I finally blurted, "Did someone put you up to dating me? Because this feels a little uneven."

He frowned. For a moment, his face became positively discombobulated. "I don't do things because someone tells me to," he said defensively. "And I don't see anything uneven about this."

"How are you today, sir?" Pippa calls out to a customer who's just come in, breaking me from my thoughts. I quickly hide my pint of ice cream and stuff my textbook into my backpack, but it turns out I don't need to worry about the boss catching us—it's just Sal, a regular, in here to buy his daily can of cat food for his fourteen-year-old Siamese.

38

I follow Pippa toward the register as she rings Sal up. After the guy leaves, she asks again why I'm having doubts about Marcus.

"He just seems too good to be true," I say. "Life isn't this easy. This kind of guy doesn't just drop into your world, you know?"

"Tell me about it," Pippa says, rolling her eyes. "But for you, he has! So go with it!"

I peer distractedly around the store. When you come into Pet Planet, the floor tile just beyond the door spells out *Dan's*. The boss never changed it; I'm assuming it was the name of the place before it changed hands, and maybe the pet store used to be a bar. I picture what Dan's was like back in the day: a smoky eatery where jazz bands played and everyone drank gimlets, maybe. I like the idea of that.

"Did your high school boyfriend ever mutter weird things to you?" I dare to ask Pippa. "Things he didn't think you heard?"

Pippa appraises my expression. "What did Marcus say?"

"Nothing," I say quickly.

Pippa looks worried. "No, really. Was it derogatory? *Sexual?* You don't have to consent to anything you don't want to do."

"I know." I shouldn't have opened this can of worms. "Never mind. I thought I heard him say something. But it probably was just in my head."

Pippa's eyebrows shoot up. "What did you think you heard him say?"

I swallow hard. "Never mind. Forget it."

The front door's bells chime again. A figure steps inside and looks around. My gaze passes over the guy's face at first, but then I freeze.

Pippa sees him too and grabs my wrist. "Did you call him?"

"No!" I say through clenched teeth, confounded.

Marcus smiles bemusedly at a large bin of Christmas-themed dog toys. Then, his gaze swings over to the two of us. He brightens. "Hey! There you are!"

"Marcus!" I try to sound pleasantly surprised, but instead I feel caught. I pray he hasn't heard anything I've just said to Pippa. "W-What are you doing all the way down here?"

"Just want to see where you work." Marcus nods approvingly at a basket of dog bones. "Kip likes that kind, too." Kip is his dog. He lives with Marcus's father because the building Marcus moved into while at Columbia doesn't take pets.

Then he notices Pippa. "Hey. How are you?"

"Hey, Marcus," Pippa says in a fluttery voice. "Um, we were just talking about the party." She glances at me cautiously as if to say, again, *You all right?*

I nod. But for some reason, my throat feels scratchy and dry. My heart is pounding.

Marcus turns to me. "Have a sec, Casey? Maybe . . . outside? I know it's freezing . . ."

I stiffen. Have I done something wrong? This has to be about last night. He thinks there's something wrong with me.

"We could go to the back," I decide. "It's quiet there."

Pippa shoots me another concerned glance, but I smile as if everything's okay.

Still, my legs are wobbly as I walk toward the back of the store. He's going to break up with me. It's got to be that. He's just being chivalrous and polite by doing it in person. That voice I heard yesterday?

Maybe it was a premonition. Maybe it was my mom, watching me—warning me. The hurt is coming. I guess I should steel myself.

We pass a row of tropical fish tanks. I point out a tank full of mice. "We named that big, white one Algernon."

"Weird name," Marcus murmurs.

"From the book. You know, *Flowers for Algernon*? The mouse? Such a good story, right?"

But Marcus still looks confused. I let it drop. He isn't a reader.

Jeremy's office is the best option, but Pippa's got the key. So I open the door to the dog wash room instead. "Don't worry, floor isn't wet."

Marcus looks around at the tiled walls, giant showerhead, and industrial-strength blow-dryers. "Very nice. If I were a dog, I'd feel like I was in a spa."

"Well, you'd be in the minority." I flip on the lights. "Most dogs hate coming here." Then I turn to face him. "Um, I had fun yesterday, by the way. It was a dream. Thank you for inviting me. Again." I'm babbling.

"Of course." Marcus shuffles his feet. Stares at the floor. My heart starts to bang even faster. I wish he'd just pull off the Band-Aid. "So I was a little worried about you. With the dizziness."

"Oh. I was just overwhelmed. The dancing . . . that champagne." I shrug. "I really had a wonderful time. Tell your father, too, by the way. It was so nice to meet him. And Miranda! She was lovely."

One corner of his mouth curls into a relieved smile. "Miranda adored you. And so did my dad. He's hard to please. And he actually gave me the go-ahead, which is why I came down here to tell you in person."

I search his face. *Go-ahead* . . . for what?

Marcus takes a breath. "Would you like to join us in Turks and Caicos for New Year's? Normally, it's just a family thing, but my dad said it's okay if I invite you along."

I blink at him. "Huh?"

"Turks and Caicos?" He smiles hopefully. "It's an island in the Caribbean?"

"I know where Turks and Caicos is," I say slowly. My heart's banging for a different reason. "I'm just . . . wait, really?"

"You don't have other plans?" Marcus looks crushed. "I should have asked before just assuming . . ."

"No," I interrupt. "And, I mean, if I did, I'd cancel them." It's starting to sink in. I vaguely remember reading an article about the Coleman compound in Turks and Caicos. It is literally that—a compound. With like twenty bedrooms and a staff.

"Th-Thank you," I stammer. "That would be wonderful—if you're sure."

"'Course I'm sure." Marcus beams. "I'll pay for everything. The flight—all of it. You don't have to worry about a thing." Then his smile turns coy. "And actually, that's not all. This is also presumptuous—so you can totally say no—but my father is going to call you."

"*Me?* Why?"

"He wanted to take you up on interning for the company."

I rear back. "Take me up?" I repeat slowly.

"Didn't you send him your resume? He said you did."

"I . . ." I pause. Did I? I'd sent out tons of resumes for internships at the beginning of this year. The problem is, tons of other people want an internship in publishing as well. Half the time, when I call about an internship role, the role has already been taken.

"Look, you can tell him no—I mean, the book side is so commercial, and I don't know if it would interest you, and the magazines are great, but if you want something brainier—"

"Hold on a second," I interrupt. "Of course I want to. The big reason I'm still in New York at all is to snag an internship in publishing." I'd thought long and hard about leaving the city after everything happened with my dad and Fran. Starting fresh somewhere else. Getting rid of all the toxicity. But being close to the field I wanted to eventually work in outweighed that. Doing something in publishing is my dream.

"Well, then, great." Marcus shrugs good-naturedly. "He'll get in touch."

Then I realize that maybe I sound too happy. Like Coleman Media is the only reason why I'm dating Marcus. I don't want to be seen as an opportunist. "Are you sure, though? I mean, I'm sure there are more qualified people . . . with better resumes . . . I don't want to jump some sort of internship line."

Marcus shrugs. "Don't feel guilty. And besides." He touches my cheek. "He thinks you're very qualified. Which I'm sure you are."

My heart flutters. I try to understand what I've just been presented with: an amazing New Year's trip . . . and the promise of an internship. An *in*. Don't get me wrong, that first day I met Marcus, after I went home and googled him and found out who he was connected to, I did wonder if maybe I could hit him up for a contact inside Coleman. But it didn't feel right. This, though . . .

This could change everything.

"So now are you glad I came down to your funny little pet store?" Marcus asks as he pulls me close.

"This store isn't funny," I say, mock offended. "And you'd better not think I'm quitting if I start interning. Even if I get a job at Coleman, I'm still loyal to Pet Planet until my dying breath."

"I love a woman who's loyal," Marcus teases, squeezing my hands.

Love. And then, even better, he leans in to kiss me. I lean in, too, feeling my body relax, letting the mix of adrenaline and euphoria mingle in my veins. Our lips touch, and I shut my eyes. But then . . .

You've been a bad girl.

The voice rockets through me. But it isn't Marcus—or Marcus saying it now, anyway. It is a man's voice, though. Maybe his. In the future. Or in the past. Something I'm forgetting. Something my subconscious is warning me about.

I feign a cough so I can break away. Is that it? Should I be scared?

"Casey?" Marcus sounds worried again.

I bite down hard on the inside of my cheek. No. *No.* I will *not* freak out. There's got to be an explanation for this.

I regain my bearings and wrap my arms around Marcus's neck again. "Sorry," I tell him. "Just a tickle."

We lean to kiss again. But the moment our lips touch, I feel a snap of electricity. This time, I see something—a memory?

A hand sliding around your waist. Someone pulling you backward. You try to scream, but someone's hand is pressed over your mouth. And a voice in your ear. A man's voice.

Maybe Marcus's.

"Shh. You've been a bad girl."

I let out a whimper and break away once more. *What the hell is happening?*

"Casey," Marcus is saying from what seems like down a long, long tunnel. "Casey. Are you okay?"

I stare down at myself. I've shot away from him, now standing pressed up against the wall across the room. My lips are trembling so badly I can't form any words. I'm suddenly afraid that the vision I saw, the vision that somehow implanted itself in my brain just now, is going to happen. I expect Marcus to shoot forward and grab me just like in the premonition. I expect him to silence me with his palm. I'm ready for him to tell me that I've been bad, even though that makes absolutely no sense.

"Casey," Marcus says again. "What is it?"

I can't let that happen. I need to save myself. "I-I have to go," I sputter.

And then I run.

THREE

"This stop, Southold!" a voice calls.

A woman conductor in a fitted navy suit appears at the front of the Long Island Rail Road car, unlatches a door, and opens it wide for the exiting passengers. Cold December air spills down the aisle, stinging my face. I pull my scarf over my nose.

The car empties. When I look around, I'm the last person in the seats. As if reading my mind, the conductor eyes me as she shuts the door.

"Avon Shores is next. Twenty minutes."

I nod like I know where I'm going. But really, I don't have a clue.

It's later in the afternoon, nearly evening. I've spent the past few hours walking the city streets, trying to calm down. I couldn't bring myself to go to my evening class. I even considered going to the campus Health Services, but I didn't know how to explain what was going on. I've also ignored the persistent phone calls from Marcus, hating that I don't have the strength to answer or the words to explain.

You've been a bad girl. And the vision—what am I to make of that? Was that Marcus? Am I having a flashback of something I've repressed—with him?

Or am I seeing the future?

It can't be real. It must be some kind of flare of anxiety, my brain playing tricks on me as a means of self-protection. I think of the girls at the party: Bronwyn's long eyelashes and silky blond hair; Shay's tiny dress. I think of the whispers she and Shay exchanged when I walked away. It's going to be an uphill battle trying to prove my worth to Marcus's crowd. Maybe I'm scared and am trying to protect myself. The person I loved most in the world—my mom—left me, and I don't want to repeat the experience with anyone else.

Maybe Pippa's right—maybe this is stress. As I walked, I thought about the five exams I had in the next week. Between working and Marcus, I wasn't as prepared as I wanted to be—and I'm usually someone who's very, *very* prepared. Maybe my subconscious is making up outlandish lies to divert my attention from Marcus for a while so I can study.

That had to be it.

Still, I was too scattered to go back to the dorm. I needed somewhere quiet, somewhere I could think. As a sign for 31st Street came into view, I hit on the idea of taking a trip to one of the beaches on the Long Island Rail Road. The water and waves always calmed me, and the beach would be dead this time of year. A change of scenery would help me focus on studying. It was perfect, actually—I was carrying my textbooks anyway, and my laptop; the rest of my materials were online. And no one can fault me for wanting to study.

It was the nerdiest college getaway ever.

At the station, when I looked at an LIRR map to peruse my options, the answer came. Avon Shores—Avon is my mother's maiden name. It felt like a sign. It's a small seaside community popular in the summer. Standing in line for a ticket, I looked up motel options, and lo and behold, there was one called the Wayfarer, on the same block as the beach, that had vacancies.

It felt preordained.

I had enough cash saved from Pet Planet to afford a few nights. I booked it on the spot. Done and done.

Now, the train clacks on, rushing toward a beach I know nothing about. I fidget nervously with my scarf. Another worry strikes me. I reach for my phone, and this time, I call Pippa.

"Oh thank God, you're alive," she blurts.

"You've been texting me this whole time. Of course I'm alive."

"That could have been your kidnapper posing as you. You ran out of the store like you were possessed! I was worried!" She pauses. "What did Marcus say? If he's hurting you, somehow, I'll kill him."

"He's not hurting me." *Yet*, I think. But then I push that thought away. It isn't true.

"Listen," I add. "I need you to be my alibi for a little bit."

"Alibi? Are you going to commit a crime?"

"No. But I'm going to text Marcus about leaving the city. I'm going to say I'm overwhelmed with finals and need some time to study—which is true. I'm also going to say you offered for me to stay at your parents' beach house in Jersey to study."

"My parents don't have a beach house in Jersey."

"*I* know that, but Marcus doesn't. Just go with it. I'm actually going to Avon Shores instead—on Long Island."

"But why do you have to lie, Casey? This makes me think you *are* hiding from him. And what am I supposed to say about not telling him this in the first place?"

The train sways, and I hold on to the handle on the top of the seat to steady myself. "Say I asked you not to. I just needed a few days of really buckling down, and I was afraid he'd be a distraction. I'm not hiding from him. Really."

"Are you sure?" Pippa sounds worried. "Why can't you tell me about what he said?"

"I just need to get hold of my anxiety. It's a huge deal that I'm dating Marcus. I'm losing track of classes. I need to get my head together."

"But all alone? Are you sure?"

I'm not really sure about anything. I've also never taken a trip alone. But I try not to worry about that. "I'll be fine. I promise. Anyway, will you do that if he calls again? It's just for a day or so."

"Just . . . you'd tell me if it was something serious, right? Something with Marcus?"

"I promise."

Pippa sighs. "I'll keep your secret. But I want you to explain yourself as soon as you're ready, okay? Let's just hope Avon Shores is everything you're looking for."

"Let's hope," I agree, just as the sign for Avon Shores comes into view.

Here goes nothing.

●●●

The disguises I wear aren't limited to just when I'm in Manhattan. On the train, I'm impersonal, efficient, patient Casey. A girl who knows her own mind. It helps drown out the nervous thrum in my gut.

As I'm getting ready to leave the train, a response comes through from the text I'd sent to Marcus. I'd told him the canned excuse I'd talked through with Pippa, but he doesn't seem satisfied.

Sure we can't talk about it? Sure everything's fine?

I answer

Totally. Sorry, I always get like this about exams. Be back soon! Jersey sure is pretty this time of year!

I punctuate it with some x's and o's.

I don't like lying. I've told Marcus other truths, even sad truths, about my mom's accident; and about my cold, unforgiving stepmother; and about how Fran had nudged me out of the house this summer.

Marcus has been forthcoming with me, too. He's told me all about his old girlfriend, Caroline, who he'd dated since they were both fifteen and in boarding school. They wanted different things, he told me, though he didn't elaborate on what those things were. He also said his father didn't like her. Why, he'd never known.

He told me about the loneliness of growing up with a distant, resentful mother and a workaholic dad. His mom isn't in New York anymore—Faye took off when he was twelve. Apparently, she lives in Europe now. Life was hard for him with just his dad. He always worried his dad blamed him for his mother leaving. He also was never sure if his dad completely respected him. This one time, he told me, his father had given him these engraved letter openers he'd had specially made by some samurai sword maker in Japan. Roland Coleman was giving them out as corporate gifts, but he had too many, so he said that Marcus could have a few of them "to give out to people he wanted to impress." Marcus had been so flattered that his father had entrusted him with letter openers made by a samurai sword master. He only gave one away and kept the rest, figuring they'd appreciate in value. Later, though, when his father visited his apartment, he'd spied the coveted boxes and asked why Marcus still had them. Marcus said he felt they were too valuable to give away. His father had let out a cruel guffaw. "You bought that line about the samurai sword maker? I picked up those things from a wholesale store in New Jersey. Just slapped on a different label." He'd shook his head in disappointment. "If you were an ice fisher, I bet I could sell you ice cubes."

Marcus had been so hurt, he told me. So humiliated. Often, he told me, he feels like he has no family in his corner—except maybe Miranda, who really does care about him like he's her son. He even said that once, about a year or so after his mom left and when his dad was traveling all over the world on business and leaving him alone with various nannies, Marcus had the family's driver take him down to where Miranda lived in Greenwich Village. He sent the driver away and stood outside Miranda's brownstone, working up his nerve. He wanted to ask Miranda if he could move in with her. She wasn't married and had no children, but she'd always treated him so kindly. Maybe she'd like to adopt him.

But then he chickened out. It was a dumb idea, he thought. She'd most certainly say no. So he took the subway home, and that was that.

If he could admit those sorts of things, I have no reason to doubt he's being anything but honest with me now. He *wants* me as part of his life. He's a good person. And what do I do? Sneak away. Lie. Conceal.

But then, it's for the greater good. Because what's happening now, in my head? The voice, those visions? I need to come back when I feel steadier. When I've studied. When I'm ready to face life again.

I pull my bag higher on my shoulder as I step onto the train platform. The air is dead silent except for the sounds of the whipping wind. Since this is the end of the train line, there are a few trains sitting idle on other tracks. I climb the stairs and assess the empty ticket booth and shuttered newsstand.

When I step out on the sidewalk, a line of dark shops greets me. They are all summer-themed—Rick's Surf Emporium, Sand & Sea Accessories, and then an Italian ice shop with a sign in the window that reads "Reopening in June." A deli on the corner boasts a few shabby Christmas trees lined up where fruit bins would normally be. I'm surprised when I intuit correctly that the shop after the deli will be one that makes and sells fudge. But then, it's a beach town. It's probably a prerequisite that there's a shop here that makes sugary stuff.

I'm the only person at the crosswalk. It seems kind of silly to even wait for a walk sign, as there's no traffic. I look at my phone, trying to find where the Wayfarer motel, where I've booked my room, might be. The map app directs me to walk east.

The town seems to be built on a grid system, the streets running straight and true, the stilted houses painted muted pastels. As I'm crossing another road, I catch sight of someone stepping out of a building down the block. It's a lanky guy with an explosion of dark curls. He doesn't see me, doesn't even look my way, but something jolts through me. It's almost like I know him. Except that's impossible.

I pull up my collar and march on, trying to shake it off.

The Wayfarer Motel is made of dingy white stucco. There's a dented Coke machine next to the front entrance and a shabby gate that presumably leads to a pool. I'm dubious as I go through the door marked Office, as it's hanging crookedly on its hinges.

In the office, a woman with stringy blond hair wearing a T-shirt from *The Big Lebowski* movie printed with the saying "The Dude Abides" works the front desk. The TV she's watching, tuned to *Dr. Oz*, is one of those old, bulky units with rabbit ears—I've rarely seen one up close. I have sunglasses on, which I hope will make me seem older, but she doesn't bother to ask for ID anyway—only for the cash.

As soon as I hand it over, I regret it. The lobby smells like mildew. Do I *want* to spend a night here?

"Strange time to be taking a beach vacation," she says as she places my twenties in a drawer, perhaps reading my mind. "You shoulda gotten a place at the other side of the island. Better views."

"This is an island?" I ask, surprised. I hadn't noticed that on the map or when I'd come in on the train.

"You didn't notice the causeway bridge? Train goes right past it." She turns her back and peruses a wall of keys. "But like I said, other side is better. Walk over there if you can stand the cold. That's where you find the houses for the big bucks." She hands me a key with a smirk. "Givin' you the honeymoon suite upstairs. Great view. Three nights. No upcharge."

"Uh, thanks?" I stare at the keychain—it's made of a sticky laminate material that seems like a hotbed for bacteria.

The woman gives me instructions on how to get to my room, which includes climbing a set of rickety outdoor stairs to the second level. Before I leave, she gives me a strange look. "Have we met before?"

"Pretty sure that's a no," I state.

She crosses her arms. "Huh. Guess you just have one of those faces."

I head to my room. The railing is lined with flimsy silver tinsel. I flick the edge of a piece with my fingers and feel a nostalgic pang.

My mother adored tinsel. She loved decorating for Christmas, full stop. After she died, my father didn't have the heart to even bring out the decorations that year. I didn't challenge him on it. I didn't want to look at all the ornaments she'd chosen, either.

My mom's death is such a hole in my mind. I was eleven. One minute, it was a clear November Saturday morning. The two of us were in her car heading toward the city. I was eleven, but I was small for my age, so I was still sitting in the back. I don't remember where we were going. Funny, what details don't make it through.

I buckled myself in. My mother slid into the driver's seat and started the engine. She hit some buttons on the car stereo, and our favorite song from *Tosca* blared. We didn't sing the real Italian words, only approximations of them, the proper notes. A few blocks into the drive, she met my gaze in the rearview mirror.

"Isn't this song the best?" she swooned. She had explained to me that the character in the opera had been given one hour to live. He'd declined seeing a priest, instead choosing to write one last letter to the woman he adores, Tosca.

"So romantic," I sighed.

And then, something flashed out of the corner of my eye to the right.

Next thing I knew, I was sitting on the edge of my bed at home in an itchy black dress I hated. My father loomed in the doorway. I was disoriented. I stared down at my dress, not remembering putting it on. I asked him why mom was making me wear a dress—were we going to church?

My father's expression crumpled. He told me my mother and I had been in an accident. The car plunged into the Gowanus

Canal, a particularly polluted waterway in the city. I was thrown from the vehicle, so I didn't make it into the water, instead landing on the pavement with a concussion. I'd been in the hospital, remember? It was days later. Even worse, he'd told me all this already. Now he had to tell me again.

But I didn't remember any of that.

And then my dad told me the worst part. My mother . . . Well, she was in the water when the car sank. She couldn't get out of the car in time. She was gone.

I didn't believe him. I had no memories of this. My mother was a careful driver; it was hard to believe she'd crash through a guard rail into a body of water as disgusting and polluted as the Gowanus. I asked my father again and again if he was lying. He said he wished he was. I also noticed him looking at me strangely in those days after it happened. He kept saying, "Are you sure you don't remember what happened?"

But if I remembered what happened, I would have told him. It was just . . . *gone.*

The only imprint from the experience was I suddenly developed a deep and all-powerful fear of riding in a car. Even for my mother's funeral—no casket, and these awful prayer cards with her name in flowery script—I insisted to my father that we walk the twenty-odd blocks. He was grieving, though, and nothing made sense anyway, so he complied.

It was so hard to look at anything of my mom's for a while after that—her clothes, her handwriting on the calendar, and definitely those Christmas ornaments. Her life felt so . . . interrupted.

One minute, we were singing. The next . . . gone? Down there in the water. Sunk, in that car. I hadn't gotten to say goodbye.

The following year, my dad and I went out and bought all new Christmas stuff—a tabletop tree, new ornaments, new lights. We tried to make a go of it, but there was always an undercurrent of sadness, a feeling of *why bother?* Still, we tried to forge a life on our own. We did pizza nights, trips to Coney Island. Dad was a little uptight and reserved, but he was kind and tenderhearted, and we were bound together by our deep, sad love and grief for my mom.

Also around that time, it became clear that school was too easy for me. I was tested for the gifted program, and the teachers determined I could skip not one grade, but two. My dad was proud, but he deliberated long and hard over whether this was the right choice. I'd endured a lot of upheaval; being in a class with thirteen-year-olds as a puny eleven-year-old might scare the shit out of me. We decided that I'd be pulled out of class to take certain subjects with the older kids—reading, math—but I'd stay with my grade for everything else.

For a while, we hobbled along. School was great. Learning was my salve. I was still deeply sad, but there were moments when I could forget. I thought my dad was happy—enough—but it turns out he was lonely. He had no one to talk to—it wasn't like the two of us were having great conversations. Right around the month I turned twelve, Fran started popping into his social calendar.

Fran and my dad had worked together at the small financial planning firm in Bensonhurst, and I'd known her forever. My mother used to gently poke fun at her, saying she was a stick-in-the-mud, teasing that she had a thing for my dad. One time, we all went to a holiday party Fran was throwing at her apartment, which wasn't that far from our own. I made the mistake of spilling a whole glass of red punch on Fran's carpet. Fran stopped in the middle of a conversation and ran for cleaner in the kitchen, then got down on her hands and knees, in the middle of the party, and started frantically scrubbing. Her large butt jutted into the air. Her mouth was a permanent frown.

"I mean, come on," my mother said later, trying to make me feel better. "It wasn't even that nice of a rug. She didn't have to make you feel bad in front of everyone."

It never crossed my mind that my father would ever date after my mom, and certainly not someone like prickly, domineering Fran. And marry her? My mind was blown.

From the moment she came into our lives, Fran wasn't thrilled about me. She put a lot of rules in place with me, and I became headstrong and defiant. I had tantrums most twelve-year-olds had already outgrown. I deliberately broke her rules. Within a year, arguments devolved into Fran sending me to my room and telling me to calm down and then slamming her own bedroom door and loudly crying. I've mostly blocked that out; I don't like thinking about it. But I didn't want a new mother. I resented Fran for trying to be one.

I still did well in school—by this time, I was in high school, officially moving ahead two grades. Learning was still my escape, though I barely had any social life. Still, I was able to graduate a full two years early, and with my impressive test scores, I earned scholarships to various colleges. I chose NYU for a few reasons—one, the goal to work in publishing, but two, there was my father's health. He'd dropped twenty pounds seemingly overnight the spring of my senior year. He also developed a cough that wouldn't go away. After badgering him to go to the doctor, he finally went. Later, I found out he'd been subjected to a barrage of tests, even a biopsy. When he returned home, he looked gray and shaken. He'd received a diagnosis: throat cancer that had metastasized into several nearby lymph nodes.

He started chemo. I tried to help, but I was busy getting used to my freshman year at college. The summer between freshman and sophomore years, I fell ill. A flu, I guess. The days were a blur. I barely have any memory of it. I'm assuming I stayed in my bedroom in the apartment, trying to keep away from my dad. But when I started to feel better and the fog cleared, I heard Fran whispering to my dad in the kitchen. "That was way too much," she said. "I think we need a new plan."

"I know, and I'm sorry," my father said weakly. "Should we talk to her about it? Finally?"

"No!" Fran said sharply. "What's that going to solve?"

I didn't know what my dad meant. Tell me about what? Something about his diagnosis? Then, Fran then came into my room. She told me that she'd called NYU and arranged for me to stay in the dorms for my sophomore year. I was startled. All because I was sick? I knew to be careful about germs. Chemo made people immune compromised, I got that. And from what I'd gathered, he hadn't picked up my bug. Fran hadn't either.

I pushed back. Fran's expression was pinched. "Right now, having you here is just not working for us, Casey. I'm sorry."

Up the flight of stairs, the door to my motel suite features a heart-shaped sign that reads "Honeymoon" in swirly letters. I jam the key into the old-fashioned lock. It sticks for a moment, then gives.

A short hallway leads me into a small, dark, dusty-smelling front room. I flip on lights, drop my heavy backpack on the ground, and look around, taking in an efficiency kitchen and a small blue couch with a big amoeba-shaped stain on a cushion. A door leads to a room with a lumpy-looking queen-sized bed. Another door leads to a clean-enough bathroom. Two giant windows look out to the water. The sun is sinking lower into the sky, but I can still see the waves rolling in gently.

I suddenly feel the need to be outside. Studying can wait a few minutes.

I change into sneakers and walk out my door again and down the tinsel-adorned stairs. The chilly wind bites my cheeks. I pull my coat around me as I head toward the dead end of the street. I go past the empty bike racks, tidy garbage cans, and Beach Rules signs to a small walkway that leads to the sand.

There's no one on the beach. The tide is far out, leaving behind rocks and shells. A few brave seagulls peck at things in the tide pools. I start down the wooden stairway and head over the walkway that leads across the dunes.

I stand stiffly, the wind blowing directly into my face. I wonder if I look ridiculous, the only person outside on such a cold day. I picture someone coming upon me. Marcus. Pippa. Fran. I imagine my stepmother sitting at my dad's bedside right now, feeding him soup, portioning his pills. I imagine her disapproving frown, the deep wrinkles in her forehead. In my mind's eye, I can see her using my mother's towels and linens and forks and frying pans like they're hers. It's always curdled my stomach.

The waves crash. Gulls squawk, bickering over a scrap of food. I think I hear a helicopter, but when I open my eyes, the sky is empty. I must have imagined it.

But then I hear the helicopter sound again. With it, a strange vision unfurls in the landscape of my mind.

> You're sitting on a couch. A helicopter thwap-thwap-thwaps outside. You look out and wonder, are they coming for me?
>
> And then a makeup artist stands over you. "Perfect."

My eyes spring open. Did I just doze off? Was that a dream? But if it was, it's left an intensely vivid imprint behind.

Or maybe it was another vision like at the pet store . . . because it rolls on like a movie.

> You look down at yourself: you're in a lace wedding dress. An older woman walks in, saying you look nervous. You spring up and head for the door. "Maybe I'll just step outside," you say.
>
> You retreat to a large patio. It's part of the enormous house where you've been staying, a blue-gray colonial that sits right on the beach with a spectacular view of

the waves. On the patio, you feel your heartbeat slow.
You stare into the water until your eyes blur with tears.

A whitecap crashes out at the sandbar. I hug my body tightly, a shiver traveling down my back. I can't identify the people speaking to me. I've never been in a house like that, either—in the pictures I've seen of Marcus's family's Hamptons estate, the only thing that compares, the place is painted white.

And then I'm sucked back into the vision.

You stand on the patio, your fingertips outstretched.
The smell of honeysuckle and wild rosemary is on the
wind. You glance at a long, dark steel pier to your right.
It stretches far into the water, disappearing into the fog.
Next, you look down at something you've pulled out of a
clutch purse. It's a picture of a guy. He smiles up at you.
You stifle a sob. Your heart hurts.

I press my hand to my cheek and spin around. Reeds on the dunes dance and wave. When I turn back, I stare at the motel's ugly façade, grounding me back to the present. *Breathe*, I tell myself, but my body feels tingly and full of antsy, toxic energy. *You're not there. You're here.*

Who is the guy in the photograph? He seems familiar, and yet I've never seen his face. One thing's for sure: he's definitely not Marcus.

And then something happens that makes my heart freeze. As my gaze scans the Avon Shores coastline, it locks on that same pier. The same one I'd been staring at from that luxurious back porch in the vision. There it is in the distance, angular and long and completely the same. The two images, real and imagined, overlay one another until they're a perfect match.

I stagger backward. *How is that possible?* Maybe I glanced at the pier from the train and didn't realize? Maybe the pier was an image on an internet search, or on a map, somewhere else within my subconscious?

But then, when I look farther down the beach, I see something else: that monster-sized blue-gray estate, also from the vision. There's the patio where I collected my thoughts. There's the same honeysuckle bushes, the same bluffs, the same . . . everything.

I definitely didn't see that house upon coming into town. Except for in my mind, I've never seen that house in my life.

The vision starts to roll forward again in my brain like someone has pressed play. I'm unable to turn it off.

> You turn for the door to go back inside the house, your shoulders slumping. But as you reach for the knob, you sense someone behind you. There's a hand on your arm.
>
> "You've been a bad girl," someone says.
>
> You're pulled backward. You stumble. You stifle a scream, and then, all at once, you can't breathe.

I let out a small whimper and touch my throat, realizing that this newest vision has matched up with the last one with Marcus.

"No," I say aloud. "No, no, *no*." I have to pull myself out of this before it's too late . . . but the vision pounds on.

He drags you backward now, hissing in your ear. "Hurry up. Stay quiet." And then he throws you into the back of a car. The door slams, and you hear him open the front door to climb in. Your heart is pounding.

I clutch the sides of my head, trying to squeeze the thoughts away. The thoughts are so much more vivid than they were in the city. I can smell the leather interior of the car. I can feel the scratchy lace of the dress and the cold sweat at the small of my back and the dryness in my mouth. This isn't just a soft, strange little suggestion of something in my head—this is a blown-out memory slotted neatly inside my mind like a USB in a drive.

I stagger up the concrete steps back to the motel room. The wind presses against my side, sending my hip crashing into the railing. Once I'm back indoors, I collapse on the couch, my head whirling. I'm too afraid to even close my eyes. I don't know what I've seen. Was I really once in that house down the beach . . . or is this something that's going to happen, in the future, with Marcus and me? But why would I have a wedding here? And *marriage*? That's the furthest thing from my mind, period.

You feel the pillowcase being pulled off your head. Your body clenches. You whimper. You aren't going to live through this, and you know it.

"That didn't happen," I say into the room. "It *won't* happen." It's from a movie, maybe. A book I've read, spinning in my mind, conflating with my fears. That's not Marcus. That's not me.

Except I can't quite convince myself. There's something deeper inside me, telling me that all of it, every last moment of the vision I've just seen, is somehow true.

FOUR

I hurry down the sidewalk. I pass homes on stilts, a closed-up souvenir shop with a faded plastic swordfish above the door, a water tower bearing the town's name in jaunty letters. Everything I see is suddenly, oddly familiar. And not just because I saw it after getting off the train.

I feel like I've known it my whole life.

The cold wind smacks at my face, stinging my eyes. I barely notice. Every minute that passes, my memories of this place are stronger and more certain. I know, instinctively, that the street after Dune Drive will be called Sea Oats Lane. Certain signs spark disorienting familiarity: a placard for Uccello Construction, an old-school Santa in someone's front yard. When I pass a small white house with an eagle statue in the front yard, I think, *That's where Mr. Matthews lives.* Then, as though by magic, I see that very name etched into the mailbox. Except I don't know anyone named Mr. Matthews. I haven't met a soul in this town, I'm sure of it.

What the hell is happening to me?

I'm scared. I'm also no longer sure this is a message from my mom. Maybe it's something way deeper. Darker. Perhaps I was a fool to think I could handle whatever this is on my own. I'm in a strange town where I know no one, and now it seems my brain has turned against me.

Has someone slipped me drugs? Am I going to die? What if I can't make these thoughts go away? What if I'm stuck with them for life, and they only get worse and worse, blotting out everything I know?

I need to see a doctor. I need to turn this problem over to someone else. If I can just make it to help, through these next few minutes, then I'll be okay. I've googled a GP's office in town. It's in the same building as a psychologist. Perfect. Two birds, one stone.

One step in front of the other. Try not to be scared. Try not to think about it. Try not to pay attention to all the new memories roiling in your brain. Easier said than done.

Then my gaze snags on something else. A palm, sculpted from neon, glows in a window in a small, weather-beaten building across the street. "Readings," a sign declares. "Psychic Advice." Astonishingly, unlike everything else in this town, this shop is open.

A shiver travels from the base of my neck to my knees. I've never believed in psychics. I don't even read my daily horoscope like Pippa does. And yet . . .

A shadow moves across the shop's window. A face leans toward the glass from the inside. It's a woman with brown hair to her chin and broad shoulders and kind eyes. She spots me. Our gazes lock for three full, strong heartbeats at my temples. She raises her hand and makes a beckoning gesture: *Come in.*

I shake my head. The woman frowns and gestures more forcefully. I glance up and down the street, wishing I had somewhere else to go—an excuse that can drag me away. The sidewalk is empty. Not even a car passes, and there aren't any other open shops on this road.

I turn back to the window, swallowing hard. The woman still stands there, hands on her hips, waiting. My feet stay planted on the concrete. The woman disappears from the window, and I think I've been given a reprieve, but then the front door to the shop flies open. She steps under the little green awning and points across the road to the center of my chest.

"Casey," she shouts across the street. Clearly. "It's Casey, right?"

I look down at my body—am I wearing something bearing my name? Does she have facial recognition software? I look back at her, then weakly nod. She smirks as if she can read my mind—which, I mean, *can* she?

"Hurry up," she says in a no-nonsense tone. "I can help you."

I shouldn't fall for this. There are all kinds of ways she could know my name. Maybe the woman at the motel's front desk tipped her off. Maybe they're in cahoots and the hotel clerk gets a kickback. That's probably it.

And yet, there's something comforting about the psychic telling me what to do. I find myself nodding, clutching my tote closer to my body, and hurrying across the street.

Just as I'm hopping up to the opposite curb, my phone beeps. *Marcus*, reads the caller ID. There's no way I can answer—he'll hear how freaked out I sound. Is he going to throw me into a car? Kidnap me? Hurt me? Why did my brain show me that?

I hit the button to ignore the call. Then I write him a text:

Saw you called. Making some good headway with studying. Call soon!

I send it off and shut my eyes tight, dread and guilt oozing over me once more.

The psychic holds the door open for me. She says nothing, her eyes traveling over me, taking me in. "Thanks," I say as I step inside.

I look around. The waiting room is decorated like a dentist's waiting area, with three blue plastic chairs and an empty check-in desk and some bland framed paintings on the walls. A sign-in clipboard sits on the desk, but all of the entries are empty. The only sound in the room is the bubbling of a fish tank filter in the corner, though when I peer through the glass, I don't see any fish.

I turn and look at the woman more carefully. She's about fifty, in a white fisherman's sweater and black wide-legged pants. Her downturned hazel eyes and pudgy cheeks make her look more like a dental hygienist than a psychic.

Her eyebrows knit together, and her eyes widen. "Come this way. Good thing for you, my afternoon appointment canceled."

I follow her through the door and into a small office. The only items in the room are two velvet couches that face each other. I sit on one of them. My knees are trembling.

"I'm Karin," she says, pronouncing it *Car*-inn. She settles down on the opposite couch. "And *you* aren't from around here." It's not a question but a statement.

"I'm from the city," I say, trying not to be impressed by her astute observation. It's probably obvious I'm from the city.

"You've come in search of something. An answer? A person?"

I just blink at her. "I'm sorry, aren't *you* supposed to know that answer?"

"It doesn't always work like that. Why don't you tell me what's happened?"

This is clearly a quack's sleight of hand to get me to open up, but I don't care. It was one thing when I was out on the street and exposed. But I'm Karin's now, and there is something about sitting in this small room face-to-face with her that makes me feel— well, not exactly safe, but at least seen. And also, the snarls in my head have quieted for the moment—so that's something.

Also, if there's anyone who might not judge me right now, it's a psychic. I have to tell someone what's going on.

I take a deep breath and explain about the voice and the visions. And how, on the beach, everything else about Avon Shores became suddenly familiar. "It's like I've been here before, but that's not possible." Something else snaps into place as I'm saying this: I see a clear memory of this very building with its neon palm and pink shutters; it shimmers in the bright sun. Had I known it would be here all along?

Karin leans back and crosses her arms. "What do *you* think is happening?"

I let out a small, helpless moan. "I don't know. Is my boyfriend going to . . . to hurt me, somehow? Do I need to get away from him?" I swallow hard. "I can't imagine he'd do that. But I don't know what I'm seeing. I don't understand anything in the vision, or why I know this place. And I especially don't understand . . ."

"What?" Karin asks when I trail off.

I think of that guy's face in the photograph. Whose picture am I staring at, in the vision? Who is that other guy?

Will.

The name comes to my mind in a finger-snap. But I don't know anyone named Will. I have never known anyone named Will. Maybe I'll meet him in the future, too?

"Casey?" Karin nudges. "What is it?"

I try to breathe. "I need help. I don't want my boyfriend to be dangerous. I want to feel normal again. I don't want to wreck my life."

"Would you be, though?" Karin cocks her head. "Wrecking your life? If he *were* dangerous, that is. If you broke up with him."

I jerk up. "I don't think I should break up with my boyfriend just because of some random thoughts and weird images."

"So you love him, then?"

I pause. "Well, I mean, I haven't known him that long."

"Usually, with love, that doesn't matter."

I scoff. "Says who?" Karin stares at me so long I flinch. "Marcus is a great catch."

"Since when does that matter?"

I prickle with frustration. "I don't know what this has to do with anything!"

Then Karin scoots forward and takes my hands. I let her. Her hands are warm, and I know mine must be freezing. Her fingers travel over my palms, my knuckles, the pads of my fingertips. I wonder what she's searching for.

"Casey," she says after a while. "I'm going to tell you something that might sound a little shocking." She drops my hands to my lap. I can feel her gaze on me, but I don't return it. "That voice in your head? I don't think it has anything do with your boyfriend. Nor do I think that's who you're seeing in the vision."

"Oh." I sit back, not expecting this—from a psychic, no less. "Really? Well, good. That's really good!"

But she has more to say. She stares at me, her eyes wide and serious. "Have you considered that you might have ties to Avon Shores? Ties you're only now understanding?"

I curl my hands at my chest. "No. I've never been here. So unless you're saying I've been here in the future and that's what I'm seeing, you're wrong."

Karin shakes her head, her hoop earring tinkling. "I don't believe you're seeing your future." She takes a breath. "I think you're seeing your past. Your past life."

FIVE

A little while later, I'm back in the doorway of my room at the Wayfarer. A stoned-looking delivery boy drops off a pizza I don't want.

"Thanks," I murmur to him as I take the box.

"Congratulations on your wedding," he mutters back. I'm about to ask him what the hell he means, but then I realize. The Honeymoon Suite.

I place the pizza box on the counter. I've barely eaten all day. I rationalize that perhaps some of the dizziness I'm feeling might be hunger's fault. If only I could believe that.

As I open up the box and breathe in the greasy, cheesy smells, my phone starts to buzz. *Marcus*, reads the caller ID. My chest clenches. I'm in no mood to speak to him, but I've put him off all day. Reluctantly, I answer.

"There she is!" he crows. There's a lot of street noise—a grumble of a city bus, a honk of a horn. "How's Jersey? How's studying? Cramming all that knowledge in your brain?"

"Oh, absolutely," I muster. "And Jersey is . . . nice."

"Well, good."

There's a long pause. I'm so confused about what I'm supposed to think or feel about him, which makes me want to shut my eyes and hide.

"Actually, Casey . . ." Marcus starts hesitantly.

"I should go," I interrupt. "Gotta get back to it."

"Okay," he says reluctantly. "Are you sure—"

"Sorry," I add. "I miss you. I'll see you soon."

After I hang up, I press my cold fingertips into my eye sockets until I see stars. These lies are choking me.

I need to force down some food, then tease out what the hell I'm supposed to do with what Karin the psychic told me about a past life.

My past life.

But then my phone rings again. This time, it's Pippa. I watch her number flash, knowing I shouldn't answer. But then, against my better judgment, I do.

"Hey," I say.

"So?" Pippa asks. "Getting any studying done? I'm still stressed about lying to Marcus, by the way."

And then I burst into tears.

Pippa gasps. "Casey. I'm sorry. I was kidding. It's okay that I'm lying. Really."

"It's not that." My voice cracks.

And then it all spills out of me. Everything—including what the psychic told me.

"Whoa," Pippa says when I'm finished. "Casey. That's . . . *amazing.*"

"No, it's not," I argue. "It's nuts." I can't believe I've just told her. I feel so vulnerable. "I don't have time for this! I have *my* life to live! The professors aren't going to give me a break because I've apparently got another person lurking inside me!"

"Actually, maybe they will." Pippa is joking . . . kind of. "Seriously, I wish I knew who I was in a past life. I think all of us have lived lives before, but most of us have blocks that prevent us from seeing those memories. You're lucky, Casey!"

I bite my bottom lip. "So you think it's true? Couldn't there be some other reason why all of Avon Shores is suddenly as familiar?"

"I guess so. But if the psychic's right, that means you don't have to worry about Marcus. So that's good, right?"

"True." I start to peel cheese off the piece of pizza. "I still feel terrible for the girl, whoever she was. But *she's* the one with these problems—not me. It also means I'm not going to meet some mysterious man named Will whose photograph I'll cling to my breast at my wedding like it's a life buoy."

"That sounds so romantic, though." Pippa sighs dreamily. "But . . . okay, then. In that case, you can come back home. It's all good."

I walk to the window and stare out at the beach. It's dusk. The sand is just as desolate as before. "Except these visions . . . the past? It's all still in my head. And it's loud. How long will it stay here? For the rest of college? Grad school? What about when I get a job? Travel? Is this past life going to weigh in about all of that, too? Am I stuck? That's what the psychic seemed to think."

"What do you mean?"

I consider what Karin told me. "You need to listen to what your past life is trying to tell you through these visions. Only then, once you understand them, will she leave you alone."

"But what if I can't understand them?" I asked her.

"You will." Karin seemed so certain. "Perhaps you're already halfway there. Perhaps the lesson you need to learn *does* have to do with your boyfriend."

"So . . . Marcus is wrong for you?" Pippa asks after I explain this. "Sorry, Casey, I'm having a hard time keeping up."

I groan. *Tell me about it.* "Karin said that maybe Marcus isn't right for me. Not because he's going to hurt me, more because there's someone else out there who's more . . . perfect, I guess? And maybe that's what this past life is trying to tell me, and maybe that's what I'm supposed to understand."

"Hmm. And what do *you* think?"

I consider the tough questions Karin asked. If I loved Marcus. If it would be such a bad thing if we broke up. Is love supposed to come so quickly, though? Why does everyone keep asking me that?

I shake my head vigorously as though to reset my thoughts. "I'm not basing my relationship decisions on what a psychic tells me. But still, I do sort of want to know what this past life wants me to figure out. Because Karin seemed pretty determined, based on her past clients, that whoever I was before had a message."

"Huh," Pippa says. "I wonder why you've never heard from her until now?"

"I know." Then again, maybe it was going to Avon Shores that opened the floodgates. Past Life Girl was getting married here, it seemed like. Maybe she's from the area. Maybe all the familiar surroundings triggered something in my brain.

Then again, I actually got the first visions before I came here. So maybe that doesn't fit.

"It would be useful if you knew your past life's name," Pippa says. "We could look her up. See what she's all about. And not to scare you, Casey, but she's probably dead. You realize that, right?"

You've been a bad girl. I shiver. "I understand how reincarnation works."

"Do you see anything else about her in those visions? Anything that could give us a clue?"

"She was getting married really young."

"So maybe she lived a while ago. The fifties, the sixties?"

"Hmm." The other women in the vision didn't seem particularly old-fashioned. "Oh, and she either regularly visited Avon Shores, or she's from here. And her fiancé's family has a lot of money—they own or owned this estate at the end of the island."

"Ooh, fancy. What was his name?"

I shake my head. "No idea." Nowhere in the memories I've been given are there any references to a fiancé's name—or anyone's name, for that matter.

Except for Will. The guy in the photo.

He shimmers in my mind again. His light eyes. His beaming smile. My body warms. I know inherently he isn't the husband-to-be. A new vision comes to me:

It's earlier. The sun is higher. You've already put on that lacy dress you'll wear later, but luckily, you have a little time.

Well. Not me. *Her.* But it feels like me, too. It's hard to separate the two of us.

You stand in a dark hallway in that same house, holding a flip-style cell phone to your ear. You type in a number like you're not quite sure how to use the thing. The line rings, rings, rings, and then a choppy recording comes on. A man's raspy voice announces that no one is home. After the beep, you stand there for a moment before finding your voice.

"Will," you say. "It's . . . it's me. Becky. And . . . I miss you."

"Becky," I whisper, sitting up straighter.

"What?" Pippa asks.

I grip the phone. "I-I think the person I was in a past life was named Becky. And . . . and she was using a flip cell phone. When were those popular—2003, 2004?"

"I think so." Pippa sounds excited. "Whoa. That wasn't even that long ago. And . . . did you have another vision just now?"

I look around. The motel suite is cold. I'm sitting here in the dark with a piece of greasy pizza halfway to my lips.

"I think?" I swallow hard. This is so disorienting, switching from past to present. "It was the same girl, maybe the same day. In a hallway this time. Same house."

"And her name's Becky? What about her last name?"

"I . . . don't know."

But then I gasp, realizing something. *Becky.* That name.

I sink to the couch. My limbs are vibrating. "Karin gave me some articles to read. I looked through a few of them. This one talked about how sometimes, a reincarnated soul has a way of speaking in its new life. There are stories of little kids speaking foreign languages they've never been exposed to, or a story about this little boy who knew everything about being a firefighter in New York City, which made his mother think he'd been one of the firemen killed in 9/11. The theory is that it's the reincarnated soul speaking through them."

"Did Becky speak other languages?" Pippa asks excitedly. "Is that why you did so well in freshman Italian?"

"I don't know, but the article also says that kids sometimes spoke about people they'd never met, or knew the names of relatives who were long dead without having any prior knowledge about them. That's happened to me. With Becky. Kind of."

I close my eyes, remembering being seven years old. While all of the other kids in the neighborhood were running through the streets or gallivanting on the playground, I sat at the kitchen table, drawing pictures and writing stories. I was like a machine with those stories, cranking out pages and pages a day, dividing the story into separate chapters just like the chapter books I'd started reading. Along with everything else, I was a precocious reader, already reading at a much higher level.

My mother marveled over those stories. She kept them safe in a hutch in the closet. It's been a long time since I've thought about them, and I certainly haven't looked at them in years, but I remember they were often about a little girl who was going on a long journey across a desert. *Sand*. Like the beach.

And I always named my character the same thing. *Becky*.

"Whoa," Pippa whispers when I tell her about this.

"I still name characters Becky," I say breathlessly. "It's like my default. I've never really questioned why—just thought it was one of my writing quirks."

"Do you think you've ever written anything true about her life? Like . . . maybe she's channeled her experiences through you? Maybe you've written about what happened to her? Who took her that day? How she died?"

I rack my brain, thinking of the short fiction I'd written recently where Becky's name appeared. The latest story was more of a contemplative piece, a girl riding the subway all day without getting off because she was grieving for her mother. But that's *my* story—I'd just used Becky as a name.

Then I think about stories I wrote when I was younger where Becky popped up. That first one featured Becky traversing the desert on a camel—the desert *could* be the beach, I suppose. But there certainly isn't a kidnapping plot.

I remember another story, too: a girl named Becky deciding that she'd like to play the tuba, but people make fun of her for it. Again, that's a reflection of my life at the time: *I* wanted to play the tuba, but my peers talked me out of it, saying the tuba was for a particular type of boy who has hefty lungs.

"I don't think so," I tell Pippa. "But do you think she was trying to speak through me, though? Make her presence known?"

"This can't be a coincidence. You lived this person's life, Casey. She's *in* you."

I consider this. Maybe it's more than just me using Becky's name in stories. I wonder if this has anything to do with how easily I learned to read—learned to do everything, in fact. Perhaps I already had the innate knowledge from Becky. As a child, adults often looked at me curiously, commenting, *She's such an old soul. So mature for her age.* Maybe that's even why Fran found me so strange.

It's like they could tell, without actually knowing, that this wasn't my first time around the block.

Out of nowhere, a new vision rushes in:

Glass rains inward. Your head hits the back of the seat hard. Someone is screaming near you, but you can barely hear because everything explodes. You're in water, suddenly. You struggle at the door handle, desperate to wrench it open. It doesn't budge.

I jolt up. What the hell?

But the memory rushes on.

The car starts to fill. Your dress is getting soaked. That same voice screams and screams. You stare up, realizing the car is sinking.

Now the water is at chest level. Now it's touching your nose. You wrench at the door, but the handle still won't budge.

"Oh my God," I whisper.

"What?" Pippa cries. "What's going on?"

"Now I'm seeing . . ." What am I seeing? Is this my mother's accident? The one where she . . . in the water . . . ?

Except *I* wasn't in that car. I'd been thrown out when it hit the guard rail. I'm seeing this person—this other me. I flash there again:

You're flailing, desperate to smash a window. You tip your head up, sucking in air.

"Becky!" someone tries to yell, their voice garbled underwater. "Becky!"

"Oh my God," I whisper. Could this be true? Is this how Becky died? And she's in a wedding dress—is it the same day? And Becky was in a car accident . . . a lot like the one that killed my mom.

"Casey?" Pippa calls again. "Are you still there? Talk to me."

I tell her—or I try to, anyway. My story is met with a series of gasps. "God," Pippa whispers. "That's . . . eerie."

I feel shaken. I have no idea if what I've seen is real, although it feels . . . palpable. "I wish this is something I could look up," I say. "Just to see if there's some kind of story . . . and when it was. A record."

"Try," Pippa orders me. "Do a Google search. Or here—I will." I hear her typing. "Becky . . . crash . . . water?" There's a pause. "Hmm. Not finding anything. But that doesn't mean it didn't happen."

My hands tremble. Now that I've been given that memory, I can't unsee it. And the more time that passes, the more the memory settles into my mind, I feel convinced: I am seeing the last day of someone's life. *Becky's* life.

I think about what Karin said: Past lives only hang around when a loop isn't closed. When they're still yearning for something, or when something is unfinished.

Something in Becky's life is unfinished. But what?

"Will," I whisper, the answer coming to me from somewhere mysterious and deep.

"Will?" Pippa's voice lifts. "Are you having a memory about him now, too?"

"No. But . . . I think Will is the key. I think he's what Becky misses. Or wants. Or . . . needs?"

"What do you mean?"

I have no idea what I mean. Words are just spewing out of me from a place I can't explain. But as I shut my eyes, the vision I'd experienced earlier—standing on that patio, the guy in the photo, someone grabbing me from behind—pounds like a sledgehammer. If anything, it's gotten more vivid.

I'm suddenly so full of longing and sadness I can't breathe. Except the longing isn't for someone *I* know—it's for this Will person. The guy *Becky* knew. Her desire for him washes over me like warm water in a shower. Grief comes next—bottomless grief, the grief of being separated for eternity. *I've* never felt this way before. It's like a door has opened and there's a whole new wing to my house I've never explored. It's a sudden rush of *Oh, is this what it's supposed to be? This is love?*

The love in the opera. Devastating, desperate love. Will elicited some bombastic feelings in Becky—but for some reason, they came apart. And now they're separated for eternity.

Find Will a voice says. *Find Will!*

"I have to go," I tell Pippa suddenly.

"What?" Pippa sounds flabbergasted. "No, Casey, wait! I'm worried! All of this has to be so overwhelming. Are you going to be okay? Maybe I should come out there . . . We could figure this out together."

"I'm fine," I assure her, even though I have no idea if it's true. But I need to get off the phone. "I promise," I add. "I'll call you in the morning. There's just something I need to do right now."

"You're leaving the motel?"

I don't answer that, saying a halting goodbye instead.

When I hang up, I pace. My mind feels jumbled. Becky is sapping me dry. But I keep hearing those instructions. *Find Will. Find Will.*

But how do I find a guy I've never met? Should I look up every person named Will in the state? Might he find me through some secret energy field, or perhaps by my aura? Should I wear a sign around my neck saying *Hey, are you my past self's true love who for some reason she didn't marry?* I mean, I guess I have *some* sense of what he looks like: blond hair, light eyes. Like a pro baseball player. A camp counselor. Except he would be almost twenty years older. A full-grown man.

And what happens if I do find him? What, will Becky just . . . just stop speaking to me, then? Let me go on as myself? And what am I supposed to say to Will? *Hey, so I'm this girl you were once in love with. Sorry if I look a little different!*

Use your intuition, a voice tells me. If Becky's really inside me, then maybe she knows where Will is. I close my eyes. *Come on. Give me an address. That number you called on the day of your wedding. Something.*

Something catches in my mind from earlier. I stop and draw in a breath. There was something I'd seen out of the corner of my eye. A person.

Have I already seen Will?

But . . . no. There's no way. The person I'm thinking of looks nothing like the person in my visions.

But the idea keeps pinging. I slide on shoes. It's probably nothing, but I just have to see.

It's dark out, but my feet seem to know which streets to take, which turns to make, angling away from the water and toward the center of town. Soon enough, I'm back at that low-slung building I'd noticed earlier. It's a house that also seems to house a business, with professional-style landscaping and a six-car parking lot. A streetlamp beams down. A single business is advertised in the front window: Carson Veterinary Care.

I stand there, deliberating, and then I feel a jump in my chest. What am I doing? The weight of it sinks in. I picture Marcus watching me, trying to understand my actions. This would break his heart. If he even tried to understand what I'm doing.

I turn and step off the porch. I'll go back to the motel and pack up. I need to live *my* life, not Becky's. Whoever she even is.

Then there's a *whoosh* behind me as a door to the vet's office opens. Milliseconds before I turn, I know it's going to be the same person from before. The same young, tall, gangly, curly-haired stranger I'd had a weird feeling about.

And then, it is. He's younger than I ever thought—close to my age. So it can't be right. Will would be in his thirties.

I back up, certain I've got it wrong, just as he stops, noticing me on his porch. "Can I help . . ." he starts, but then he trails off when he sees it's me. "Oh."

We stare at each other. My heart starts to pound. Another vision plays in my mind, opens up:

You're standing together, holding hands, dancing long into the night. "I'm going, but I'll be back," he says.

But you shake your head, a fat tear falling down your cheek.

"Wait for me," he begs. "Promise you'll wait."

The guy on the porch breathes in and brings his hand to his mouth almost like he's seen this vision, too.

"Oh my God," he whispers. "It's *you*."

SIX

There's a ringing sound in my ears. Obviously I didn't hear this correctly. Obviously. This guy doesn't know me, and I don't know him.

I stare at the guy, taking in just how different he is from the flash of Will I remember from the photo. This person's features are big: big eyes, long eyelashes, prominent nose. His fingers are long. His feet in their skater-style shoes look enormous. His jeans hang on him in a way that indicates he's probably one of those guys who can eat anything he wants and never gain weight.

And his *hair*. It's the hair of hair commercials, bouncing curls that seem to have a life of their own, lifting many inches off his forehead. I want to touch it.

And yet, all put together, he's not unattractive. In fact, I can't stop staring at him. His exuberant, baffled smile doesn't hurt, either.

And then he says it again. "You're here—again. I can't believe this."

I draw in a breath. This is impossible. The world doesn't work this way. Past lives aren't really a thing. And also, why is this guy—this guy I sought out—looking at me like he knows who I am? Even like he . . . adores me? This isn't Will. It can't be. And yet, in the same breath, I somehow feel like it is.

I step back, blinking hard. "I'm sorry. We . . . know each other?"

He laughs. "Of course we do." He shakes his head. "I'd never forget you. Ever."

My head swims. Just because I rushed down here, looking for something—I never thought I'd actually find it. *Careful what you wish for*, I think.

"Will?" I whisper experimentally.

Surprise flashes across his face, but then he smiles. "Will," he says in a faraway voice. "Yes. Right. Or Jake. Either one. And . . ." He narrows his eyes. "And you're . . ."

"Casey," I say.

He nods, but he looks unsatisfied. "But that's not what I called you. Not then."

I blink. I clear my throat, daring to ask, realizing how unlikely this all is . . . but also going with it. "Did you, um, call me Becky?"

His eyes light up. Before I know what's happening, he steps forward and touches my hand with those long, sinewy fingers. His touch isn't dangerous. It doesn't fill me with discomfort. His fingers feel right against my skin. *Really* right.

"Becky," he whispers. "I've been looking for you. I pretty much gave up. It's not like the universe makes it easy, you know?"

The universe? Is he talking about . . . fate? Past lives? I fight off the notion, snapping back to myself, pulling my fingers to my chest. I need to be Casey again. And not just Casey, but the rational Casey who is too smart for believing in this nonsense.

"When did we meet?" I ask. "I'm a little . . . spotty with the details."

His forehead wrinkles. "I saw you across that room. And I just knew. I know, I know, everyone always tells me I'm so dramatic and I should just cut it out and whatever, but like . . . I thought you did, too. You seemed so happy . . ."

I stare at him. And suddenly, a new image flickers in my mind.

> Your jeans are low-slung on your hips. There's a huge crowd tonight, and the air is humid with bodies. This is the first of these you've been through, and you kind of want to leave. This isn't your scene. You're one of those people who get filled up by a night home alone, not a night around complete strangers.

The room I'm seeing is both utterly familiar and utterly unfamiliar. I've never been there before. Just like I've never been to this beach town.

> A disco ball glitters overhead. Someone elbows you, and you jerk away. But then, it seems like the crowd parts. Someone is watching you from the bleachers. You stand up straighter, knowing him and not knowing

him. Tingles course down your arms. Before you know what's happening, he's starting toward you. Blond. Smiling. Shining.

You take in his rolling gait, his broad shoulders, his hesitant smile. He's nervous, but he's also determined.

"You're Becky, right?" he says. "I'm Will. I've been wanting to meet you since eighth grade."

"I've been wanting to meet you since eighth grade," I whisper. It almost comes out like a question. Like I don't quite believe it myself.

"What's that?" Jake asks.

I'm jolted back to the present. I feel sweaty and breathless like I've run laps around the block. My head is thrumming. And here is Jake, dark and not light, wiry and not muscled. In a rational brain, he is not Will. And yet I feel I know him.

Jake is still talking. "I feel terrible about how things ended. I didn't want it to be the end. I looked and looked for answers. Combed the earth for you, it felt like." He breathes out a laugh. "And here, on a random Tuesday, you wind up on my porch! Pretty amazing early Christmas present."

"What happened to me?" I whisper. But I don't mean me. I mean Becky. Trapped in that car. The water rising. The desperation. Could that be what he's talking about? He felt terrible about how Becky died?

Jake's lips part, but I can't hear his words. The memory of the accident washes over me again. A car is hitting the bridge. First,

I'm eleven, and it's my mom. Then, it's Becky's memory. The car sinks. Becky holds her breath, her lungs burning. My lungs are burning. I can't tell us apart.

"Hey." Jake's face registers alarm. He steps closer. "You okay?"

His voice sounds far away. Muddled. Black spots form in front of my eyes. This is all too much. These visions, this new person, even all the new downloads of Becky's life slotting into my brain. One person can't handle all of this. I feel my legs crumple. I vaguely hear Jake calling me, though the sound is muffled like I'm underwater.

Underwater. I'm in that sinking car again. Or no—*Becky's* in that car. Pulling at the door handle. Desperately trying to get free. Someone else is in the car, too, equally struggling, but when I try to turn Becky's head, it doesn't budge.

The water fills. Becky's legs—my legs—thrash. I can feel how desperately she wants to live. As the water covers her head, she opens her mouth to silently scream. Water flows in. Her heartbeat thuds in her throat. She knows she isn't going to make it. And as her vision starts to black out, mine does, too.

And then I feel nothing.

●●●

When I wake, I'm lying on a twin bed in a dark room. There's one window to my left. The blinds are half drawn, and there's moonlight shining through the slats. Several bookcases line an opposite wall, all of them stuffed with books. And there are movie posters everywhere: *The Usual Suspects*, *Grease*, *Moulin Rouge*. There's a TV, a DVD player, a tangle of stereo wires. Something angular lurks in the corner—an electric guitar on a stand. Next to it is a keyboard. Next to that is a set of drums. Someone could start a band in this room. Outside, a car hisses past, and I can hear the faint thump of bass from the radio.

I shoot up, adrenaline coursing through me. I have no idea where I am, but everything rushes back: The beach. The psychic. The visions. Becky. Will.

My legs are heavy, and for a moment, I worry they're bound to the bedposts. *I've been captured. By . . . by that guy! That one on the street!*

I screech. A chair scrapes, and someone leaps up. A light snaps on, and there he is again. *Will.* No. The other guy. Jake. He stands over me, his eyes wide.

"Hey," he says, breathless. "It's okay. You're safe. I'm here."

"Where am I?" I thrash my legs, thinking they'll be bound. They aren't. "Where have you taken me?"

"You're in my apartment. This is my room. I live above the building I was coming out of. The vet's office."

"What?" I can't stop hyperventilating. "W-Why am I in your bed?"

"Because you passed out. In the parking lot. Remember?"

I blink hard. The vision of the sinking car had come back. And then, everything had gone fuzzy. I don't remember anything after that.

"I carried you up," Jake explains. "But I promise, no funny business happened. I'm only in here to make sure you keep breathing. I didn't want to just leave you outside. Temperature's dropping."

"Oh." I press my hands to my face. My cheeks still feel cold. Maybe I haven't been lying here for very long.

Jake gestures around the room. "Place isn't much, especially not for a city girl, and I apologize for all the movie posters. They're kind of my thing, though. I was into some of them in high school, and it's hard to let go of the memories."

I squint. "H-How did you know I lived in the city?"

"You . . . told me." He smiles wryly. "Oh, and I also went through your wallet."

I shoot up, horrified, but he raises his hands in surrender. "Kidding! Sorry. Bad joke."

"I don't remember telling you I lived in the city," I mumble. I rifle through the words we'd said to each other before I passed out. Maybe I did?

He looks at me with concern. "You hit your head. I tried to catch you—but you fell so fast. I mean, look, I'm all for swooning and drama, and I've dreamed of a girl fainting the moment I come back into her life, but not like this." He chuckles at his own joke. "I was debating whether to take you to the emergency room, but to be honest, the ER out here is notoriously understaffed. We would have had to wait hours."

I touch my temple and feel a ripple of pain. It's scary how much it hurts. I think of my empty dorm room. All my exams. The textbooks waiting for me at the Wayfarer. I've wasted a whole day of studying with this nonsense. This is inappropriate. I shouldn't be in some stranger's bedroom in some random beach town.

I try to sit up. "I need to leave."

"I'm not sure you should." Jake shifts awkwardly. "You're probably better off staying put with your head and all. At least until tomorrow."

"I have a motel room. The Wayfarer. The Honeymoon Suite."

"Honeymoon Suite?" He looks disappointed.

"It's just me. I was studying. My things are there."

"What are you doing out here at all?" he asks. "I wanted to ask you that before you passed out."

"Studying," I explain again—didn't I just say that? "I need to get back to it."

Though, truthfully, I can't imagine studying at the moment. My brain feels like oatmeal. Experimentally, I touch my forehead again. What if I did permanent damage?

"Listen," Jake says. "Full disclosure? My mom looked in on you while you were sleeping. She's a vet, but she has some nurse training as well. She says you should just rest." He ducks his head sheepishly. "I share this place with her. Like I said, I'm doing a gap year. Working at the vet's office. Trying to save up for my big break."

Like I said? He told me this, too? How much of our conversation have I forgotten?

"You'll like my mom," Jake is saying. "I've told her all about you."

I shift my legs against the cool, silky sheets. What has he told her? Any explanation would likely sound unthinkable to anyone not going through this . . . this whatever it is. Past-life trauma? Visions of your dead self? I don't even know what to call it.

I'm filled with so many questions. I don't know what to believe. How can Jake be Will? How can I even know about Will—and how can he?

And yet there must be something to this. I was drawn straight to Jake, and he was drawn straight to me. He knew we'd met before. He seems to know me . . . and in a strange way, I feel like I know him, too.

"Listen," I say, sitting up slightly. "The last time we saw each other—what we were talking about it before I passed out . . ."

"Hold up." He raises his hand to cut me off. "We don't need to go there. It upset you so much this first time around . . ." He laughs nervously. "I'd rather you feel better. And then we can go through everything. Okay?"

He says it with such authority. And admittedly, I do feel confused—and exhausted. Taking a little while to rest doesn't sound like a bad plan. When was the last time I'd had a decent night's sleep?

"Okay," I say. "I guess I could rest a bit." My head is feeling dizzier by the second.

Jake seems relieved. "Do you need anything? Water? Food? I can put something on for you?" He glances at the TV across from me, and then at the bed. "I'll sleep on the couch. I mean, obviously. I'm a good guy, in case you've forgotten."

I know, I almost say. And even though I've tried to block it out, the newest image I've been given breezes through my head again. Will walking up to Becky at that dance, saying he had wanted to meet her since eighth grade. There was something comforting about his presence. No arrogance. No self-assured male bravado. He was a good guy. Safe.

"I think I'll just close my eyes," I tell him. "And . . . thank you. For this."

"Are you kidding? Thank *you*."

His gaze pauses on me a moment, his expression awed and maybe even lovestruck. But then he seems to snap himself out of it, perhaps realizing he doesn't want to scare me. Well—scare me more than I'm already scared.

"Holler if you need anything," Jake adds, stepping toward the door. He bites his lip shyly, almost like he's hoping I'm going to ask him to stay for a little while. And crazily enough, I almost do it.

But then Marcus snaps back into my mind. I have a boyfriend! A boyfriend who would probably not like this one bit. I consider texting him, getting ahead of the guilty feelings that are sure to come. But maybe that would invite more questions. I decide to tell Marcus about my fainting spell later. Or maybe never.

Fatigue weighs on me. I've never felt this tired. Reconciling with one's past life, I decide, wears a person out. My eyelids close fast, and my thoughts are skittering in all directions, not quite making sense. I pull Jake's blankets to my chin.

"Good night, Will," I murmur.

Jake gets that bemused smile again. "Right. *Will*. And good night . . . Becky."

I sink back into the pillow, thinking drifting half-thoughts about the bizarre day. This morning, I was in the city. Now I'm here, knowing—well, knowing a lot of strange stuff. There's a part of me that wants to return to the time when I was ignorantly bliss-ful, fearing only that the bizarre voices and images I'd heard and seen were trying to sabotage my relationship with Marcus. But there's also a part of me that's glad about what I know now. There's even a part of me that's glad I know about Becky, as unconceivable as it all is.

And there's a part of me that is curious about Jake, too.

Sleep seizes me, blurring my anxieties, even blotting out the visions. But then a thought wrenches me awake. A thought so startling—so obvious—that I sit up in bed and stare, wide-eyed, into the darkness.

Say I'm Becky. And because she's a past life, that means Becky had most certainly died—violently, it seems, in a car crash into the water. As illogical as it sounds, say Jake is somehow Will reincarnated. But if that's true, I've overlooked something obvious.

If Jake is Will, then that means Will is dead, too.

SEVEN

The following morning, I wake to my phone ringing. It jolts me from sleep, but I don't have the same disoriented sensation that had rocked me when I came to in Jake's bed the day before. I've probably woken up six times in the night already, each time taking in the movie posters and the collection of instruments with the same fresh terror. It's worn off. I know where I am. It still doesn't make it normal.

My head hurts, and I'm groggy, and I know I'm going to feel exhausted today, but at least I feel rooted in reality.

Sort of.

I look at the screen, worried it's Marcus. An unfamiliar 212 number greets me. No one I know has scored a 212 number. That's an old school, hard-won Manhattan area code practically from yesteryear.

When I hear a booming, authoritative voice on the other line, I nearly drop the phone from shock. "Is this Casey? Roland Coleman here. Marcus's father?"

I jolt up and pull my shirt around me as though Roland Coleman can see exactly where I am. Roland Coleman is calling me. *Roland Coleman.* A terrifying thought rushes in: What if he knows I'm in a strange guy's house? Maybe Roland is more protective of his son than Marcus lets on. Maybe he can just tell I'm bad news and he's looking for a way to prove it.

"Hi, Mr. Coleman," I say, trying to keep the quiver out of my voice.

"No need with the Mr. Coleman stuff," he says. "Call me Roland. Not when I hear you're coming to Turks and Caicos with us! Really looking forward to that."

I've nearly forgotten about the holiday invitation. It feels like it happened a million years ago. "Yeah. Me too."

"Anyway, I was calling to set up a meeting with my assistant for a possible internship position. If you're still interested."

My brain is whirring. Does Roland Coleman usually make personal calls to potential interns? "I'd love the opportunity," I add. "Thank you for thinking of me."

"Marcus has told me how bright you are. I don't know if he mentioned this, but I attended college at sixteen as well."

I shift on the mattress. Jake's mattress—I notice, for the first time, that his sheets are printed with images from Star Wars. I had the same sheets in my bed before I moved to the dorms. I used to love those movies.

"Can you stop by today, by any chance?" Roland Coleman says, which makes me feel terrible that I'm staring at another guy's bed sheets. "We could have a chat?"

"Today?" I stare out the window. Avon Shores is just as desolate and gray as it was yesterday. Even the town's holiday decorations are depressing: ratty tinsel wrapped around light posts, ancient-looking bells and stars attached to telephone poles. "Um, I'm not in the city at the moment."

"Oh? Where are you?"

"Avon"—I catch myself—"Jersey. Sorry, Avalon, New Jersey. Beach town. A friend's house." The words come out staccato. "Studying—I've got five exams. But they'll be over in a week. Then I'll be back."

"Got it. We'll talk in a week, then. We don't need to have a set time. Just drop in. You met Miranda, right? She can make the arrangements."

"That sounds great." I square my shoulders. "Thank you."

I press the red button to end the call and then hold my forehead like I'm afraid my brain is going to leak out of my skull. *Get a grip*, I tell myself. Talk about a wake-up call. I need to focus. I have to live my current life. School. Studying. Exams. Internships. Marcus. I've done what Becky asked—I've reconnected with Will in his current form. He's here. In someone else's body. Done.

I shut my eyes, figuring Becky's going to weigh in with some sort of comment or memory. No voices come. No visions. Nothing.

I open my eyes again and smile. Maybe it's over, then. Maybe I have done what she wants. I found Jake, who used to be Will. Maybe that's all Becky needed. To see him again. A version of him, anyway.

Relieved, I slide out of bed and tiptoe into the apartment's small hallway. I smell coffee brewing. Slinging my bag over my shoulder, I head toward what I think is the exit, passing through a curious curtain of beads hanging from the hallway ceiling. They rattle together, dripping across my shoulders. I pause on them, realizing that Jake probably had to pull me through these same beads last night to get me to his room. I have no memory of that.

Past the beads, I take in a living room filled with mismatched velvet furniture, a cabinet with tiny drawers that looks like it should belong in a library, and what I think is a genuine bearskin rug on the floor. A giant print of a single tarot card—the Hanged Man—is framed over the couch. A quick peek at the bookshelves: I see *Auras and You*, *The Runes*, and *Crystals and Other Elements*. On top of that library cabinet are a few tiny bottles of what look like tinctures and a ceramic mortar and pestle, along with about twenty differently shaped candles.

This is what Karin the psychic's office should look like.

"Hello?"

I spin around to see a slight woman in a caftan coming out of a small galley kitchen. She holds a silver coffee pot in one hand, and she has streaks of pink and blue in her hair.

"Becky, is it?" she asks.

I feel heat rise to my cheeks. "Casey, actually."

"Right, right, sorry." She extends her hand. It's adorned with silver rings. "Connie."

Another relief: I don't recognize Connie. I don't automatically know her, as I seem have an intrinsic knowledge so much else of this town. Her downturned eyes are warm and comforting.

She's around my height—just a little over five feet—and has the same wild, curly hair that Jake does.

"Want coffee?" Connie asks.

"Actually, I have to run. I have a lot of schoolwork. Thanks for letting me stay, though. Jake said you checked on me after I fainted—thanks for that." I remember she's a nurse. She doesn't *seem* like a nurse.

Connie looks chagrined. "Jake will be disappointed you're going. He's been looking for you for a while."

I run my tongue over my teeth. How did Jake explain any of this to his mom? But then I look around the room again. Connie seems like someone who'd very willingly accept the concept of past lives. She'd probably celebrate the fact that Jake had found someone from a life he'd once lived.

Did they sit around, chatting about it? Did Connie know about Becky, too? The thought makes me a little squirmy.

"Jake's on a supply run," Connie goes on, breaking me from my thoughts. "We're running low on rabies vaccines. A pharmacy inland has some extra, so he's gone to get them." She rolls her eyes. "We all know he'd rather be auditioning, but he made a promise to stick this out for a year and help with the clinic. Besides, he has a way with animals."

I nod, though I have no idea what she's talking about. Auditioning? Why does she assume I know anything about that?

We stand there awkwardly for a beat. Then I turn to the door. "I have so many tests coming up—I need to get to it. Tell him I'll be in touch?" I rip off a scrap of paper from a receipt in my bag and scribble my cell number. "Tell him to call me."

Connie nods. I thank her one more time and duck for the nearest door. Which turns out to be a coat closet. After Connie directs me, I find the real door, and then I'm outside.

I can smell the water. Gulls flap and cry overhead. The street is quiet, but it's not an eerie quiet. I'm surprised how comforted I feel, actually—almost like Avon Shores is more of a home to me than Brooklyn ever was, especially after my mom died. I glance at the doorway I just went through, feeling a guilty pang that I'm leaving Jake without saying goodbye.

There's a lot we could talk about, admittedly. And with my realization that Will has also died, I'm filled with more questions. I wonder what Jake knows about Will's life. From how nonchalantly he and his mom talked about it, it seems like it could be something he's known for a while—versus my situation, which I only found out yesterday. I envy him if he has more answers and clarity. As much as I don't want Becky to dominate my life, it would be nice to know who she was and what happened to her. Especially on that final day she was alive.

That sinking car. Her panic. Her regret. Does Jake know about that?

I pause on the sidewalk, conflicted. The way the island curves, I can see all the way to the other side from this vantage point—including the pier and big blue-gray house near the water. Just looking at it sends an uneasy sense of déjà vu through me. Is it possible the house still has the same owner? The early 2000s weren't that long ago. Maybe if I just walked over there, looked at a name on a mailbox, it could jog a magic keyword that would unlock a Google search that would explain what happened the day of Becky's accident.

The Wayfarer and my books are to the right. The big blue-gray mansion is to the left. My watch says it's not even ten a.m. I have the whole day—and tomorrow—to cram. Maybe I can clear this up in an hour or two.

Maybe I can put this all to rest.

●●●

Not surprisingly, I somehow know my way over to the other side of the island by instinct. I even know which little coffee shop will be open this time of year. I stop in, recognizing the older man behind the counter, knowing that his name will be Christopher before even glancing at his name tag. The strangest thing is that this isn't quite as alarming as it was yesterday. Funny how even the weirdest occurrence can become second nature.

Steam curls from the top of the coffee cup. My breath comes out in puffs in the cold air. Fifteen minutes into my walk, my phone buzzes again, and I fumble for it. This time, it is Marcus. This time, I answer.

"Are you okay?" He sounds on edge. "Where are you?"

I try to laugh. "You know where I am."

"Jersey?"

I feel a pang of guilt. "Same place."

"How'd you sleep?"

My skin prickles. Is that a loaded question? Could he know that I didn't sleep where I was supposed to?

But that's impossible. Of course Marcus doesn't know. And anyway, nothing even happened at Jake's house. All we did was look at each other. We barely even talked.

"Slept great," I chirp. "The wave sounds help."

When Marcus speaks again, there's a catch in his voice. "Do you mind coming back? I really want to see you. I really want to . . ." He breaks off, taking in a ragged breath.

I skirt around a woman pushing a baby carriage. I've never heard Marcus sound so needy. I try to picture him sitting in his apartment. He doesn't live in the dorms like an ordinary Columbia student—his father rented him the top floor of a beautiful brownstone. It's been recently renovated with gleaming hardwood floors and a roof deck. Most of the furniture in the place costs as much as a used car, and his king bed alone is the size of the dorm room Pippa and I share. Gray fabric padded hardboard, sleek lines, the sheets always crisp and white and a zillion thread count. Then I think of Jake's bed I just woke up in. Those endearing Star Wars sheets. Those flattened pillows.

I stop myself. What am I doing?

"I need to finish studying, and then I'll come back," I say briskly. "I need to stick to this, okay? This is just how I am."

"But why can't you study here?"

"Because. I'm sorry, Marcus. I'll be back soon, okay?"

Marcus sighs. "Casey . . ."

It sounds like he's going to start begging again. I cut him off. "I gotta go! Getting another call."

I hang up, then rub my eyes. *Way to sound innocent.* Could Marcus have detected I was lying? Maybe I should tell him the truth? Only, I wouldn't even know where to start. He wouldn't believe me about Becky. Reincarnation doesn't really seem like something the Coleman family would buy into, period.

I stop short and look up. Suddenly, I'm right in front of the blue-gray house. Another instance of my body knowing where to go even while my brain's elsewhere.

The house looms above me. It's set back from the road on a thick bed of grass and raised up on a majestic stone wall. There's a circular driveway out front with a flagpole in the center and a small gazebo off to the left. The house has blue-gray siding and bright white shutters, its black roof providing a sharp and attractive contrast. Off to both sides of the property are covered porch areas, and there's a front porch, too, with several heavy white rocking chairs and an abundance of potted plants. I stare at the rocking chair, and a flash comes to me.

You're sitting on that chair, trying to think, trying to breathe. Maybe you should call Will's house, you think. Maybe you should do it, just to see, just to try.

I blink hard. Was this from the same day? I remember that Becky *did* end up calling Will—on that new cell phone of hers. There was no answer.

I glance around, realizing something else. Did Will live near here, too? Or was Avon Shores familiar to Becky only because she—or the man she was going to marry—was from this place?

I turn back to the house. At this time of year, the trees and bushes are bare, but I swear I can detect the scent of wisteria in my nostrils. A flash rips through me:

Walking next to him as you walk up the front steps. "It smells amazing."

The voice is close, nearly tickling the hairs around my eardrums. As hard as I fight in the memory, I can't see whose hand Becky is holding. Not Will's, though. Someone else's. The guy this house belongs to?

I peer around for a mailbox. There isn't one. Even if there was the owner's name printed somewhere, who's to say it would be the same owner as before?

"Casey?"

I wheel around, startled. An old wood-paneled station wagon with rust around the wheel wells lurks at the curb. The driver's window cranks down a little farther, and Jake leans out, peering at me curiously.

I draw back in horror. "How did you know I'd be here?"

Jake smiles sheepishly. "I took the bridge that's closer to this side of the island. Just as I was getting off, my mom called. Said you left. Although she also said you went in the opposite direction of the Wayfarer." He shrugs. "Took a guess that I'd find you here. Coming back to the scene of the crime, huh?"

A frisson goes through me. Jake came looking for me. His mom was spying on where I went after I left her house. Jake knew to find me here. He said *the scene of the crime.*

The place where Becky was kidnapped, he means. Or maybe where she was going to get married.

Jake is staring. There's something so swoon-worthy about his deep-set eyes and earnest smile. I'm drawn to an . . . essence, maybe, a deep vibration I can't explain. Or maybe I can explain it. Maybe it's because of Becky.

"You were really going to leave without saying goodbye?" Jake sounds hurt. "I mean, I get it—you have to study. But I'd love to talk with you. As friends," he adds quickly. "If that's not too weird. I mean, maybe this is being presumptuous, but I have to think that there's a tiny part of you that chose to come to Avon Shores to study because of me?"

I think of the textbooks still in my backpack at the Wayfarer. I can't bomb my exams. Being good at school is my whole identity. And if I bomb my exams, Marcus Coleman would likely not offer me an internship. My whole life would implode.

I look at him helplessly. "I'm sorry. I have so much work to do."

Jake nods. "At least let me buy you an early lunch. There's this amazing spot near here. The owner is old and cranky and hates everyone and sometimes throws peanut shells at people's heads."

I twist my mouth. "You're really selling me on the place."

"Yeah, but he makes the best burgers on the Eastern Seaboard. And I'm including the city in that statement."

When I glance back at the blue-gray mansion, the floral smell no longer wafts in my nostrils. It's just a big-ass house, nothing more. I am in the present now, and in the present, I realize that I am weak with hunger. Besides those few nervous bites of pizza, I last ate—when?

I turn back to Jake's arm dangling casually out the window. Something about his long, sinewy fingers sends a warm feeling through me.

"Are we able to walk there?" I ask, feeling a ribbon of hope.

Jake grins. "Sure. Nice morning for it."

An hour with him can't hurt. And not so deeply inside me, I can feel Becky prodding, suddenly back again.

Saying, *Go.*

EIGHT

When we walk into Woody's, I'm not assaulted with the familiar, which makes me think that perhaps this is a place Becky never frequented. It's clear Woody's existed in the early 2000s—I take in the weathered plaque on the front door that reads "Established 1966." But perhaps this wasn't really Becky's or her fiancé's cup of tea. Whoever her fiancé was.

Because it certainly is a very specific flavor of tea in here. On the walls are old license plates, wrinkled fishing maps, and various crisscrossed wooden fishing poles, some of them with sharp, rusty hooks still attached. The floor is littered with peanut shells and sawdust, so much that it sticks to the soles of my shoes.

"They ever think of sweeping in here?" I murmur.

Jake eyes me. "You ever been to McSorley's in the city?"

I squint at that name. It's familiar, but I'm not sure why.

"It isn't far from NYU," Jake adds. "East Seventh Street, I think? Really old bar. They only serve two types of beer—light and dark. There's sawdust all over the floor there, too—pretty sure Woody took it as inspiration for this place. It's featured in this great book about Manhattan called—"

"Up in the Old Hotel!" I blurt.

Jake's smile stretches wider. "You've read it?"

No wonder the bar's name was familiar. The book is by the journalist Joseph Mitchell, and it chronicled interesting characters around the city in the 1940s and 1950s—including McSorley's. I loved books about New York City from that time period, but I'd never met anyone else who'd even heard of the book.

"I read those stories over and over when I was in high school. I feel like the city isn't like that anymore. It's so slick now. Everyone is the same." I cock my head. "How do you know about it? I've never met anyone else who's read that book."

Jake pauses to think. "Sometimes, when I'm at the library, there are certain books I'm just drawn to. I go with it. I've learned about a lot of strange subjects that way."

"I do the same thing," I murmur. "One of my favorite games when I was younger was going to the library and just randomly walking into a section and seeing what caught my eye. I never went for the books on the display shelves."

"Same!" Jake says.

We share a smile. There's that deep, magnetized pull again. Why had I picked up that book about McSorley's? Was it my choice, or had Becky guided me? Maybe she and Will used to read it together. Maybe they even went to the bar together, in the early 2000s, once they were old enough.

I clear my throat. Can I ask Jake about Will? I want to. No one else I've met shares this predicament. No one else understands.

But then I sense a presence behind us. A balding man with tufts of white hair above his ears and bushy white eyebrows glares at us through watery blue eyes.

"Woody!" Jake says cheerfully. "How are you, my man? Table for two?"

Woody grunts and points to a bistro-style table with two mismatched bar-height chairs. We head over and sit. The old man practically hurls menus at us.

"Thank you!" Jake sings. He points to me. "This is my friend. Casey." He quickly glances at me. "Or would you rather be called Becky?"

"Casey is great," I say, noticing that Woody doesn't seem to give a shit what I'm called. It's amazing we can get drink orders out of him. I say I'll just have water, but Jake orders a Dr Pepper. Woody grunts and points at a soda dispenser in the corner as if to say *Get it yourself.*

Jake cheerfully unfolds himself from the seat and lopes over, filling a paper cup with water and another with soda. As he brings them both back to the table, I watch as the Dr Pepper bubbles rise to the surface. Something about its distinct smell ignites another tiny fire in my brain.

> You sit across from each other, and Will orders a Dr Pepper. You watch as he slurps it down nervously and then orders another, drinking it just as fast. You giggle at how unsure he seems. You tell him he's going to have to pee a lot the rest of the night. The tips of his ears turn red.

"Have you always liked Dr Pepper?" I ask.

"Oh yeah. It's my kryptonite." He sucks more through the straw.

Because of Will? I wonder. I wonder if I drink what Becky drank, eat what Becky ate. Bacon sandwiches, despite otherwise being mostly a vegetarian? Those weird wrapped cakes at bodega checkout lines? Hot sauce on everything? Chocolate milk?

"So, you sleep okay?" Jake asks, puncturing my thoughts. He stirs the ice cubes in his drink.

"Uh-huh." I look at him coyly. "I like your bed sheets, by the way. I had the same ones when I was growing up."

"Oh shit." Jake grimaces. "I was hoping you didn't notice. I've had those sheets since I was, like, nine."

"Same." I clear my throat. "I watched all the movies."

"For sure. It was all so magical to me. I even liked Jar Jar Binks. I know everyone else hated that guy, but he really resonated with me."

"Me too!" I cry. Something hits me: The Star Wars movie with Jar Jar came out in the late nineties. I wonder if Becky saw it. Maybe she and Will watched it together.

Am I going to dwell on every cultural reference this way?

"And, um, I met your mom," I add. "She seemed nice."

"Right!" Jake's eyes light up, but then he grimaces. "I hope she didn't force her mushroom tea on you. It's god-awful."

I shake my head. "Luckily, no. She has an interesting decorating style. Does she know Karin, by any chance?"

"The psychic?" Jake looks taken aback. "How do you know her?"

"I . . ." I feel like it should be obvious. Isn't one of a psychic's jobs talking about past lives? But I just shrug, muttering something about seeing her sign on the storefront. "I didn't think Avon Shores was big enough for two psychics."

"Oh, my mom isn't psychic." Jake waves his hand. "She's a vet, remember? She's just fascinated with all that stuff on an amateur level."

"But she knows about us," I say carefully.

This seems to surprise Jake. His cheeks turn pink. "Well, yeah. I hope that's okay . . ."

Is it okay? I have no idea.

I clear my throat and look at Jake. "So about . . . us. The past—our past."

A worried expression crosses Jake's features. He stares into his drink. "Seriously. We don't have to talk about it."

"I won't pass out again. I promise."

Jake fiddles with a napkin. "The thing is, *I* might."

I sit back. "Really?"

On the TV, a man dressed in a Santa suit gets excited over an electronics sale. *Ho, ho, ho.*

"Look," Jake says. "I've had a lot of anxiety thinking about all of . . . that. It's been really hard for me, too."

My lips part. I nod, encouraging him on.

"I want to think about it, but . . . it's hard to look it in the eye, you know? My mom is so good at talking me through the anxiety. And this is the thing she always says—the past is the past. And now is now. It's better to live in the present than dwell on what happened—or what didn't happen."

I'm frowning . . . and nodding . . . and frowning again. I'm disappointed he doesn't want to go there—yet—but I also respect his feelings. Just because I want to know more about a past life doesn't mean I can just ask any old question I want. Jake is traumatized. It's possible Jake's seen more of Will's life than I've seen of Becky's. Even scarier stuff than what I've seen.

It's possible he's seen Will's death.

"Anyway." Jake turns the menu over. "Is that okay if we don't, like, rehash quite yet? If we just kind of stick to who we are now? I still want to know who you are, Casey. There's so much I have no idea about. So, like, maybe we can go forward—not back?"

"Sure," I say, nodding. I'm disappointed that he doesn't want to talk about what I find to be the most interesting trait we have in common . . . but I can live with it. Maybe, in time, I can earn his trust . . . and we *will* talk about it.

My thoughts screech to a halt. I'm thinking about Jake like I'm going to know him going forward. Like there will be more conversations after this. But, I mean, I can have a friend, can't I? Is that really so out of the question?

Woody returns, this time with an apron tied around his waist and a small notepad in his gnarled hands. Jake glances at me. "I recommend a burger. They're the best."

"Sounds great."

As Woody ambles back to the kitchen again—I wonder if he's a one-man show in there, as I haven't heard any other voices—Jake smiles at me. "So. Besides reading a ton and studying a ton, what else are you all about?"

I laugh. "How much detail do you want?"

He rubs his hands together greedily. "You can go as far back as elementary school if you want. As far back as birth."

I twist my mouth. "I thought you didn't want to talk about the past."

"I meant our past. Not yours." He leans on his elbows. "So. I bet you were the smartest in your grade."

"I was."

"Oh yeah?" he teases. "How smart?"

I tell him about being moved into higher reading and math levels as soon as I started school. How reading and math came so easily to me, and I felt confused when others struggled because it all seemed so simple.

"Always came easy to me, too," Jake said. "I think I was reading at four, maybe? Most kids I know didn't pick it up until they were nearly seven."

"You know why," I say. "It's because . . ."

But then I trail off. Jake doesn't want to talk about when he was Will. Will's knowledge might have seeped into him, and while that's unbelievably cool, I'd made a promise not to talk about it right now. I can't break that within the first five minutes.

Woody reappears with two plates. *That was fast*, I think, but the food looks fresh. Jake tries to thank the man, but he turns with a grumble back to the kitchen.

"You're going to love these," he says as he reaches for a shaker.

I crunch into my food. I try not to eat much red meat, but I have to admit, the burger is delicious. I grab a fry next, and it's perfectly crispy, perfectly salted. I can already feel my body gaining strength, thanking me for eating. This is the first time in a while that I've felt relaxed enough to eat. Ever since I started hearing the voice in my head, I've been so tightly wound, practically too afraid to breathe.

I tell him about how I wrote story after story as a little kid, yearning to be an author as early as third grade. Jake says he liked to draw at that age, and like me, he was the kid who stayed indoors, doodling, instead of playing sports with other kids. I admit that I don't draw much.

"The only thing I remember drawing was this cartoon of a pyramid in my journal, and it was related to writing. At the top were published authors. At the bottom was me, just floundering around." I pop another fry into my mouth, then duck my head. "Sorry, you don't want to hear about drawings I made in third grade."

"Who says?" Jake asks. "What third grader even knows the concept of a published author?"

My cheeks blaze. Have I ever told anyone about that silly cartoon before? I'm not sure I even showed it to my mother. She encouraged me every step of the way, even when I couldn't figure out how to move from chapter one to chapter two. "Just keep writing," she'd always say.

My chest feels tight with grief. I look up at Jake, trying to refocus. *Dwell on the present, not the past.*

"So what are you up to now?" I ask Jake. "You, um, work at the vet's office? And what else?"

"Uh, don't you remember me telling you?" Jake tilts his head. "Straight guy, Broadway dreams?"

How much did we chat about before I fainted, anyway? I shrug noncommittally, asking Jake to repeat the story. He explains that he likes drawing, but he loves theater. "Ever since I was a little kid, I've been performing," he says. "I love playing characters. I love telling stories. I feel more natural on a stage than I do in real life."

I nod. "I create versions of myself for different situations in real life."

"Same." Jake folds his hands. "It makes it easier, doesn't it?" But then he sits back. "So does that mean you're playing a part for me right now?"

"I mean . . ." I think for a moment. Am I? I don't really feel like I am, astonishingly. Not at all.

Then Jake tells me that he was in most of the plays through high school, many of them musicals. He rattles off a sampling of songs from some of the shows he performed— Henry Higgins in *My Fair Lady* and Curly McLain from *Oklahoma!* When he starts singing a new song from a more modern musical, I feel familiar tingles again. I know the words, but not because I've ever seen the play. When I close my eyes, I'm in Becky's body again, listening as someone sings them to her.

You look up at him and applaud. "Thank you, Will," you gush. "That is and will forever be my favorite song."

When I come back to myself, I feel flushed. And when I look at Jake, he appears even cuter than before. I look away quickly.

Jake explains that he'd love to go to school for theater—maybe even NYU. But he needs to save up some cash, which is why he took a year off.

"Working at the vet's with my mom isn't so bad," he says. "The locals love us. Of course, you get the snotty rich people from this side of the island who are kind of bitchy with their pets—but even they were okay." He crunches a fry. "In the summer, I also had a job working with a diving instructor. The rich people were real jerks. They think they're slumming it, using a local instructor instead of, say, learning to dive on their trip to Turks and Caicos."

I shift. *Turks and Caicos.* Is it a coincidence he chose the island Marcus's family goes to? But it must be, because he keeps going, seemingly unaware. "You would like scuba. It's so quiet down there. So beautiful. My mind is so clear. It's like I understand everything."

"That does sound nice," I admit. "Except I'd be afraid of the tank failing. Drowning."

"I get that," Jake says, meaningfulness creeping into his voice.

We lock eyes for a moment, and I feel another shiver. Does Jake know because he knows that Becky drowned? Flashes of that memory assault my brain once more. That sinking car. Pounding on the window, desperate to escape. The water filling, filling . . .

"And what about you?" Jake's voice pierces through the vision. "Second year of college, right? How's it going?"

I talk about the dorms and Pippa, my overwhelming course load, but also my need to support myself. My silly job at the pet store as well as my previous jobs before that. Jake laughs that, for a few weeks, I'd worked for Greenpeace, shouting at people on the street to get them to sign petitions. "You wouldn't believe how angry passersby get at the sight of someone handing out flyers about whales in trouble. They don't have to yell at me!"

"The summer after my junior year, I went door-to-door selling knives," Jake admits. "I had to contact all my mom's friends and then go over to their houses and give them this demonstration of how the knives could cut through a penny and slice a tomato."

"There's no way I could do that," I say.

"Me neither. I hate talking in front of people," Jake admits.

"Same!" I cry. "And I could never sell things. If someone doesn't want something, I'd just be like, okay, that's cool, not gonna push."

"And yet you worked for Greenpeace?" Jake crosses his arms.

"And yet you perform onstage?" I shoot back.

"Touché," Jake admits. "But the stage is different. On the stage, I can be someone else."

"My situations were different, too. Greenpeace was just shouting stuff. I didn't have to sell the message. At the pet store, too—people come in knowing what they want. Mostly, all I have to do is direct them to the aisle that sells stuff for fish tanks or dog food."

This gets us on the topic of pets, though it gives me another pang—when my mother was alive, we had pets in abundance, but after she passed, animals were too much for my father. Jake says it was the opposite in his family—when his dad was around, pets were off-limits, even though his parents were both vets. He got too attached, he said. It was just too emotional to have pets.

"Where's your dad now?" I ask.

Jake looks away. "Pancreatic cancer. I was ten. It sucked."

A hand flutters to my mouth. "Same with my mom. I mean—not cancer. A car crash. It, um, went over a guard rail. She didn't make it."

"Yeah," Jake says softly.

And again, I feel off-kilter. Is he saying *yeah* because I told him this before I passed out? Is he saying *yeah* because he somehow knows that I've lost someone, too? Or is *yeah* just something you say?

"What was she like?" Jake asks next.

I feel my eyes misting with tears. "It's hard to talk about."

He nods. "Got it. But you can, if you want to. You can talk about anything."

"Thanks," I whisper.

He looks at me carefully, shaking his head in wonder. "God, Casey. It's amazing you're . . . here. I still think you came back for me." Then he stops. "Or is that being presumptuous? For all I know, maybe you have a boyfriend."

I stare at the piles of shavings on the floor. They're almost too artful just to be curls of wood. They look like little sculptures. *Tell him yes*, my brain screams. *Of course you have a boyfriend.*

And yet my mouth doesn't move to form the words. With a snap, I'm not me anymore, I'm Becky, and we're back at that dance, sitting across from each other, Will sipping his Dr Pepper, the two of us enamored.

"Do you have a boyfriend? Because every guy in here is checking you out."

You blush. "No."

"Would you like a boyfriend?" Will's eyes sparkle playfully. A smile spreads across his lips.

Jake says something I haven't caught. I blink hard, asking him to repeat it. "I was just saying that we'd better get you to your books." He taps his watch. "You, my dear, have some studying to do."

I nod and stand from the chair. I'm shaky. Why didn't I take my chance to tell him about Marcus? What's wrong with me? I could still say something, though. Jake would find it odd, but there's still an opportunity to come clean. I don't lie about this stuff. That isn't fair to anyone.

And yet I can't do it. I say nothing as I sling my bag over my shoulder and stomp through the peanut shells and shavings. I say nothing as Jake holds the door for me to exit the restaurant. I say nothing as we joke about how Woody had only communicated in grunts.

"Ironically, Woody is a ladies' man," Jake says. "Mom's always seeing him out with different women at this bar nearby. Can you even imagine what his dating profile would be?"

"Grunt grunt, grunt grunt grunt," I joke. "Likes grunting and stomping around."

"Looking for someone who also likes grunting, peanut shavings, and a general sour disposition," Jake adds, chuckling. "And, oh my God, his profile picture?"

"It would be one giant frown!"

I still say nothing about Marcus as we walk back to to the blue-gray house, where Jake's car is parked. I say nothing as he pauses at the door, offering to drive me back but also seeming to understand when I balk about getting in. Instead of telling him about Marcus, I spit out an even more vulnerable truth: that I avoid riding in cars at all costs and have been pretty successful at it since the car accident.

"Wow," Jake says admiringly, slamming the car door shut again. "Years and years without riding in a car?"

"I've done it, on rare occasions. But if I can avoid it, I do."

"Well then, I'll walk you all the way," Jake says.

I say nothing about Marcus during our stroll through Avon Shores. We talk about other things—friends, movies we love, places we'd like to visit someday. After a while, the moral urge to confess dissipates. I rationalize that it would be weird to tell Jake about Marcus at this point. And what does it matter? We're two people who know each other on a different level. It's what it feels like, anyway. I've never had such easy conversation with a person before—not even Pippa. I feel like I could never run out of things to say. And when Jake's hand brushes against mine, sparks fly through me.

I don't pull away immediately. Part of me wants to pull him closer and not let go. I can feel the temptation creeping closer. It's an out-of-body experience, this person I'm being today, this other life I'm temporarily living. In fact, as we walk, I feel more and more like I'm someone else entirely. Becky, maybe. Whoever she is.

I wonder if Jake feels more like Will, too. And we've found each other, and we're settling in again, and this is the most right thing in the world.

When we reach the Wayfarer, the tip of Jake's nose has turned red, and he's shivering. "I hate that you have to walk all the way back to your car," I tell him.

He waves a hand. "Builds character."

Silence passes. We stare at each other again. I almost want to invite him in. Almost. But the rational part of my brain screams *Study!*

"Anyway," I say. "I guess I should get to it."

"I guess so."

Jake shifts. I stare at a crack in the pavement. When I peek at him again, he's looking at me intensely. He wants to kiss me. I can feel it. And the thing is, I want to kiss him, too. He steps closer. My heart starts to pound.

But at the last moment, I let out an embarrassed laugh and pivot toward the stairs that lead to the Honeymoon Suite.

"I have so many chapters to review," I say.

"Of course," Jake says quickly, stepping back. "Totally."

"But thank you for lunch."

Jake nods, looking at me hungrily. I turn away. If I look at him for another second, I'll dive into his arms.

"And you have my number," I mumble as I lurch away.

"Already texted you mine," Jake answers.

I take a few steps and glance over my shoulder. Jake raises a hand in goodbye. And then, one more piece of memory swims to me, though it's garbled and hard to understand.

> You're hurrying away. Will's face peers at you through the crowd. Call me, he begs. Please, please call me.
>
> And you nod. You nod as someone drags you out of the room, your feet stumbling under you, your whole body aching to stay here, with him, with Will.

I snap back, wondering who was pulling Becky from him. The boyfriend? This mystery guy she was supposed to marry? Regardless, the boyfriend wasn't the one Becky wanted. Not really.

Seems like Becky and I have way more in common than I realize.

NINE

I flip to the final chapter of the material for my art history exam. I've reviewed nearly two hundred pages of text, and my brain feels like mush. But I have at least another hour of studying to do.

I feel more in control. Calmer. I've set up a schedule for myself: tomorrow morning, advanced calc. Tomorrow afternoon, Shakespeare. The other two exams are other writing courses where I've already read the novels several times before, so I'm pretty sure I have a handle on any random question the professor might ask.

I've got this.

My phone buzzes. I grab for it, wondering if it's Pippa. Shortly after I got back to the Wayfarer, I called her with an update. I owed her that, as the last time we spoke was the day before. The squeals on Pippa's end—after she chewed me out for not checking in sooner—numbered in the hundreds.

"Oh my God, Casey, he sounds adorable," she gushed. "You really think he's Becky's Will?"

"I mean . . ." It sounds so strange to say out loud. Do I? Then again, how else does any of this make sense?

"You're not going to try to talk me out of this?" I asked Pippa. "You're not going to try to tell me that what I'm doing is wrong because of Marcus?"

"Casey, if I'm going to be honest, I've never heard you this . . . alive. Sure, Marcus is, like, Mr. Eligible, but that isn't the end-all, be-all. You sound like how I did when I was with James."

Her love from high school. I try to humor her. "Really? You can tell?"

"Totally. So? What are you going to do?"

It terrified me to make any rash decisions. I didn't answer.

"Follow your heart," Pippa said after the silence. And then there was a *click* on her end. "Huh. I gotta take this. Some number I don't recognize."

So now, as my phone rings again, I figure it's Pippa calling me back. Instead, it's a text. From Marcus.

Hear there's an ice storm coming for Jersey. You okay?

I glance out the window. The sky is gray, but there's no precipitation, nor has my check on the weather app alerted me to any in the future. Where I am on Long Island isn't that far from my made-up seaside home in Avalon, Jersey, but today, the coastal weather systems don't match.

What else can I do? I write back to Marcus to say that yes, there's some ice, but I'm staying indoors, and I should be fine. Marcus responds:

Sounds good. Miss you.

My fingers hover over the keyboard. I know I should write back that I miss him, too. I know I should write back *something*. But whenever I picture Marcus's face, I see Jake's instead.

I squeeze my eyes shut. I barely know Jake. So, okay, he was ridiculously easy to talk to and totally endearing. We seem to have similar interests and contexts. And it was adorable that when I said I had a perpetual fear of riding in cars because of my mother's accident, he'd just rolled with it like it was totally normal.

And I did want to kiss him before he left. Badly.

I wonder what he's doing right now. I picture his Star Wars sheets, still in a jumble from when I'd slept in them. I smile as I hear his confident voice singing those lines from *Les Mis*. I giggle at the notion of his mother brewing disgusting mushroom tea to go with their dinner.

Another buzz from my phone. Marcus:

Case? You there?

Marcus's previous text, the *Miss you*, has gone unanswered. I grit my teeth.

I need to stop thinking about Jake.

Sorry, yeah.

I write back.

Miss you too.

A few hours later, I've made my way through reviewing the rest of the artists I'm supposed to know for the exam and even skimmed through *Twelfth Night* and the notes about themes. I allow myself a few minutes to zone out on the couch. It's strange being by myself. I'm not sure if I've ever been so alone for so many days. The motel is so silent, too. I might venture a guess that I'm the only person staying at the Wayfarer.

I rise, the silence suddenly bothersome. I need some air. I wonder if Becky didn't like being alone, either. That moment of her standing on the porch flashes back to me: she was alone then. She'd seemed desperate to escape those people inside, people whose identities I still don't know. I can practically feel her hair blowing against my face from the wind as she stepped out onto that porch. That's when she'd looked at the picture. Will's picture. But then she'd stubbornly put him out of her mind.

> You shrug your shoulders, tuck the photo back in your purse, and turn to go inside. It's time. Time to grow up. Time to let go. Time to forget your past and your winsome, blue-flame-hot, first love. True, pure, timeless love, like what you had—it isn't realistic. This new path? It's a good one. A safe one. It will set you up for life.

But who was the person she planned to marry? I have no idea.

I'm about to open the front door when my fingers freeze. If I twist my neck just so, I have a partial view of the outside through the

SARA SHEPARD

big windows that look out onto the beach—the small landing, the railing with the tinsel, part of the concrete stairs. Something is there. I can tell because a shadow is there that shouldn't be. I draw back, confused and uncertain.

Is it something? Or someone?

My skin prickles. I check the door to make sure it's locked. It is. I peek out the blinds again. Is someone on the stairs? House-keeping, maybe? Does housekeeping usually come at night?

And yet they aren't moving. They face the landing. These stairs lead to the Honeymoon Suite alone—nowhere else. Perhaps someone has stopped here at random? Maybe they meant to go up one of the other staircases? I'd noticed two more leading to other suites on the side of the building that doesn't face the ocean. If I open my door, perhaps they'll move along?

But something is telling me not to open the door. I draw my hand away from the knob. This doesn't seem right.

I move back to the couch, feeling like a trapped animal. I pick up the room's phone and dial 0 for the front desk, but it just rings and rings. Is anyone on this property at night? That can't be safe.

I try again—still nothing. Should I try another room? The police? And say . . . what? *Hello, someone is lurking outside my motel room?* It's not a crime to stand on a flight of stairs.

The memory pounds at me.

As you reach for the knob, you sense someone coming up from the wooden walkway. You freeze just as a hand slithers around your waist. You're pulled backward, your feet lifting off the ground, your lungs suddenly crushed flat. You try to scream, but a hand presses over your mouth.

"You've been a bad girl," a voice says in your ear.

I swallow hard. Becky knew a split second before it happened that someone was coming for her. This feels familiar in terrible ways. I try to tell myself it isn't—there's no reason someone would be after me—but the fear from the past is mixing with the strangeness in the present. I tiptoe to the door once more and peer out the blinds.

The shadow is gone.

Quietly, I open the door a crack. Silence. Emptiness. No bodies lurking. No sounds of footsteps heading down the stairs. The night is eerily still—no barking dogs, no swish of cars, even the tide is quiet.

Did I imagine it?

I shut the door and twist the lock. The fear is palpable— a squirmy feeling in the pit of my stomach. Someone was outside my door. And now they're not. And I don't want to be alone.

I reach for my phone, wondering who to call. The logical choices would be Marcus, or maybe Pippa. Except the city seems so far away—at least an hour's drive. They aren't who I want, anyway.

I'm weak with relief that I thought to key his number into my phone. He answers quickly, almost like he knew I'd be calling.

"Five minutes," Jake says, after I explain what's going on. "Wait for me at your door."

I stare hard into the empty parking lot. A circle of light from the streetlamp illuminates the sidewalk. No one is there.

It takes Jake three minutes, not five—as if he was literally waiting by the door, keys in hand, hoping I'd call. My heart hammers as I hear tires squeal in the parking lot. Then I hear footsteps on the stairs. I open the door wide this time, and it's him. He stops and looks at me. His mouth wobbles. Then he takes the rest of the stairs, walking right up to me until we are almost touching. Our exhalations make white puffs in the air.

"Are you okay?" he breathes.

I nod. And then gulp. "Yeah."

His mouth twitches again. His eyes search mine. And then, by some unseen force—by Becky—I give him the slightest of encouraging nods.

He takes me into his arms. When our lips touch, it's warm and soft and sends thrills down my spine. I press myself farther into him, wanting to be as close as possible. And though no flashes of Becky and Will doing this exact same thing appear, it doesn't matter—I know they have. And to be honest, I want to experience it all my own. I want to kiss and kiss Jake until the end of time.

I let go.

TEN

An hour later, Jake and I are lying on top of the covers, staring into each other's eyes. It's been a while since either of us has spoken, and yet, I don't feel awkward. I also don't feel strange that I'm only in my bra and jeans or that Jake is shirtless. I'm the type of girl who doesn't move very fast with these types of things. I'm modest—not for any body-shame sort of reasons, more because it's how I'm wired. But I feel free with my skin showing. Comfortable.

My lips are sore from kissing. My body thrums from the excitement. Jake and I have kissed a hundred times if not more, and each one has felt exactly right. And yet. I curl my hands against my chest. I'm turned on my side on the pillow, looking at Jake. The lights are off, but the streetlamp creates a faint glow in the room, illuminating our faces.

"This isn't like me," I say.

"I know," Jake answers quickly. He blinks worriedly. "Do . . . do you want me to leave?"

"No!" I say it forcefully. "I just mean . . . this isn't something I normally do. I wanted you to know that."

"You think it's something *I* normally do?" Jake laughs. "I haven't had a girlfriend since Caitlin Hodges in eleventh grade. Did I mention Caitlin? I swear I did."

"You haven't mentioned Caitlin, no."

Jake shifts on the pillow. "It wasn't a particularly memorable relationship. But I had to get to know Caitlin for years before I put the moves on her. You, Casey? You just . . . do something to me."

"Well." I clear my throat. "We sort of have known each other for years."

A wrinkle forms on Jake's brow. "How do you fig—"

A creak stops him midsentence. We look at each other. It sounds like it was coming from the walkway outside.

Slowly, Jake rises from the bed and peers out the window. "I don't see anything," he says. "Wait, are you actually afraid of being alone? Here I thought it was just a ruse to get me to come over."

"It was and it wasn't. I really did think I saw something. It freaked me out."

"Just call me your knight in shining armor." Jake settles back onto the bed and traces the edge of my shoulder with his fingertip. I dare to hold eye contact. A swoop of passion rushes through me.

I want to kiss him again, but before I do, I add, "I don't feel like this is real. And I don't quite feel like myself."

"Whoever you are, I'm here for it." Jake looks at me carefully, an eyebrow raised. Moonlight dapples against his cheek. "So do you feel more like . . . Becky, then?"

The sound of her name from his lips sends tingles through me. "Kind of."

Jake edges closer so that our bodies are almost touching. His breath is hot and sweet on my cheek. "You can be Becky with me. I won't stand in your way."

I press my lips to his. But it isn't me kissing him—not entirely. It's her, too. Becky, kissing Will. I feel tendrils of her personality creep into my own. She was . . . sweet, I think. Hopeful. But also spunky. Up for anything.

I see flashes of her and Will laughing. Becky throwing a water balloon at Will's head and hooting with laughter. Becky dancing on a wooden boardwalk to an old Destiny's Child song—something I'm way too inhibited to do. Becky was charming and effervescent and fun, qualities I know I sometimes lack. I'm always Careful Casey, endlessly stumbling over what to say, Second-Guessing Casey, never sure if she's good enough.

I close my eyes, letting Becky's essence cover over me like a second skin. If she's in me, if she's always been with me, then maybe it's okay to be more like her. I want to whoop. I want to do that stupid Destiny's Child dance.

But mostly, I want to kiss Jake, and so I do. I kiss and kiss and kiss him, and we fall asleep, wrapped in each other's arms. I know, in my heart, that when we wake, we'll start to untangle our past in a more meaningful way. How we knew each other. What happened to us. Why our past selves haven't left. And how amazing it is that we found each other again. I will convince Jake to open up, and I'll get over my fears, too, and the world will split open, ripe and bountiful and brimming with promise.

And I can't wait.

● ● ●

The next time my eyes snap open, I'm disoriented. It's deeply dark in the room. Middle-of-the-night dark. The blinds are closed. There are goose bumps on my skin—I'm still topless except for my bra, and I fell asleep on top of the covers.

Next to me, Jake snores on his back, one arm thrown over his face. I wonder if he's told his mom where he'll be tonight. I wonder what woke me up.

I get my answer: a creak, somewhere close. I sit up. There it is again: another creak, but this time maybe not coming from the window. It's coming from somewhere else.

"Jake?" I whisper.

One of his feet splays to the side, and he lets out another adorable snore.

I slip off the bed and pad to the door. The light in the main room is off. I try to get a sense of my surroundings. Straight ahead of me are the windows that face the beach. To the right is the kitchenette. To my left is the couch where I'd been studying. Beyond that down a small hall is the front door that leads to the stairs. The sound of the waves can be heard through the floor-to-ceiling windows, muffling all other sounds. How could I have heard a creak over that racket? Maybe it is all in my head?

My vision adjusts, trying to make sense of the shadows. Everything is a varying shade of dark, dark gray. I take a step, the tip of my foot hitting something soft. *The couch.* I whirl around, peering for the bedroom door, wishing I'd brought my phone with its lighted screen. Actually, I have no idea where I'd left my phone last. Did I bring it down the hall with me when I went to let Jake in? Do I remember anything after meeting Jake . . . besides kissing Jake?

Creak.

My ears perk up. I stare in the general direction of the front door. The noises from the outside are louder than normal. The kind of loud you'd experience when a door was wide open.

Did I leave the door open?

I fumble to my right and left, trying to find the wall and then a light switch, but I only swipe air. Gritting my teeth, I take another step forward, my arms outstretched like a zombie. Jake and I were so involved in each other, so blinded by what we were doing . . . maybe the door has been standing open for hours.

Creak. Then comes another sound. A little puff of air. Like breathing.

I freeze. The waves pound. Is someone in the Honeymoon Suite? I think of the sounds I'd heard before Jake arrived. The sense someone was lurking. Only, who knows I'm here? Pippa. That's it.

Maybe it's someone else who has a room at the Wayfarer. Someone accidentally stumbling into this unit instead of their own. Only, I think of the empty parking lot. It doesn't seem likely.

"Hello?" I whisper.

No answer. But I swear I can sense a presence. Someone has gone very still. I glance over my shoulder, praying for Jake to wake up. He's read my mind in so many other instances—maybe he will now, too.

But nothing moves from the bedroom. I hear another snore.

I pivot back around and peer down the hallway. Do I dare venture closer? What if someone is waiting? What if I bump straight into them and . . . and they hurt me?

"Hello?" I make my voice steady. Reaching out, my fingers touch stucco, and I lunge forward, grabbing onto a wall. My hand hits the edge of a picture frame, and I draw back too late. I've bumped it hard enough that the frame crashes to the floor, glass shattering anywhere. Now I run the risk of stepping on glass in bare feet in the darkness.

But maybe I can use that to my advantage. I kneel down, carefully feeling for glass pieces beneath me. My fingers close on a large shard.

"Don't come any closer," I warn. "Or I'll hurt you."

To my horror, there's another puff of breath. And as I blink, some of the shadows rearrange into something that makes sense. A figure, lurking near the door, just as I suspected. My heart starts to pound.

"Who's there? What do you want? I'll hurt you, you know. Stay away."

The figure is in constant motion. There's a rummaging sound like they're looking for something in a bag. My hand curls around the piece of glass, but then I think of something disheartening. What if they have something more powerful? A knife, a gun? And all I've got is this sharp little triangle of glass.

I wheel around to the shape near the door. "Just please—go away!"

The rummaging continues. And then, a beam of light pierces through the darkness. I shield my eyes, but not before I see the figure backlit before me. The person is in a dark hoodie. They shine what I now realize is a phone flashlight along the wall, beaming it straight on me. I shriek, feeling trapped.

"Go away!" I scream. "Go the fuck away!"

"Casey," a calm voice says. "Calm down."

I blink. Jake? But no. It's a woman's voice.

"Casey," the voice repeats. "It's okay."

A light snaps on. Before me is the ruined picture frame and a zillion pieces of broken glass. For a moment, all I see is the blood running from my palm, dripping to the carpet. I think the intruder has done it, somehow, but then I realize it's from the piece of glass I'm holding.

My gaze lifts to the intruder. The person now stands at the light switch, staring at me with palms lifted and a guilty—but not that guilty—look on her face. I know her. But I don't understand.

"F-Fran?" I whisper.

My stepmother swallows awkwardly. "It's going to be okay. Just come with us."

"Us?" I whisper.

And that's when I realize the second figure huddled by the door, arms wrapped tightly around his chest. He lifts his gaze to mine and says, in a small voice, "The door was open, Casey. And she's right. You need to come."

Marcus.

ELEVEN

I shift my gaze between the two of them. Their eyes look hollow, their mouths ghostly gashes. They're dressed in heavy puffer coats, Fran's much dowdier and cheaper than Marcus's. Marcus wears the trendy vinyl snow boots we bought together at the sporting goods store on Lexington Avenue. A keychain flashes in his palm—he brought his Acura, a car that's mostly kept in an expensive underground garage in the city.

"W-What are you doing here? How do you even know each other?" I explode.

"Casey, it's okay," Fran says. "We're just here to help. We just need you to stay calm."

"Help?" I take another step from them. "You scared the shit out of me!" Then I realize something. "Was that you lurking on my stairs?" I check their hands for weapons. All at once, I wonder if those old warnings in my head about Marcus were true. Not Becky's voice at all. Maybe my intuition.

Fran shakes her head. "We came as fast as we could, as soon as we knew." She glances at Marcus. "We were so worried."

"Worried?" Because I'm cheating on Marcus? What does that have to do with Fran?

Then I hear the door open. "Casey?" Jake calls sleepily. "What are you . . ."

He comes to a stop. Even in the darkness, I can see Fran's mouth grow pinched and Marcus's jaw tighten. Intuitively, I know that Jake is still in his boxers. Looking down, I realize that up top, I'm still in my pink bra—and only my pink bra. I hurriedly cover myself.

"This is who I've been telling you about, Marcus," Fran growls. "This is exactly what I thought would happen."

"Whoa, whoa." Jake raises his hands, his gaze on Fran. "What's going on here?"

"You stay away from her, man," Marcus warns.

Jake squints at him. "Sorry, what do you know about Casey?"

"I'm her boyfriend," Marcus insists. "And you're taking advantage of her."

Jake turns to me, his eyes wide with surprise. I feel exposed— and it's not just the bra thing. *Boyfriend.* I can tell it's swirling in his head.

I turn back to Fran and Marcus. "Why are you spying on me? What right do either of you have to be here? W-Who told you where I was?"

"Not in Jersey, that's for sure," Marcus says quietly.

I feel a pinch of guilt. "Sorry. But that doesn't explain—"

"Your roommate told me," Fran interrupts. "She didn't want to, but we had an understanding. I said it was for the best.

And then Marcus reached out, too. Also concerned. We came together."

My mouth drops open. "Pippa sent you here? You had an . . . *understanding*?"

"Once I realized you were going to be roommates, I asked Pippa to get in touch with me if you ever left the city unexpectedly."

I stare at her. "Why the hell does it matter where I go? I thought you were happy to be rid of me."

Fran's throat bobs. "Casey. You've done this before. *Exactly* this. Same town. Same motel. Same everything."

I shake my head. This makes no sense. "I've never been to Avon Shores."

"Yes, you have," Fran says. "Except last time, you stayed in one of the rooms downstairs. That's the only difference."

"That's impossible!"

Fran glances at Marcus. "Now do you see what I mean?"

Marcus bites his bottom lip. His gaze dances between Jake and me. No one says a freaking word. Not even Jake, who, I suddenly notice, hasn't asked who Fran is. It's almost like he knows her.

"What the hell is going on?" I explode. "Why are you all acting like . . ." I realize I don't even have the words to explain how they're acting. I turn to Jake. "Tell her! I've never been to Avon Shores before! Why are you just standing there?"

Jake's mouth opens, but no sound comes out. He narrows his eyes, and then makes a strange noise at the back of his throat.

"But Casey. I mean, of course you've been to Avon Shores. This summer? When we first met?" He laughs uncertainly. Pushes his hand through his hair. "How did you think I knew you, otherwise?"

I feel like I've dropped through the floor. My brain literally stalls for a beat, unable to process this. "Wait. What?"

Jake shifts nervously. "I saw you across the room. You saw me. You came right over. I thought . . . I thought it was . . ."

"Love at first sight?" Fran asks wearily.

I'm spiraling down a hole. No. *No.* That's Becky's memory, not mine. I call up the vision: that bustling room, that retro music, and spying Will across the room. Our eyes meeting. Him coming over.

Except suddenly, the face isn't Will's. In my mind, his blond hair shifts to dark, curly locks. He grows several inches. Even his walk is bouncier, less athletic.

It's Jake's face now.

More memories twist and morph. It's Jake singing *Les Mis* to me, not Will singing to Becky. It's Jake sipping Dr Pepper, not Will. It's Jake and me kissing feverishly—and only Jake and me.

I clutch the sides of my head. When I turn to Jake, he's stricken. "Why didn't you say something?" I demand.

"You should have," Fran snaps. "Casey never remembers."

"Huh?" I whip my head back to her.

Jake says, at the same time, "I'm sorry. But, I mean, if you didn't think we met then, when did you think we met?"

I swallow hard. The answer should be obvious. I thought we were on the same wavelength. But now, saying we were kindred spirits in a past life sounds ludicrous.

"But why would I forget that?" I whisper.

"Because," Fran says. She sounds weary . . . but maybe not exasperated. "You were Becky."

The name ripples like it's a living thing. My mind goes still. I notice a muscle in Jake's cheek twitch. He looks like he wants to run from the room.

"H-How do you know about Becky?" I ask Fran.

Fran looks at Jake. "I warned you."

"That's what you were trying to warn me about?" Jake squeaks. "I mean, you just sort of came in . . . and took her . . ."

"And said to stay away from her," Fran adds. "That it's complicated. That she doesn't know who she is."

Jake blinks. "But I didn't . . . I thought you were just being . . ."

"A bitch?" Fran sighs. "Irrational? That I was trying to keep Casey from having a life?"

"What about Becky?" I screech. "How do you know Becky?"

Fran reaches for me. "Casey. Becky is *you.*"

"I-I know," I stammer. "But how do *you* know?" I click through my memory. Had I called Fran in the past two days and not realized? Had she bugged this motel room?

Fran shakes her head vehemently. "It always happens like this—the few times I've seen it, anyway. Becky starts as a voice in your head. Or sometimes it's a memory. Did it happen that way again? Did you have memories of things that were disorienting? It didn't feel like your life?"

My gaze flits to Marcus. I run my fingers down my face to make sure it's still there. I think of the strange visions that came to me at the party. "I mean, yes, but . . ."

"Then," Fran interrupts loudly, "you move on to more substantial memories. You think you need to act. You go looking for things. Answers. You display irrational, out-of-character behavior. Like, for example, coming to a certain beach town." She glances behind me at Jake, and then her eyes lower. "Seems we're at that stage at the moment."

My mouth is dry.

"And then," Fran continues, "You forget who you are, Casey. You become her completely. You turn into Becky. You think she is you."

"No." I shake my head. "I . . . I know she's not me. I do."

"You've been doing it all your life." It's like Fran doesn't hear me. "I thought home was a trigger—still living with all the memories of your mother, the trauma of it . . . it's why I encouraged you to move to the dorms. Getting away—I thought it would help. Again."

I scoff. "You made me move to the dorms because of that flu I had. Because you thought I was reckless and would infect Dad."

Fran frowns. "You didn't have a flu. You had an episode. As Becky." A variety of emotions cross her features, but her voice isn't accusatory. "You came to this town, searching for a memory you were sure was real. It took us forever to find you. Thank God I realized we could track you on your phone."

There are confused tears in my eyes. "But I didn't come to Avon Shores this summer." Except then I look at Jake. He just said I did. "Why don't I remember?"

"I just told you." Fran's voice is tender now, which knocks me even more off-kilter. "You never remember what you do when you're acting as Becky."

"I'm not acting as Becky," I insist. "I have no idea where you're getting that from—how you even know about her. Becky is—"

"An alternate personality," Fran interrupts. "A young woman you've created when you feel overwhelmed, or scared, or guilty. A girl who's carefree and romantic, always in search of her long-lost love, Will."

"Excuse me?" I shriek. I can't breathe. "No. Becky was a person. Not a . . . a figment." I glance at Jake. "She lived before I did. I'm her, but I'm also not her! I thought you understood."

Jake's lips part. He looks cornered . . . and definitely not like he understands.

Fran is wrong. They're all wrong. Becky lived, and now she's gone, but she lives on in me. How else do I know everything about Avon Shores? How did I know where to walk, people's names, all of it?

Except then it hits me. Do I know about Avon Shores because I came to Avon Shores this summer? A trip I do . . . and don't . . . remember?

I blink hard. I stare at my still-bleeding palm. I start to shake.

"It's called dissociative personality disorder," Fran says quietly. "People develop it, sometimes, after they've experienced trauma—they disassociate themselves, form another person inside them called an alter to escape into. Your doctor suggested you developed your Becky alter after the accident, but it's actually not true. You were Becky long before that."

"I don't have a doctor!" Except when I close my eyes, a flash comes. *A balding man in a sterile office. The sun streaming in, hot against the side of my face. My head pounding with exhaustion.*

"Becky only seems to resurface when you're going through difficult stuff," Fran goes on. "For a while, she didn't show up at all—it's unclear why she's started to poke through again. Your therapy worked for a long, long time. Marcus and I were talking about it on the drive here—it's probably your course load, a job, living in the city, all of it."

"The promise of an internship," Marcus says. "Dating me. It's too much."

"My life isn't too much," I say weakly. "I can handle it. I'm fine." I point to my books stacked on the side table. "I-I was studying. Getting ready. I'm good."

Fran looks heartbroken. "But you're hearing voices again, aren't you? And you're having visions?" I look away. "And you've reached out to the same person from before. You're having the same memories." Then she frowns at Jake. "You should go now. Please."

"Oh." Jake shifts awkwardly. "Um . . . I mean, I'd rather—"

"Please," Fran says abruptly. "This is a family matter."

I can feel Jake looking my way, but I'm too humiliated to meet his gaze. Finally, he disappears into the bedroom. A moment later, he returns, now wearing his T-shirt, coat, and shoes.

His head is down as he walks to the door. As he passes Marcus, I notice how much taller Jake is. Still, Marcus puffs out his chest. He seems more substantial, somehow.

"Little bit predatory, dude," Marcus says under his breath.

Jake stops and looks back at me. "Casey, I didn't think I was being . . ." he starts, but then slaps his hands to his sides. "I'm sorry. I . . . I didn't know. I didn't put it together. Really."

My eyes blur with tears. There are so many things I want to ask him, but I don't have the words. The memories of meeting Jake swim in the same brackish waters as the memories I thought were Becky's. I still can't figure out if they're the same memories or different ones. I go back to the vision of seeing Will across the room of that crowded party—but now it's Jake's face. Jake's eyes. Jake's hair.

The memory keeps going. I rolled up to him, interrupting a conversation he was having with other people. *"It's me," I said, taking him by surprise.*

"Hi, me." Jake smiled flirtatiously. Achingly flirtatiously. "Does me have a name? Or are you just me?"

"It's Becky."

Now, I go limp. Did I really introduce myself as Becky? Is that all this is?

I stare around the Honeymoon Suite. My books are scattered across the coffee table. The air smells of watermelon hand soap. How clear-eyed I've been since Jake and I kissed hours before. Jake felt like my person. I was edging toward embracing that. And, okay, it sucks that Marcus . . . discovered us, but he was bound to figure it out at some point.

What if I'd been moving toward this same conclusion last time, too? What if, I don't know, I just have a sense Jake and I are meant to be, and that's why I keep coming here? Even if Becky doesn't really exist, it doesn't mean I haven't found my person.

"What's so wrong with having someone else's voice inside me?" I dare to ask Fran. "Especially if she's leading me to happiness?"

Marcus sighs. He sounds hurt. I don't mean to hurt him. But I have to be honest.

"Casey," Fran says softly. "Remaining as Becky too long . . . it's led to some terrible consequences." She swallows. "She takes a dark turn. She makes you reckless. Once, it was even grabbing the wheel of a car."

I scoff. "I don't know how to drive!"

"You weren't the driver."

I stare at her. She looks wrecked. Then I burst out laughing. "What are you talking about?"

She glances over her shoulder then. "Actually, there's someone who might be able to explain." She whispers something to Marcus. It almost sounds like *get him*.

Marcus nods and disappears out of the suite. I stare at Fran. "Where's he going?"

Fran doesn't answer.

Soon, there are slow footsteps on the landing. When a gray, stooped man steps through the door—tightly clutching Marcus's arm—I almost don't recognize him as my father.

My mouth drops open. "Are you well enough to be here?"

"I'm okay," Dad says, though his voice is ragged and thin, far fainter than it used to be. His eyes are sunken. His skin has double the wrinkles. He's wearing pajamas and walks with stiff legs, and he looks like he's ninety years old.

When he gazes at me, his smile is sad. "Marcus has told me a little of what's been going on."

"Is this true?" I whisper. "Everything they're saying—is it true?"

He lets out a deep sigh. "Yes, honey. Becky's been with you a lot of your life. Your mother and I thought she was an imaginary friend. She wasn't harmful, until . . ."

He trails off, looking pained. "Until what?" I ask.

My father shakes his head and glances at Fran. She shrugs.

He takes a breath. "There was an eyewitness at the scene of the car accident. The one with you and your mother. And someone says they saw you . . . lean forward, to the front seat. Grab the steering wheel from her. Turn it . . . toward the bridge."

I stiffen, slowly understanding. "I wouldn't do that," I whisper.

He raise his palms. "Then, when I came to you in the hospital, you were talking as Becky. She wasn't just next to you anymore; she *was* you. And you kept saying . . . *she* kept saying . . . that she had to do it. She had to turn the wheel."

My heart bangs. I try to swallow, but bile rises in my throat. "No. I don't remember any of this. Why didn't you tell me?"

He stares at the floor. "I didn't want you to know."

"You didn't want me to know that you think I caused my mother's death?" I clutch the sides of my head. Is this possible? "There's no way I would have done that! And who was this eyewitness? How do we not know they're lying?"

My father looks at me sadly. "Why would someone lie?"

Tears stream down my face. "But I loved her. And . . . and what?" I swallow down a sob. "You're saying Becky killed her? You're saying, what, Becky is . . . evil?" I glance at Marcus, who's still standing there, staring at all of us with pity. I hate that he's witnessing this.

"Something was clearly wrong," Fran says quietly.

I whip around to her. "You weren't there."

"Casey," my father warns. "I've told Fran about it many times. She's helped with you, through the years. We thought, we hoped, this might fade away. Like I said, we hadn't heard from Becky for a long time. But it's clear you're not healed, still."

I squeeze my eyes shut. I still can't believe it. Images from that last day with my mom flash into my mind. Her playing that aria over the car stereo. The reflection of her in the rearview mirror as she smiled. I can't fathom lurching forward and wrenching the wheel.

But there's so much I don't remember from then—the moment of the crash, the days after it, all of my time in the hospital. Could I have become Becky, somehow? Like maybe her life twisted up in mine? Could someone have seen me through the window doing the unthinkable? But why?

How well do I really know myself? Could I do something like that?

Fran breathes in raggedly. "Let us get you help. Please."

I shake my head, not wanting to believe any of this. The panic is rising. My heart is beating hard in my chest. But then, my arms fall to my sides. I can feel the struggle seeping out of me. *You don't know yourself. Maybe you're a danger.*

"Okay," I say. Because I don't know what else to say. And I let them take my hands and lead me out of the suite. Away from the beach. Away from my life.

PART TWO

TWELVE

"Checkmate," I say, moving my pawn one square up the board.

My opponent, Charlie, groans. "Tell me again. You really never played chess until you came here?"

"Never interested me."

"You could've been the captain of your school's team."

Charlie rubs his temples, his chestnut hair falling over his forehead. Despite being pale, despite the circles under his eyes, and despite the fact that he's usually wearing the same Columbia hoodie and plaid pajama pants, Charlie is attractive and really smart. He's been a good friend to me since I've come to Chadwick Pond.

"Another game?" Charlie asks.

I shake my head. "I think I need to get my thoughts together before my session."

"Gotcha," Charlie says.

His gaze wanders around the room, searching for someone else he can play with. Charlie's the first person who will tell you that chess is one of the few things that calms him down. He has an agitated mind, and though he's trying to work through it, he knows his limitations.

I guess we all do here.

It's a new disguise I'm wearing: the disguise of the patient of Chadwick Pond, a residency program for teens and young adults struggling with mental illnesses or behavioral issues. Or maybe it's not a disguise at all. It's what I'm realizing—all those disguises I wore before, all those different versions of myself, alters maybe, coping mechanisms.

And this Casey, it's just me. Stripped down. Vulnerable.

A little sad. Actually, a lot sad.

I'm not sad that I'm getting help. I mean, okay, at first I was angry. Really angry. I didn't want to give up my life. I had exams—and I'd studied so hard. I had my job at Pet Planet. I had Pippa—though, admittedly, I was furious with her.

But then, *poof*, none of that mattered. I was excused from school. A moving company was hired to pack up my things from my dorm. Excuses were made to my boss at the pet store. The world just . . . stopped.

For the first week, I was still sure everyone was lying. It just didn't seem possible. Not that I had a mental illness—I staunchly believe that mental illness is no different than childhood leukemia, or diabetes, or a brain tumor. It's something we can't control. Even if my mother hadn't been in that car accident, I likely still might be this way, as my father says Becky has been around since I was very young. I'm not a bad person for retreating into safe corners in my mind and even making things up to comfort myself.

But I couldn't believe that my mental illness is *this*. Becky. She seemed so . . . separate from me. Nor did I want to think that Becky made me do irrational things, even dangerous things. Take trips I don't remember. Wrench a steering wheel, sending my mom's car into incoming traffic.

Killing my mother.

It destroyed me. I didn't want to believe my mind had tricked me so viciously. It astonishes me that my brain just wiped out the moments where I'd stepped into Becky's shoes, where my personality shifted into her personality, where we bled into each other. And I questioned why. Why is this happening to me, of all people? Why do I have to be struggling? And why would Becky want to hurt the person I loved the most in the world?

My therapist, John, decided to try hypnosis sessions to see if he could draw Becky out. Session after session, though, nothing happened. I was put into a relaxed state, I said some stuff, and then I came back to full consciousness with John smiling a thin, disappointed smile.

Except one day, all that changed.

John recorded all my sessions, and we both reviewed them when they were over. This time, he was excited for me to see what had happened. On the screen, I watched as John gave me some instructions and my head bobbed into my neck, deeply relaxed. John gave some more guided meditation prompts. He wanted me to go deep within myself, see who I really was. He said I should welcome all parts of myself . . . and that he'd welcome those parts, too.

Then he paused the video and pointed at the screen. "See how your features relax? There."

I leaned in. Sure enough, my jaw had slackened. The Casey on the screen opened her eyes again, and her smile was no longer a grimace. Even when I spoke, my voice was a little more high-pitched. I was someone else.

"Hi," the someone else said.

"Who am I talking to?" the John in the video asked.

The girl on the screen smiled. "Becky." Her voice was floaty, calm.

I pressed my hand to my mouth.

"How are you doing, Becky?" John asked cheerfully.

Becky smiled brightly. "Good, I guess." She looked around, annoyed. "But where's Will?"

I bit down hard on my bottom lip until I drew blood.

"Who's Will, Becky?" John asked in the video.

Becky smiled sweetly. "My true love. Seriously, where is he? He *was* here. We were together. I'd like to see him again."

"Maybe we could talk about the accident instead?"

Becky's eyes widened. "Why do you want to talk about that?"

"Because it's important. Do you remember the accident with Casey's mom. Near the canal? In the car? You know Casey, right? And her mom? You want to tell me why you did it?"

Becky became agitated. "No. *That's* not the accident."

"Yes, it is. Stay with me. The Gowanus Canal. Can you explain what was going through your mind? It's okay. No one is mad. We just want to help. We want to understand."

Becky shook her head. "I wasn't in *that* car," she kept saying. "You've got it wrong. That's not my accident." But she couldn't explain. She retreated shortly after that. And then it was over.

John turned the video off and looked at me. "So. Who's Will?"

I lowered my eyes. "It doesn't matter. Apparently he's not real, either."

John held up a hand. "Even so. Will represents something. Something that you, as Becky, need very badly." He shifted in his chair. "Are you sure you don't want to talk about any neglect you'd felt as a child? Trauma?"

"The only trauma I endured was my mother dying," I said through gritted teeth. "Before that, my childhood was great."

"Do you remember Will in your early iterations of Becky? When she was more of an imaginary friend, a character in your stories?"

I shrugged. "The Becky in my stories never had a friend named Will."

"So when did Will come into the picture, then?"

"Just recently, I think." I waved my hands. "A few months ago? When I was at the beach the first time, maybe? But it's not like I remember that trip, so I can't say for sure."

John rubbed his beard. "Perhaps Will is your security blanket. He represents love. Stability."

"Why would I fabricate this whole marriage plot between Becky and someone else, then?" I asked. "In the story I created in my head, Becky doesn't even get engaged to Will. So I made up this whole scene before her wedding; she's marrying someone else. So, what, I'm sabotaging my subconscious, too?"

"Who's this other person she's marrying?"

I slapped the couch cushions. "Someone else who doesn't exist, I assume!"

"That person must represent something, too. Tell me more about this wedding story you've created."

I walked him through the visions. "The last thing I see"—I catch myself—"*imagine*, is someone's grabbing her from behind. Attacking Becky."

"Ah. Maybe *you're* attacking her."

"No." I sat up straighter. "I'm the one *being* attacked."

John regarded me. "There are two of you, though. There's you, Casey, and your alter, Becky. Remember, those who have dissociative personality disorder are never aware of their alter personalities—Becky is aware of you, but not the other way around. That explains why you have gaps in memory."

I frowned. "But I *am* aware of who Becky is. As myself. I've seen her memories. They feel like hers, not mine."

John smiled sadly. "Do you know anything about her, though? Or do you just think you do?"

I felt so turned around. Becky seemed like a distinct person from me, with her own life and tragedy. But it was true: I barely knew anything about her. And it was hard to know whether those were her details or my own, spun differently in my muddled head.

"Perhaps subconsciously you understand that Becky isn't real," John went on. "And you understand that she's holding you back—and even more, that she's dangerous. You want to be whole. Safe. Now do you see how it could be you grabbing her from behind in that memory? You're playing both parts?"

I blinked. *Was* I the one doing the grabbing? That's who I've been scared of this whole time—myself? I think of the voice from the dream: *You've been a bad girl.* So I'd been warning the part of myself that was Becky? I felt like I'd broken my brain.

I felt so weak. So defeated. So confused. Becky was within me. A fabrication, nothing more. I just needed to accept it.

John and I also tried immersion therapy to get me over my fear of riding in a car. We took John's car and went for simple outings, only a mile or so away. The first time, I shook in the back seat. I couldn't regulate my body temperature. Strange visions kept flashing in my mind. It got so bad that John had to pull over so he could talk to me.

"What are you seeing?" he prompted. "Is it the accident?"

"Yes," I whispered.

"Tell me."

But I couldn't. I wasn't seeing the accident I'd experienced with my mother. I was seeing that other car going over another bridge—with me still inside. I saw the car filling with water. I felt someone squeezing my hand as we sank. I was *in* that car. Or Becky was.

Or neither of us was.

The memory is a delusion—that was what John explained. A twisted version of the real accident I'd endured with my mom, a version where I put myself in the car with her, a version where I made both of us drown. "You're seeing it because you feel guilty," he said gently. "You wanted to die with her that day. You still blame yourself."

"I guess," I said, sobbing. "I guess that's right."

The mind is so powerful, I've learned. It's amazing what a bunch of neurons between your ears can convince you to believe.

●●●

As Charlie packs up the chessboard, I look out the big picture window in the game room. There's a sparkly layer of ice on the trees. A blanket of snow coats the ground, but even so, a few of the residents are traipsing around outside in boots. We're in the middle of the woods on Long Island, miles from tall buildings or subways or heavy traffic—or, for that matter, Avon Shores. Sometimes, we see a fox cut across the snowy fields. Sometimes, deer.

I can't really complain about the facilities. The food is decent and healthy, far better than the NYU dining hall, cooked by a bearded chef who rarely speaks. There's a library here, full of the kinds of books I love to read. I've gotten to write—a lot—and for once it has nothing to do with the courses I'm taking in college. Everything about the facility screams *money*, though, and that makes me uneasy.

After Fran and Marcus ambushed me at the Wayfarer, I was taken to the ER and held in a psych room. The hospital couldn't keep me—I wasn't suicidal—but in the interim, Marcus lingered in the doorway, looking spooked. Even his father showed up. That was the straw that broke the camel's back. It was beyond embarrassing to have Roland Coleman, a person I respected and wanted to impress, knowing about whatever weird mental break I was experiencing.

And even worse, Roland was so kind.

"I've talked to your family, Casey," Roland said in my little ER nook. "We'll get everything sorted out. This is nothing to be ashamed of."

They'd given me some kind of drug in the ER because I was combative; soon enough, it zonked me out. When I woke, I was told I was being taken to Chadwick Pond. Fran was with me, but not my father. Marcus had left, too. When we pulled up, I figured we were at the wrong place. The facility was like a palace: columns, a creamy white façade, rolling hills. It looked like some sort of country retreat and not a mental facility.

I turned to Fran accusingly. "Are the Colemans paying for this?"

She wouldn't meet my gaze. "Would that be so terrible?"

"I don't want them paying."

"Why?"

"Because . . ."

And then I realized. I didn't want to owe them anything. I didn't want to be with Marcus, period. And it wasn't just because he ambushed me in Avon Shores—and humiliated me. Though that didn't help matters.

It was because I didn't love him. I loved . . .

But no. *No.* I wouldn't think about who I loved instead. It hurt too badly. I was too heartbroken.

Fran made no motion to steer me away from the beautiful hospital. That filled me with guilt, too: if I didn't want the Colemans to pay, then she and my father would be footing the bill—and I doubted it was cheap. I felt guilty putting my needs over my dad's treatments. So I made a deal with myself: I would remain coupled with Marcus, but only until I left this place. It wasn't a good feeling, but I felt stuck.

Marcus has only visited me twice. Both times, I've felt like the world's worst actor, pretending we were still together. Christmas came and went. I made Marcus go on his family's trip to Turks and Caicos because, horrifyingly, he offered to not go and to stay here instead, and I couldn't bear the idea of that. It's where he is now. Where his father is, too. Maybe these hospital fees are a drop in the bucket for them, but I keep imagining an invisible tally climbing, climbing, climbing with every passing second, just like that ever-increasing national debt billboard on Sixth Avenue in the city. *I don't love you, Marcus. I don't want to be with you.* The moment I got out, I'll have to say all those things. It scares the heck out of me. It fills me with shuddering shame.

I head back to my room and shut the door. I'm in a single, just like Fran wanted for me at college. Patients aren't granted complete privacy—the doors have small windows for the nurses to see in, and we aren't allowed anything in the room that might hurt us, which means we can't even have pencils or shoelaces—though I don't really care.

I sit down, the mattress springs squeaking. Then I notice a few envelopes on my bedside table. I've gotten mail.

I reach for them. The first is a postcard from Pippa; it's a picture of the Carolina shoreline. It's taken a while for it to arrive—winter break is over. Pippa went to South Carolina for a few weeks in December, but I'm pretty sure she came back to NYU in time to celebrate New Year's. She's one of those people who go to Times Square to see the ball drop.

I get a pull in my chest, thinking about the city, college, my old life. I haven't had the strength to ask anyone if Pippa will get a new roommate, or what classes she's taking, or if someone is working my shifts at Pet Planet.

I place the card message side down on my mattress without reading it. I shouldn't be upset with Pippa. It isn't her fault I'm here. She visited me once, the very first week I came, and begged for my forgiveness.

"I didn't know the extent of what was going on," she pleaded. "And I'm sorry I didn't tell you about Fran reaching out. I just thought you were anxious, and that she was worried about you. Or maybe because you were younger? But she kept me in the dark."

I'd stared at her stonily. I knew I was being obstinate, but I couldn't bring myself to say that I forgave her. I was also so embarrassed. All those calls I'd made to Pippa recounting my visions of the past life, my florid description of the visit with the psychic, my tales of the fleeting romance with Jake. Pippa had believed me—or at least she said she did. I have no reason to think she was humoring me, laughing behind my back—but somehow, that makes it even worse. I can't help but feel a little bit ashamed. I know I shouldn't. I know Pippa doesn't think less of me. I know she just wants me to get better.

But it's also that I'm not used to being pitied. I'm the prodigy. The girl who's good at everything. The young woman who's dating Manhattan's most eligible guy. Now, I'm just someone everyone quietly feels sorry for.

The second piece of mail is in a heavy, cream-colored envelope, my name printed neatly on the front. As I slice it open, I wonder if it's from Marcus. I feel a pull of dread. Now that I've realized that I don't love him, I want a clean break.

My finger slices the cream-colored envelope. I pull out a folded piece of paper. It's a letter from my father. I stare at his shaky handwriting, made weak from his illness. *Just want to let you know, Fran and I are going up to Boston for a little while. I'm going into a treatment program there. Some experimental stuff. We are thinking of you. There's a lot I want to say to you, Casey. A lot I hope I can say to you, soon.*

The letter tells of the dates they'll be gone, what hospital the study is through, and where they're staying in the Boston area. They're leaving today, actually. *Good riddance*, I think miserably.

Because I'm mad at my father, too. Maybe most of all. I'm angry that he kept all of this from me. I'm also angry he believes it. Like I'd really hurt my mother? Like I'd really transform into Becky, Dr. Jekyll and Mr. Hyde style, and go on a rampage?

Apparently, it's exactly what he thinks, because as Fran was checking me into this place, she looked at me with intensity and said, "Casey. This place is a privilege—and not because it's pretty. You're voluntarily checking in here. And that's because we want to trust you. But if things go wrong, we'll make arrangements to send you elsewhere. Do you understand?"

If things go wrong. Then she made herself even more specific. If I morphed into Becky once more. If I went, once again, to find Will. If I did any of those things, Fran warned me, my stay would no longer be voluntary, and it certainly wouldn't be in a nice place like this.

Folding up my father's letter, I stuff it back into the envelope and shove it into the little drawer on the bedside table. There's a soft knock at the door. Maria, one of the nurses, pokes her head in, her brow furrowed with concern.

"There's someone here to see you," she whispers.

I sit up warily. "Who?" My father and Fran are in Boston. Pippa knows not to come. *Marcus?*

Maria moves a little closer, the fabric of her scrubs swishing. "It's a young man. Someone named Beau."

THIRTEEN

Beau. Why do I know that name? Something flickers at the edges, then fades.

The nurse leans forward, sensing my hesitation. "I can tell him to leave, if you want . . ."

Beau. It's needling at me. On the tip of my tongue. Why do I know someone named Beau? Has my brain shut him out? Is this someone obvious? Maybe this is my brain playing another trick on me.

All at once, I need to know who it is. "It's okay. I'll see him."

We head to the day room together. Today, it's empty save for one person sitting at the farthest table from the door. Whoever it is, this Beau guy, has his head down, a hoodie pulled tight. But as he looks up, something inside me turns to ice and wants to bolt. I instantly recognize those eyes, those soft lips, that jutting chin.

Jake.

I dig in my heels. I can't see Jake. I can't. Fran told me, in no uncertain terms, that if she caught me with Jake again, she and my father would involuntarily commit me somewhere. This place is restrictive enough. There's no way I'm going to risk it to be sent somewhere else, somewhere worse.

And yet, I've been thinking about Jake—way too much, against my better judgment. I can't stop thinking about how over-joyed he'd looked when we saw each other again outside his apartment . . . and then outside the big blue estate . . . and then when he came to see me at the Wayfarer. The expressions weren't predatory. They weren't conniving.

But he must be conniving. *I need to stay away from him.*

Maria must detect something off about my body language. She places a hand on my shoulder. "Are you okay, Casey?"

"Uh . . ." My feet stay planted. I don't know what to do.

Jake offers a weak, scared smile. I look down at myself, realizing that I'm wearing a T-shirt with holes in it and hospital-issued scrub pants. I showered this morning, but my hair is frizzy, and there's a pimple on my chin, and I'm wearing my glasses instead of contacts. Of course, I have no idea why any of this matters.

"Casey?" Maria's voice sounds far away.

"Sorry," I finally say. "It's fine."

Maybe I should just get this over with. Actually, maybe it'll be good to give Jake a piece of my mind. It's not like I have to tell Fran. She's all the way in Boston. Distracted, for once.

I keep my eyes down because I'm so scattered that I'm afraid I'll forget how to walk. Maria lays an arm on my shoulder as if to say, *it's not too late to change your mind*. But I don't give any indication, and after a moment, she says she'll be back to check on me in a little while.

And then Jake and I are alone.

"Hey," Jake says, breaking the silence. "Casey. Wow."

"Hi, *Beau*. Where'd you come up with that name?"

"Sorry." Jake sighs. "I didn't . . . it just popped into my head. I wasn't sure you'd see me, otherwise. But please stay. I just want to talk."

The day room is chilly; I wish I'd brought a sweater. I'm frustrated when my body involuntarily shudders. Jake notices. He whips off his hoodie and offers it to me.

I push it away. "No thanks."

"Take it. Seriously. It's cold as balls in here. Do they have heat in this place?"

"I don't want your shirt," I say through clenched teeth, turning toward the window. "I don't want anything from you."

He pulls the hoodie back, balling it up at his waist. I get a whiff of the fabric. It smells like Jake: surf wax, flowery detergent, and dogs. It almost knocks me senseless.

Swallowing hard, I slump into a chair. Jake bunches the hoodie on the table. It's like a centerpiece between us.

"Casey, I'm so sorry," he explodes.

I angle my body away as if to say, *I don't care.*

"I know you didn't want to see me. Though I wanted to see you sooner. The moment you left. But for a while, I had no idea where you were."

"How'd you find out?"

"Your roommate. Pippa."

"Pippa told you?" How many ways was Pippa going to betray me? Also, I can't believe she didn't give me advance warning this was happening. I think about the postcard I didn't read. Maybe she had.

Jake swallows hard. "I found her at NYU. We talked for a while. Pippa didn't know anything about what was going on with you, Casey. Just like I didn't. I swear."

I stare at the scratches on the table's surface. Someone has etched in a tic-tac-toe game. The X's won.

"I also told her about how magical the time was that we spent together. She told me about your phone calls to her when you first got to Avon Shores. About the visions . . . about Becky . . . about finding me. About Will—and how happy you were."

I'm more confounded by the second. Is Pippa reveling in my pain? Is this just a game to her? Some irresistible gossip?

"It's all bullshit," I explode. "And you knew it, and so does Pippa."

"Casey, I didn't know," Jake pleads. "How could I have known you thought we were in love in a past life! Why would I lead you on like that?"

I glare at him. "So you're cool with random girls coming up to you and asking you to call them by different names? Is that normal for you?" I wish I could remember how he'd reacted the first time I asked him to call me Becky. But aside from the few flashes of memory that had flitted in and out, I had nothing.

Jake looks chagrined. "The first time we met, you didn't say anything about past lives. You just said you wanted me to call you Becky, and you wanted to call me Will. I just went with it. I thought you just wanted to go by another name. I'm in theater,

172

Casey. Theater kids get a kick out of role-playing. We do it all the time."

I bark out a laugh. "That's your excuse? You're in theater?"

He folds his hands awkwardly. "No, you're right, I should have questioned it more. Absolutely. It's just . . . it's not like I get a lot of girls coming up to me, *period*. You swept me off my feet. That first time we met, in that big blue house? It was the best night of my life."

I frown. "What big blue house?"

"The huge one at the other side of the island. The one you were looking at when I found you in the car."

"We were in that house? Together?"

"It's a party space. There was a public event that night. Great view of the water . . ." He trails off, looking uneasy. "I figured that's why you were looking at it this time around. Like . . . reliving stuff. Reliving us."

I close my eyes. Well, that clears up that mystery. I know that house because it's where Jake and I met in the summer. Not the site of some sort of wedding gone wrong in a past life.

I breathe out a hot puff of air. "Why didn't you just tell me that we'd met before?"

"I tried. I really did. But then you fainted, and then I worried it was all too much. I was referring to it, though—I said I felt terrible how we left things. I meant your stepmom pulling you away. How I was never able to get in touch with you."

I close my eyes. I'd thought Jake meant how Becky and Will left things. Before she died.

How embarrassing.

"What . . . happened, that first time?" I ask carefully. "With you and me? I only have pieces."

Jake ducks his head. "You came into the room. I saw you immediately. I went over, and you seemed happy about that. And then we talked. Really connected. Had a great time. I was like, *who is this person?* You just seemed to . . . know me. And the weird thing was, I seemed to know you, too. Same as the second time around. We just clicked."

I stare stonily at the flecks of mica in the table. I don't want to think about us clicking.

"But then your stepmother showed up. Dragged you out. She didn't say anything about dissociative personality disorder. I didn't even know who she was, really. She just rushed in and said you had to go before you did something else stupid. She warned me to stay away from you."

"Something else stupid," I mutter bitterly. "Meaning . . . hijack a car? Steer it into the water?"

Jake's eyes widen. "Why would you say that?"

I wave my hand. I'd forgotten—he hadn't been present when my dad basically told me I'd caused my mother's death. "Forget it. No reason."

"No, really. The water. Is that a real memory?"

"I don't want to talk about it."

Jake sits back. I turn away. Out the window, some of the residents are walking into the woods with hiking poles. One of the therapists, Marjorie, does group sessions deep in the trees.

"So everything you told me, recently," I say after a while, "how you were sad about how we left things, how you'd been looking for me for a long time—it was all based on that one night in the summer?"

"Yep."

"And you didn't want to talk about our past . . . because that night upset you? Seriously?"

"Well, I didn't want to talk about it because I really was afraid you'd get upset, too. But also . . . I'm sensitive. I haven't dated a lot. And when I met you, it was the highest high. I was crushed when you left, and even more crushed when I couldn't find you." He searches my face. "But what did you think I was upset about, if not the way your stepmother dragged you out?"

I wave my hand. "Again, it doesn't matter."

"No, really. I want to know, Casey. That's why I'm here. Past lives, right? You think you lived another life before this one? Is it a memory from then?"

"Why are you so interested?" I glance at him for a second. "Because I'm a freak? Bet you've never met anyone as messed up as me? Because I had this dumb idea that you were in my past life, too?"

"I mean, yeah. I just was wondering—"

"It's not real," I say through clenched teeth. "Everything I thought I knew—it doesn't matter. That's why I'm here. I'm undoing all that. I'm understanding that I only have one life. I haven't lived another one. Those memories aren't hers poking through."

The corners of Jake's eyes turn down. He licks his lips. "Look, I should have questioned the Becky thing. I should have thought twice about you fainting. I just . . . I don't know, I would have never guessed it was something having to do with past lives."

I groan. It's like he's not hearing me. "It doesn't have to do with past lives. Becky isn't real. Apparently, I made her up."

"Are you sure?"

My head shoots up. "Of course I'm sure!"

He drums the tabletop nervously. "I said I felt like I knew you instantly. And if I'm being honest, it didn't feel like it was based on just that one day in the summer. The moment you walked into that house, it was like . . . I'd known you forever."

I bite down hard on the inside of my cheek. I can't even look at him.

"And I would never have made this connection, but sometimes I wonder . . ." He takes a breath. Shifts his weight. "When I was a little kid, we would go on walks around Avon Shores. And I'd point out storefronts and be like, 'wait, a toy store is supposed to be there.' Or, 'why is the record store gone'? My parents had no idea what I meant. But then they talked to people who'd lived in Avon Shores all their lives. Turns out, I was talking about shops that did exist. Just . . . years before I was born."

I stare at him in horror. He is not doing what I think he's doing.

"And sometimes I have these . . . flashes. Like, knowing how to drive a truck, which was impossible—I was only five or six. And I knew a few words of Spanish, and believe me, I hadn't picked it up from *Sesame Street*."

Oh my God. He is going there. Does he think this is funny?

"And I have these flashes of New York City, but older New York City. Like—the Twin Towers still standing, that sort of thing. And I also have flashes of something awful happening. A terrible, dark death."

I press my hand over my eyes. "Stop. Please."

"And my mom—I mean, you've met her. She's into all of that stuff. She used to tell me, all the time, that maybe this was some sort of reincarnation thing."

"Stop!" I screech again. "You think this is helpful? Making up some sort of bogus experience to, what, *bond* with me? You really think that's going to make me like you—or forgive you?"

Jake's eyes are wide and apologetic. "I'm not making it up. Weird things happened to me as a kid. I felt like there was some-one else . . . talking to me, sometimes. My mom, being my mom, encouraged me to explore that. She was like, *If you feel there's someone else, there probably is.*"

I shut my eyes. "I need you to leave now. I can't deal with this anymore."

Jake sits back, crosses his arms. "I wouldn't have bought any of this either, actually—I mean, this . . . presence, it was always at the back of my mind, and I didn't know what it meant. But when I met you, and then when I heard your story . . ." He trails off. "It sort of put things in perspective. Why I felt I knew you. Why you felt you knew me. I think I was Will, Casey. I really do."

I tremble with adrenaline. Every muscle in my body. "I've spent the past few weeks undoing my assumption that I had a past life. Please, *please* don't try to convince me that my hard work has been bullshit. I really can't take the roller coaster." I shake my head. "Will isn't real. Becky's part of me. Not a good part, it seems."

"Why do you keep saying that?"

I wince. Maybe I should just tell him. "She made me kill my mom."

Jake frowns. "What? How?"

"Apparently, she grabbed the wheel. Drove the car straight into the canal."

He blinks hard. It takes him a moment to speak. "You wouldn't do that."

"How do you know?" I howl. "You think you know someone, but it's not me, okay? Even *I* don't know me!" I cover my face with my hands. I will *not* cry in front of him.

Jake waits a beat. "I would never want to undo your progress, Casey. That's not why I'm here."

"You sure? Because it sounds like exactly why you're here." I desperately fight back the lump in my throat. It's too overwhelming—seeing him, listening to him. I've undone that Becky is real. I have to. It's the only way I'll be well.

"I want you to take care of yourself. But I also saw how damaged you looked when your stepmother and your dad and that . . . that preppy guy"—it takes me a moment before I realize he's referring to Marcus, and his disgusted expression sells it—"told you this was in your head."

"Of course I was devastated. You think it feels good to be told everything you believe is a lie?"

"Right. I know. And I believe in mental illness. I believe that's what this could be. But I'm also a strong proponent of not just assuming things are just in someone's head. A person can feel things beyond simple anxiety or repression, or that certain behaviors are just ways to self-soothe."

I want to stop staring at his moving mouth. I want to stop listening. But he has a point. Isn't this exactly how I've felt? And yet . . .

"I came because I think you should listen to both sides," Jake says gently. "I think Becky—and Will—I think they were real. I think they died together. But I don't want to mess up your treatment. I'm sorry for what's happened. I'll never forget you. But maybe . . . maybe I should go. Maybe that's better."

He stands up slowly. After a beat, he scoops up the hoodie and tosses it over his shoulder. As he pivots toward the door, I clear my throat. "Wait."

Jake turns, one eyebrow raised.

"What do you mean you think Becky and Will died together?" That plummeting car flashes into my mind again. The water rushing into the cabin. Becky's dress floating around her face.

Jake glances at me cautiously. "Maybe we shouldn't go down this road . . ."

I notice his hand is on the flap of his messenger bag. "What do you have?"

He bites his lip. A tennis match seems to take place in his mind—he opens his mouth, shuts it again, opens it again, not sure if he should speak.

"I found something," he finally says. "Proof."

"What do you mean?"

Slowly, he undoes the Velcro flap of his bag and pulls out a folded piece of paper. It's a photocopy of a news article from a local newspaper dated July 2005. Jake spreads it on the table, and I stare down at it, bile rising in my throat. A headline blurs before my eyes.

CAR PLUMMETS OFF BRIDGE INTO WATER, 2 PRESUMED DEAD

And in the text below, Jake has highlighted two names.

Rebecca Kinkaid.

And **William Woodson**.

CAR PLUMMETS OFF BRIDGE INTO WATER, 2 PRESUMED DEAD

Avon Shores, NY — A vehicle skidded off an intercoastal bridge ramp on Saturday, July 9, 2005, killing two people.

ABC News affiliate WAZK reports that there were no witnesses at the bridge at the time of the accident. The bridge is just off Avon Shores, spanning the marshland and connecting Avon Shores to the northeast tip of Long Island. Neighbors close to the bridge heard the crash and ran out to find a vehicle sinking in the intercoastal waterway. Rescue teams were called onto the scene, but the passenger and driver likely died upon impact.

The body of Rebecca Kinkaid, 19, of Avon Shores, was recovered two hours later. Sheriffs identified the vehicle as belonging to William Woodson, 20, also of Avon Shores. It is likely he was the driver, but his body has still not been found. Zero visibility and debris in the water have made it difficult to search the bottom.

Driver error is suspected. The vehicle was driving at a high speed from the island towns. It is speculated that the driver lost control, crashed into a guard rail, flipped the vehicle, and careened over another section of bridge into the water.

It's unclear whether alcohol was involved. "We're all so broken up about this," says Desiree Lofgren, a friend of the Kinkaid family. "It's such a tragedy."

This is an ongoing investigation.

FOURTEEN

I stare at the story for so long that my eyes start to water. "No. *No*. You wrote this. *You* did."

"It's on the internet." He shakes the paper. "Look, I started thinking about Becky being who you were in your past life and why you'd be drawn to Avon Shores. I thought about that you called me Will, and the things I'd experienced in my life. And I thought about that painful . . . intervention, or whatever it was, at the Wayfarer. How blindsided you were, how upset . . . and I wanted to make it right. I hunted around. The story is from 2005. A little over seventeen years ago. My mom's no expert, but she said that—"

I gasp. "You brought your mom into this?"

"She's impartial. But she said it's likely souls who've died but aren't ready to move on occupy new hosts—babies that are in their mother's bellies." He leans closer. "My birthday's August 6, 2005. A month after this happened."

My lips part. I start to feel dizzy. My birthday is December 28—I'd just turned eighteen, in fact, here at Chadwick Pond. Happy birthday to me.

But no. *No.* This isn't true. Jake's a psychopath. A manipulator. It's the only answer.

"I had my friend search for news about Becky's death," I tell him. "We looked up her name, a car accident, a bridge . . . we found nothing. So you're telling me that all of a sudden, this article just appears?"

"You searched for Becky?" Jake points to the printout. "The story gives her name as Rebecca. Maybe it's as simple as that. And wait—why did you search for a crash? You did know this is how they died?" His eyes widen. "That thing you said before—driving a car over a bridge? Have you seen that accident?"

I look away. "No. I'm thinking of my mom's accident. That's what I understand now."

"But that's the thing," Jake begs. "You saw Becky in a car crash over a bridge. That's pretty specific."

"It's also similar to how my mom died."

"But an article just pops up about a crash seventeen years ago—and the victims are named Becky and Will? Don't you think that's a pretty big coincidence? I'm not messing with you. I found this. I wouldn't be here to make things worse. But I really think that maybe what you've seen . . . maybe it's more than something all in your head."

"It has to be." I press my hands over my eyes. "I've just turned the corner on believing—really believing—that Becky is a component of my psyche and nothing more. This is a huge step backward."

"But are you sure that even makes sense?" Jake starts to pace. "Look, I've read about people with dissociative personality disorder. Most of them have endured abuse, trauma, things that cause them to retreat into their alters. From the way you talked to me, your life has been—"

"Pleasant?" I interrupt. "Sure. It was. Up until my mom's death. Guess I'm an outlier."

Jake looks at me pleadingly. "I think you have a gift, actually. You're able to see the life you lived before."

"Oh, so, coincidentally, you have the gift, too?" I wave my hand. "Reincarnation isn't real. End of story."

"Do you really believe that?"

I look away. I have no idea what I believe. Not really.

"I think we shared something deep and serious that transcends just this life," Jake says. "I think we still share something. Why it that not worth believing in? And don't you want to know what happened, in the end, in this accident? Maybe that's why Becky is poking through—she wants us, together, to understand?"

Frustrated tears well in my eyes. "But from what everyone is saying, Becky ruined my whole life. I need to let her go."

Jake's throat catches. After a moment, he takes the story and stuffs it clumsily into his messenger bag. "I get it. Totally get it. You need to be you."

Head down, he turns and hurries to the door. He doesn't look back. The door shuts quietly, and then he's gone.

When I look around, I'm startled to see that the day room is exactly the same as it was a few minutes ago. I want it to be drastically different. I want to rip the soda machines from their cords and break the glass. I want to upturn the tables and smash the chairs.

How dare Jake barge in here under a fake name and try to manipulate me with some bogus story? Why had I even listened? And as for this news story that's randomly popped up? It's got to be a trick. Or a terrible coincidence. It has nothing to do with my own visions of *the car sinking, and the water filling, and someone reaching out and squeezing your hand . . .*

I suck in a breath. More images flash across my mind even though I try to tamp them down.

You desperately undo your seat belt as the water fills the car. You try to roll down the window, but the crank is stuck. The water is starting to soak the edge of your dress. All at once, the vehicle goes vertical, throwing you against the back of the seat. Water gushes in through the cracked windshield, filling your lungs.

"Help!" you scream, except the words are swallowed up. And then you feel his hand squeezing yours. You turn, looking right into his terrified eyes.

It's Will. He nods calmly at you as he unbuckles his own seat belt. He squeezes your hand hard. He doesn't look afraid. He's going to save you.

I snap out of the memory, breathing hard. I'm covered in what I think is water, but then I realize it's a cold sweat. Damn

Jake for barging in here and opening that Pandora's box again. I need to shut Becky out. What I'm seeing isn't real.

And yet . . .

The memory feels palpable, visceral—not like some jumbled inversion of the accident with my mom, but a separate event. I can feel the bones in my spine pressed against the seat of the old car. I can smell the brine of the water as it gushes in, I can feel the itchy lace of a wedding dress. Is that normal? How could I be experiencing all of these things if I never actually lived through them?

But this is the most shocking part: If I'm to believe this memory, then it's Will who was driving. Will who'd caused the car to crash. On Becky's wedding day.

It must have been Will who stole Becky from that patio, then. Will who put a hand around her waist and covered her eyes. Whispered into her ear menacingly, *You've been a bad girl.*

I leap to my feet. Will's not the person I've been longing for—he's the person Becky feared. He isn't Becky's lost love. He's her killer.

I cross the day room and slam out into the hall. Jake's scarecrow form is visible as he stands at the desk, signing himself out.

"Hey," I say murderously. "You and I need to talk."

Jake's eyebrows lift in alarm. Maria peers around him. "Casey? You okay?" she asks.

"I'll be only a second." My voice is high-pitched, careering out of control. My nails dig into Jake's arm. "Outside."

It's freezing on the porch, and I'm only in a T-shirt and thin pants, but I'm so hopped up I barely feel the temperature. Jake cowers back like I'm going to start pummeling him.

"What do you remember from the day Will died?" I demand.

Jake's eyes dart. "N-Nothing. Not really. Just . . . trauma. Something scary."

"So you don't remember that Will stole Becky from her wedding? That he came up behind her and . . . assaulted her? Threw her into his car in her wedding dress and sped off as she screamed?"

Jake's eyes widen. "In her wedding dress! The story said she was going to be married. Wait, are you seeing more from that day?"

"I'm seeing that Will was Becky's murderer! He threw her into that car. The same car that goes over the bridge in that news article . . . on her wedding day."

"So you believe it." Jake looks excited. "You think it's true. That you were Becky—she's not something evil inside you, but a separate person. It's reincarnation."

"That doesn't matter. What matters is that Will—and maybe you, if you keep claiming you were Will—didn't have Becky's or my best intentions at heart. Thanks for making that abundantly clear to me." I put my hands on my hips. "What, were you angry Becky was marrying someone else? So you . . . you stole her? And sped off into the night? What did you think that was going to solve?"

"Casey." Jake puts his hands up in a halting gesture. "First of all, *I* didn't do any of those things. Will did—if he did them at all." I'm about retort, but he stops me. "But now that we've met, and based on the feelings I've had all my life, I don't think that's right. Will was a kind soul. He loved Becky. He would have died for her. It's the same way I feel about you."

I bark out a laugh. "You don't even know me!" Likely story he didn't know that Will was the cause of Becky's death. Convenient that he didn't remember Will pouncing on her.

But also: *Did Jake just say he loved me?*

"I feel like I do know you," Jake says in a small voice. "Every time we've talked, the time we've spent together . . ." He clears his throat awkwardly. "And the way we kissed . . ."

I hold up a hand. "Do *not* bring that up."

"Are you seriously telling me you haven't felt it, too?" Jake whispers. "This . . . connection? Why did you come looking for me? Why did you call me the minute you felt in danger?"

I look away.

"Don't you want to know what happened?" Jake asks quietly. "Why did they go off that bridge that day? What led them there? Why did they have to die?"

I point to his messenger bag. "Your news story says it all. Will lost control of his car. He was so furious Becky was marrying someone else that he flew of a bridge in a blind rage."

"I don't think that's it. I think there's more. Things we don't know."

"Of course you do! You think you're Will, and you don't want Will to be a bad guy." I turn to leave. "I'm glad I figured this out. It's a real turning point. I can forget Will for real, now. I can heal."

Jake catches my arm. "Casey. Come with me—just to see."

I laugh bitterly. "See what?"

"The bridge. Where they crashed. We . . . we could go together. It might . . . spark something. The truth."

"I'm not going anywhere with you."

"You don't have to speak to me for the rest of your life after this. I'll leave you alone. And I'll take full responsibility if Will really did cause that crash in a blind rage. But I think there's more, Casey. I think that's why these two souls are hanging around the earth—why they've nestled in us. They want us to right what's wrong. And also, think about this. If Becky was real, if she's . . . reincarnated, in you, then maybe she isn't some evil force making you do terrible things. Because I don't want to think that's true at all. I don't think you caused your mother's death because of some . . . spirit or abnormality."

I stare at the floor, not wanting to answer, but the pressure builds inside me. "I don't want to believe that, either," I say through gritted teeth. "I hate it with every ounce of my being."

"Then you shouldn't. You know yourself best, Casey."

"But I don't. Everyone else knows this . . . this other side of me," I protest. "A side I can't control."

He shakes his head. "It's hard to admit that what we're considering—reincarnation—is possible. But maybe it is. And maybe if we untangle this—what happened to Becky, why she's within you, all of it—then maybe we can figure out what happened with your mom. Or what didn't happen. I'm sure you don't want to go around your whole life feeling guilty for your mom's death. Or at least we can explain why you felt like you needed to do it."

"I would have never hurt my mom," I whisper. "It doesn't make sense."

"I'm not saying that figuring out Becky's story will definitely solve that," Jake says. "But don't you want to see if it can?"

I don't move for a long beat. My head is pounding.

"Come to the bridge with me. I've asked this facility about you traveling. You're checked in voluntarily. You can also check yourself out for the day."

"You asked about me?" I sputter. "You asked the nurses?"

He puts his hands together. "You can trust me. If I don't bring you back, if there's ever a moment you don't feel safe, you can call the police. Seriously." He peers at me intensely. "You don't think I don't find this hard, too? Seeing these . . . visions? This ongoing sense that there's someone else, someone wanting something, taking up space in my head, preventing me from doing things? You're the only person I can talk to about this, Casey. The only person who understands."

I cross my arms. "Go on Reddit. I'm sure there are chat rooms of people who think they've lived past lives—if you're even telling the truth."

"Yeah, but I don't want to talk to them. I want to talk to you."

Tingles go through me. I can't help it.

Jake holds up a finger. "A few hours. Just to see the bridge. Please?"

Snow has begun to fall again. We're safe under the awning, but I feel the chill in my bones. I need to get back inside before I get frostbite.

But I can feel Jake waiting. Every instinct in my body is telling me to turn him down. This still could be some elaborate pick-up line. Worse, it could be some elaborate scheme to hurt me.

I want to resist the little voice inside me nudging me to go. I hate how the news story lines up too eerily close with the visions I've seen. I hate, too, that when Jake said he thinks there's something more to Becky and Will's crash—and the crash with my mom—there's part of me that wants to believe him. But then, of course I do. I don't want to ever think I randomly steered my mom to her death. I'd rather it be a terrible freak accident then something *I* made happen.

I hate most of all that I've so quickly bought into Becky again. But I'm not believing I'm her, I tell myself. Maybe this is just another step in figuring out why I adopted the Becky persona to begin with. Maybe this last trip with Jake was putting the whole thing behind me.

It's the only explanation that straddles both worlds.

My body shudders from the cold. I let out a groan as the air seeps from my lungs.

"Fine," I say to Jake. "One day. And then it's goodbye forever."

FIFTEEN

I have to admit, I'm curious about seeing the bridge where Rebecca and Will died. Still, I'm shaky as I sign my release forms. Now that I'm eighteen, they can't legally report my release to anyone. I'm an adult. And I should feel okay because Fran is in Boston—at least for a little while. Still, I have no idea how much she checks on me. What if she regularly calls the facility? What would she do if they said I was gone? I need some sort of alibi.

And so, once again, I recruit Pippa.

It's a dangerous move. I know she didn't mean to work against me with Fran, but I'm not certain she won't tell Fran exactly what I'm up to again. On the other hand, Jake reached out to her—and she believed him, even took his side. She told him about my theories about Becky. I want to know why. It might be a bargaining chip.

"Casey," Pippa gushes when I get her on the phone during calling hours later that night. "I'm so happy you called. How is it there? How are you feeling? How was your birthday?" She pauses awkwardly at that one. How good could my birthday have been in a hospital? "Did Jake come see you?" she adds. Then she rushes on before I can even reply. "I wrote you to say he reached out— did you get it? There's something about him that's so earnest. I hope I didn't make a mistake—"

I cut her off. "First you tell on me to Fran and Marcus. But then you tell Jake all about my ideas about Becky?"

Pippa is quiet. "I didn't tell on you. I was only going on what your stepmother asked. But look, I heard how dazzled you were about Jake on the phone. Should I not have told Jake where you were so he could visit you?"

"I mean, aside from the fact that Fran specifically told me to stay away from him . . ."

Pippa gasps. "She did? Why?"

I sigh. "I guess she sees him as part of the problem. And maybe he is. He's trying to convince me that Becky is real. He has this . . . this article, about a car crash off a bridge and two people named Becky Kinkaid and Will Woodson dying."

Pippa breathes in sharply. "Isn't that what you saw in your vision?"

"Yeah. No. Maybe." I squeeze my eyes shut. "He wants me to leave the hospital for a little bit. Visit the bridge. See if it jogs any memories."

Pippa pauses a moment. "And are you okay with that?"

I have no idea. It's why I've called Pippa.

I explain to her that I'm going to sign out on a day pass with the hospital for us to visit together. I need Pippa as an alibi because Fran trusts her, and the last thing I need is Fran hightailing it back from Boston and my father's treatment to check on me. Meanwhile, I'll be visiting that bridge with Jake . . . which hopefully will be uneventful.

"But I want you to keep your phone handy," I tell her. "If I don't check in at certain times, I need you to sound the alarm."

"But you don't think Jake is dangerous, do you?"

"I need backup, that's all. This is something I need to do."

I wonder if Pippa is considering whether I'm having another Becky episode. Am I? Is this any different than the other times I've run off to Avon Shores in search of something?

"I'll do whatever you ask," Pippa says quietly. "That seems really smart. Level-headed." She swallows. "I know you have some disordered thinking or whatever. But from my perspective, I never saw it. I'm serious."

I assure her it's okay. That she has nothing to feel guilty about. I got that sense from Marcus, too—and even Jake—that they all thought they should have seen this coming. "Just say you'll help me," I add.

"Of course I'll help you," Pippa says immediately. "I won't tell a soul."

●●●

The drive south is tense. There's snow on the roads, and Jake needs to concentrate hard in order not to crash. His station wagon is old and rattly. Who knows how old the tires are. I also still hate being in a car, despite the work I've done with John over the past few weeks. Aversions can't be cured overnight, I guess.

I'm also deeply paranoid about leaving. I cast nervous glances out the window at every car that passes, afraid I'll see someone I know, someone checking up on me. I keep telling myself I'm not doing anything wrong. It's not like I've just broken out of prison. But what if Fran finds out?

"So does your mom think she was someone in a past life, too?" I break the silence.

Jake's hands are easy on the wheel. He's been careful with me since he picked me up in the parking lot, overly polite, vigilant about whether I'm comfortable enough, if the car's cabin is too hot or cold, if I need to stop to use the bathroom. This is the first time we've talked about anything real on the drive.

"She doesn't," he says. "At least not that she knows of. I don't think it's something that runs in families."

"And when did you first think you felt you'd been someone else?"

"I'm not really sure. Three years old? Four? What about you?"

I shrug. There's no way I'm talking about my Becky experiences.

Then I turn and look at him. "You know, if you felt like you had a past life, why didn't you say something when Fran ambushed me at the hotel?"

Jake looks guilty. "I was like a deer in headlights. I felt bombarded. Blown away. But I should have. I didn't defend you at all. I'm sorry for that."

We drive in silence for a while. Road signs sweep past. There are boarded-up farm stands, probably lively in the summer.

"So your stepmother's a piece of work," Jake says. "She's really controlling, huh?"

"I guess it's for my own good. It's not like my dad can help out much."

"I saw him go into the motel as I was leaving. He seemed weak. What's the prognosis?"

I tell him a little about my dad's illness, his various chemo and radiation protocols, how it's whittled him from a slightly pudgy middle-aged man to a skeleton. If my mother were still alive, she wouldn't recognize him, probably. She always said she liked that he had a belly because it made a good pillow. A lovely memory hits me sideways: a fire roaring in our living room, classical music on the stereo, me writing a story in my notebook, and my mother lying on the couch on my father's belly, looking perfectly content.

"That sounds nice," Jake murmurs.

I glare at him. Had I said that out loud? What is with me and this guy? It's like I'm a leaky faucet, blurting out any old thing.

"I shouldn't even be talking to you. I still have no idea if you're a good person."

"I am, though."

"But I'm still pissed. For lying to me, about that first trip to Avon Shores."

"I'm sorry." Jake gives me a sidelong glance. "Though you lied to me, too."

I scoff. "About what?"

He looks shocked. "Preppy guy! Your boyfriend? I looked him up, by the way." He shifts his jaw. "Marcus Coleman? No wonder you didn't want to let him go. He's a real step up."

I feel my jaw clench. I'd completely forgotten I hadn't been truthful about Marcus. I think of all the times I could have told Jake but didn't.

"So are you together?" Jake asks, his eyes on the road.

"No," I admit. "I mean . . . technically, but . . . I'm going to break it off."

Jake's expression hasn't changed. "Does he know that?"

"No."

Jake gives me a knowing look. I can feel my cheeks going red. "He has a lot going on in the city. And, okay, I'm kind of scared to do it."

"What did he think about finding me in your room?"

"He wasn't happy about you. But I don't think he believed it was legit."

Jake's lips pinch. "Right. Why would I be a threat?"

"I think it's more like he can't believe I'd drop someone like him. No one like me would give up such a good thing."

Jake wrinkles his nose. "Arrogant much?"

"He didn't say that exactly. But it's got to be the case. Because . . ." Then I trail off, clamping my mouth shut.

"Because what?"

I let out a sigh. I vomit up everything else to this guy, why not this, too? "I mean, why me? Of all the girls in the city. Rich guy? Could have anyone he wanted."

He gives me an incredulous look, then shakes his head. "What?" I ask.

"You really don't see what a catch you are?"

"Not at the moment."

He smirks, and I smirk, which is astonishing, because I know I'm still supposed to be mad.

"I'm sorry," I say softly, after a moment. "I should have told you about Marcus."

"Guess we both should have been a little more communicative."

We take a turn, and I draw in a breath. A bridge stretches in front of us. It spans the waterway with a few well-concealed houses around it on the marshland. The only thing protecting cars from the water is a low guard rail. I know without Jake even having to say anything that this is the bridge of the accident. No wonder a car flipped over this, I think. A person could, easily, just by leaning over a little too far.

And then it hits me. *I know this is the bridge.* It's like . . . inside me, in my brain. I try to tell myself that I've talked myself into that notion. From the article.

Jake maneuvers the car to the side of the road and parks. He gets out quickly, darting around to my side to open the door for me. I duck my head, not wanting to accept his chivalry, but also pleased by it.

I stare at the bridge before me. Flickers pop at the edges of my mind—but again, I resist them. It's the article's fault. But then I turn toward the right side, my eyes searching for something my brain isn't even sure of yet. My gaze lands on a faded

graffiti mark on the concrete that somehow I knew to expect.
The drawing is of the planet Saturn. Somehow I know that if I
get closer, the inscription inside it will read *To the stars*.

You point up to it. "What does it say?"

"To the stars," he answers. He has better vision
than you do. "Wonder who did it?"

I swallow hard.

Jake has walked a few paces toward the bridge. "People like to
fish off this thing. I've crossed it a million times. Had no idea it was
ever related to a past life."

"So you've gotten no flickers of an accident?"

He shakes his head. "Not really. I see . . . darkness. That's it."

I look over the guard rail. The marsh underneath us is certainly
dark. Could Jake be seeing the plunge into the water? Drowning?

But then I clamp down on the inside of my cheek. *Don't buy
into this*.

"Casey?"

Jake's voice pulls me back to earth. I take a ragged breath.
He's standing on the bridge now, but I'm not sure I want to take
another step.

"So?" he asks. "Getting any feelings?"

I shrug. "No."

He walks off the bridge again, and we sit down on a bench
nearby. It's a pretty spot—the water probably glistens in the summer, and the way the bridge is situated, it looks like you're driving

into a total horizon of trees. Across the water, a series of vacant docks gently bob. I bet there are boats all along here in the summer, people sitting on those docks, dogs swimming for tennis balls.

Zap. A memory breaks through. I try to hold on to it, but it's like a balloon floating away. Something about a dog? A dock? Was Becky here before other than the crash? She must have been. The news article says she was from a neighboring town. She probably knew all these secret bridges and spots.

Zap. This time, more light comes in.

Hands over your eyes. You stumble backward. Someone whispers in your ear, "*You've been a bad girl.*"

"No," I whisper. I don't want to see that memory again.

"Casey?" Jake asks, sitting straighter. "You okay?"

I fight hard to banish the memory.

He's dragging you backward now, a blindfold over your eyes. "Hurry up. Stay quiet." He throws you into the back of the car, the one with the stiff leather.

"No," I say again, this time in a moan. The leather. It's definitely the same car that crashed. Will's car.

The door slams. Your heart is pounding.

And then, the blindfold pulls away. The sunlight stings your eyes. You gasp to breathe. A face comes into focus. He's got one hand on the steering wheel, and he's definitely got a foot on the gas, but he's also looking at you with mischief and joy and relief.

"Will!"

You feel tears prick your eyes and then roll down your cheeks. "Will!" you say again, jolting forward. He's driving, but he hasn't buckled you into the back—he has only put you there because your dress is so huge. You press your face against his back, feeling the rush of intense love you always feel when you're near him. The tears keep coming.

"You came," you blubber. "Took you long enough."

"Told you I would," Will says.

A car rumbles over the bridge, breaking me from the vision. Jake is staring at me. He holds his body stiff as though he isn't sure what I might say.

"You . . . went somewhere," he whispers. "Did you see the accident? Are you . . . okay?"

My throat feels dry. That person clapping his hands over Becky's eyes—that was Will. I was right. He kidnapped her. He threw her into that car.

But Becky wanted him to. She'd been elated.

"What?" Jake demands. "Casey, seriously, what is it?" He looks worried. "Is Will a bad guy? I swear to God, Casey, if that's the case, I am so sorry for leading you down this road, and I'll never—"

"No," I interrupt. And then I start to laugh. "Will took her from the wedding, but she was happy about it. Thrilled."

Jake blinks. "Are you sure?"

I nod. "He threw her into a car. Drove off like a maniac. But . . . but she said, *You came.* And he answered, *Told you I would.* He sounds like he has a screw loose . . . though in the best way."

We stare at each other. Behind us, the marsh grass shifts with a gust of wind. This is where Becky died. Will was in the car with her. And they were driving . . . away. Away from Becky's wedding. But what happened from A to B? How and why did they crash? Who was Becky marrying, anyway?

And what does this mean for Jake . . . and me?

My voice cracks when I speak next. "If Jake didn't deliberately crash the car, what happened? Why were they driving so fast? How did they end up in the water?" I pinch the bridge of my nose, trying to conjure a memory. Nothing comes. "If they were escaping a wedding, who's to say someone wasn't coming after them?"

Jake's eyes widen. "That's what I was thinking."

"I mean, it could have been an accident. Maybe they were being careless and drove onto the bridge too fast. Misjudged. But . . ."

"But why would Becky and Will still be hanging around, inside us?" Jake interrupts. His eyes shine excitedly. "They want us to know something, Casey. Something about how they died."

I bite my lip and nod. Could it be possible?

Jake steps toward me. This time, when he takes my hand, I let him. My heart pounds hard. My mouth feels dry.

"What do you want to do?" he asks. "I can take you back to the hospital if you want. And if you want to forget all about this . . . I'll drop it."

I close my eyes. What do I want? I want to understand what's happening. I want validation. I also want the freedom to travel freely through the world again, no longer under supervision, no longer considered a danger. I don't feel dangerous.

But then, what? Becky is real? A soul, not an alter personality? And if that's true, does that mean Becky doesn't mean me harm?

If it's true, maybe Becky didn't wrench that steering wheel, sending my mother to her grave? I need to know, I realize. I need to know for sure.

I look at Jake. I want to spend more time with him. I can't help wanting that. It's like I'm pulled to him in the same way he's pulled to me. I look down at our hands. Our fingers are still entwined. I hadn't even realized we were touching.

"I think," I say, taking a huge breath, "I think we follow the string. I think we see where it leads."

Jake exhales, sounding relieved. "That's what I want, too."

SIXTEEN

That night, I'm installed under Jake's Star Wars sheets again. The blinds are drawn. Whenever I hear a noise, I feel a jolt of anxiety. Is it unthinkable that I'm back in Avon Shores—in Jake's house? Is it also unthinkable that no one has called to check on me? So far, Pippa's lie has held. Fran thinks I'm with her. She's still in Boston with my dad.

Still, I don't like lying. The whole thing makes me hideously uneasy.

There's a knock on the door. Jake pokes his head in.

"Where have you been?" I ask. Jake said he had to run out "for a second." That was an hour ago.

"Researching," he says. He looks down at the laptop next to me. "Have you found anything about Becky?"

My job has been to google Rebecca Kinkaid and William Woodson. I hadn't found much online, though. Becky's name called up so many other Rebecca Kinkaids—lawyers, teachers, yogis, a woman interviewed on the TV news. I navigated pages and pages of Google, but the only story I found about my Becky was the one that had been written after she died.

No family, either. No hits anywhere. I've written emails to the high school, at least looking for Becky's grades, her parents' names, her after-college plans, but since it's after hours, I haven't heard anything. It's unclear if they'll give that stuff to me anyway. It might be private information. It was also eighteen years ago.

Will Woodson brought up a few more hits online. There was a picture of him from the 2002 Avon Shores High School basketball championship as he made a winning shot. It's eerie, staring at that black-and-white image on the screen. I see a face I somehow know without ever laying eyes on. But when I scoured the article, all it talked about was how many points Will had scored. The article didn't say anything about if he was going to college or what he planned to do with his life.

I also looked up a Woodson listing in Avon Shores. There were public records of a Woodson family living at 3208 Dune Avenue, but when I found the property on Google Maps, there was only an empty lot. The house had been demolished.

I bring up mostly dead-end searches. Jake smiles slyly. "Well, got a surprise for you."

He pulls a book from his backpack and plops it on the mattress. "Avon Shores High School" reads the cover. It's dated 2003.

I gasp. "Where did you get this?"

"Uh, I went to Avon Shores. And I happen to be friends with the teacher-advisor for yearbook, who's still there—I mean, I only graduated last year, unlike some of us." He gives me a coy look. "Mrs. Rao let me borrow this, no questions asked." He pats his backpack. "Found Becky's, too. She graduated the following year—2004."

"She was getting married in 2005." I make a face. Who would be married at nineteen? "Do you have records of who her parents were?"

"I asked Mrs. Rao. She said the school records might not go back that far, as they've changed computer systems—but she's looking into it."

We crack open the yearbook. I find Will's picture right away. He's handsome in his senior portrait. Jake stares at him for a while. His lips purse.

I clear my throat. "Do you feel like him?"

"Definitely don't look like him," he says, laughing. He runs a hand through his wild curls—which, compared to Will's crew cut, is pretty much the exact opposite. "He's so different than I am."

I flip forward to the juniors, finding Becky. She's got a wide smile, big eyes, and flipped-up hair with unfortunate early 2000s chunky highlights. I get a shiver when I look at her—*Am I you?*— but like Jake, it isn't an instant connection. It's a weird thing, the idea that you have knowledge of this other person's life inside you, maybe even influencing you. Does it make me gifted, like Jake says—or less interesting, because I'm less me?

"But look," Jake says. He flips forward a few pages to the candid section and jabs one of the images with his thumb. There, among smiling field hockey players, a bunch of boys mugging out the window of a school bus, and a lonely girl looking ambushed in front of a water fountain, is a couple holding hands down the hall.

My heart seizes. It's Becky. And Will.

"So they were a couple," I breathe.

I stare into Becky's eyes. Her smile is huge. Her fingers are tightly clasped around Will's. He's grinning, too. They look so . . . happy.

Then I look up at Jake. He's watching me, too. A lump forms in my throat. I can feel how badly he wants to touch me—and I feel the same thing. It's like electricity. Inevitability.

And it's tempting. So tempting. Being in his room again, looking at all of his things—it makes me realize how much I've wanted this.

I cough and look down, trying to get my head back in the game. "Why did Becky agree to marry someone else, do you think? What happened?"

"I don't know," Jake says. "I scoured this whole thing for a clue. The year Will graduated, he and Becky were together. I don't know how it went wrong."

Jake's phone buzzes, startling both of us. I sit up straighter. "Who is it?" Fran's name flashes through my mind.

Jake presses a button on the screen. "Don't be mad, but—"

"Mad?" I interrupt. "Why?" Has he called Fran?

A door slams. Jake looks over his shoulder, and I follow his gaze. His mom stands in the hallway.

"Oh," I say quietly.

Connie looks sheepish. "I'm sorry, Casey. I know you'd rather I not know you're here, but I can help, I think."

"Mom moved to Avon Shores when Will and Becky were still alive," Jake says. "She says she didn't know them, but she remembers that crash. She might be able to direct us to the right places to search for things."

I kind of feel like I'm betraying Fran even more than before. So far, I've shut her out—but here's another mother, someone I barely know. I could see her feeling slighted.

Still, I shrug and gesture for her to come into the room. Connie settles on Jake's bed. "I heard what happened. Are you okay?"

"There were a lot of things I needed to work through."

"But I believe you," she says in a fiery voice. "I believe both of you. Whatever's going on—it can't necessarily be explained by science or medicine or some sort of brain scan."

"So did you know them at all?" I ask her, wanting to get the subject off of my possible mental illness. "Becky and Will?"

Connie shakes her head. "I'd just moved to Avon Shores shortly before they died. We set up our vet practice. Will and Becky were high school kids, really. I think they'd just graduated, right?"

"Will did in 2003," Jake reports. "Becky graduated in 2004."

"Yes. And the crash was in 2005. I was pregnant," his mom says. "So I was a little distracted. But I remember that crash. It wasn't long before I gave birth to Jake."

"Right," I say quietly. It's a weird notion. Am I really to believe that Will's soul floated into Connie's brand-new baby? Same for me, too: I was born only a few months later. But why had Becky chosen me?

"Do you remember any rumors about the crash?" Jake asks. "Like . . . why it happened? What might have motivated it?"

Connie shakes her head. "I thought it was unbelievable that a car flipped over that low bridge. The speed limit is twenty-five at the most. They must have been driving really fast." She shifts, thinking of something. "Some people suggested that maybe there were drugs involved."

"Drugs?" Jake frowns. "I don't do drugs."

"You're not Will," I tell him.

But it doesn't sit right with me, either. From my memories, Will didn't seem on drugs.

Then I get a flash:

> His hands steady on the steering wheel. The trees passing out the window. Sticking your hand out, feeling the breeze.

The car wasn't moving that quickly. Will wasn't speeding . . . at least not at first. Then I see something else. Just a tiny moment.

> Something catches your eye to the right. A flash of silver, suddenly appearing from the side road. You grab his arm. "Will!"

I blink. When I look over, Jake is staring at me. He can read me so well. He knows I've had another vision. But I have no idea what it means.

I turn back to Connie. "Becky was supposed to be married that day."

"Yes." Connie's eyes light up. "I remember that."

"Except she was driving away with a guy who wasn't her fiancé," Jake says. "Do you remember that part, too?"

Connie's eyes narrow. "It was so long ago . . ."

"Do you know who she was marrying?" I press. "It might have been whoever owned the big blue-gray house on the other side of Avon Shores."

"I know that house for sure. And the name of the owners at the time is on the tip of my tongue. They're in construction, I think? Built a lot of stuff around here. I never knew them—like I said, we were so new to the area. Even since then, I'm not sure I've had any interaction with that family. As far as I know, they don't have pets."

"Construction," I repeat, contemplating this. "Do you think they still own the big house? Or live around town? And are they still in business?"

"I think so." But she doesn't look certain. "It was so long ago. I wish I remembered more."

Construction. Signs I'd noticed around Avon Shores shimmer into my mind, including one I'd seen on my frantic walk to the psychic. It was large, a banner across an apartment complex. And it bore a picture of a bird in flight. The company's name means bird, except it was in another language . . .

I sift through the various languages I'd taken through the years. Four years of French in middle school. Japanese in my junior year. The online courses I took in Swedish just for fun. No. It's from the college course I took last year in Italian.

"Uccello?" I blurt.

Connie's eyes light up. "Uccello Construction! Definitely a company around here."

"They're a family?" I ask. "On the island?"

Jake seizes the yearbook and starts flipping. "There's something about that name . . ."

He turns to the senior pictures again. Our gazes light on Will, but then we move two letters back in the alphabet, only a few photos away. Then Jake draws in a breath.

He points to a picture of a beefy, grinning guy with squinty eyes and a white smile. Beau Uccello is the name beneath the face.

I clamp my hand over Jake's. "Beau." That's what Jake called himself when he came to see me at Chadwick Lake. "Did you know?"

"Not consciously."

We stare at each other a beat, then look back down at the pictures. Is this Becky's fiancé? Two boys, nearly side by side. One of them the man Becky loved. One of them the man Becky was to marry.

Until it all went wrong.

SEVENTEEN

The name Beau Uccello opens up a floodgate of information. Unlike Will Woodson, whose name only popped up in that basketball article, Beau Uccello was all over the internet, past and present. Homecoming king. Football quarterback. A representative for student government at some kind of local Long Island awards event. There are photos of him standing next to an older man, presumably his father, at various ribbon-cutting ceremonies at Uccello Construction projects around Avon Shores and other beach towns.

The Uccello business is a bit famous, too: We find out that Beau's father passed away unexpectedly when Beau was seventeen—not even out of high school yet—and that Beau had stepped in while in college and helped with the family business. Eventually, he took over. A local magazine interviewed him in February 2004; he said that he felt "poised" to be a young head of a construction company because he'd been by his father's side all his life.

I stare at his picture. He's a big guy with a square face and a smile that's more like a smirk. Definitely not Becky's type.

But then, what do I know what Becky's type was?

"The guy hasn't done bad for himself," Jake mumbles as we walk up an Avon Shores side street the next morning. He points to a giant, half-built beachfront property in front of us. "Seems like every new place in Avon Shores is built by Uccello still."

I pull up the collar of the jacket Jake lent me. I feel exposed, walking around Avon Shores like this. Every time I look around, I swear I sense a shadow, watching. "So he's still in business, then."

"Looks that way." Last night, we pulled up a few more profiles of Beau, now an adult in his thirties. He's still got that smirk, and he's lost a little hair, but he doesn't look that different.

"Is he married? Does he have kids?" I asked.

But as we pored over more recent articles, it's unclear. Everything we found was a business profile, not a puff piece about Beau's life. It's hard to know what he's even interested in, actually, besides running a business.

Now, Jake studies the phone number on the Uccello sign and taps it into his phone. The call brings us to a main switchboard for the company. He puts it on speaker, and we listen. "Welcome to Uccello Construction," says a pleasant female voice. But unlike some businesses, there isn't a prompt for a company directory—only a "Dial zero if you want to leave a message."

I look at Jake. "There's no way we're going to leave a message for Beau Uccello saying we're the reincarnated versions of Will Woodson and Becky Kinkaid."

"Understood," Jake says, pressing end.

We've learned that outing ourselves as the hosts for past lives might be a little trickier than we thought. That's because this morning, the two of us visited Karin the psychic again. I'd told Jake all about how I'd talked to her the first time and that she'd given me some ground rules. These days, Karin felt as close to an expert as we could find, and we needed some ground rules.

Karin seemed surprised to see me. But she didn't seem surprised that I'd bought into the notion about past lives. "Nothing else made sense, did it?" she said.

Then she looked at both of us. "Amazing that you both found each other, though. Seems like a one in a million shot."

I smiled shyly. Then Jake asked, "So why do you think we're seeing what we're seeing? And what do these two people want with us?"

"As I told Casey, there's probably something unfinished in their lives," Karin said. "Beyond them dying young."

"Their love was unfinished?" Jake suggested. "Or is it about the accident? Like, why it happened?"

"Maybe."

"Okay, so how can we go about getting more answers? Can we reach out to their families?"

Karin balked. "I'm not sure that would be my first point of entry. When working with other clients who have past life experiences, finding family members who have lost someone important to them—and saying *you* are that someone important now—doesn't always go over well. A lot of families take it hard. Some get offended. Most don't believe you."

"Oh," I said, feeling disappointed. I wasn't expecting a hero's welcome or anything, but meeting a family member might be kind of nice.

"To protect yourselves, I'd tell as few people as possible at first. Find another way to get your information without revealing who you are and what you know."

"And, like, how does this all work?" Jake asked. "In your previous experience, do people's past lives . . . stay with them, forever?"

"Some do. Others fade. Others leave entirely. It's all about why they found you in the first place." Karin thought a moment. "Oftentimes, past lives connect with us easier when we're younger. Closer to being born. We're more open to the experience. As we age and lay down our own memories, they tend to fade. Maybe they show up in dreams, in déjà vu moments, but that's it."

"Why do you think I sometimes blocked out moments where I remembered Becky?" I asked, thinking of the last time I'd visited Avon Shores.

Karin wasn't sure about this at all. "I've never heard of someone blocking out an experience. Unless it was traumatic, perhaps. Or unless you were drugged."

I'd paused hard at that one. My mother's accident was traumatic—that could explain why I blocked that out. But meeting Jake? The alternative was just as confusing. Who could have drugged me? Fran?

Actually, maybe that made a lot of sense. I thought I'd had a flu. I'd felt so groggy during that time. What if Fran had been giving me something? Maybe not for nefarious reasons—maybe she was just afraid of what she'd heard about Becky and that I'd do something to hurt myself.

Anyway, Karin went on, as much as we wanted to know the truth—and as much as Will and Becky are begging for it—we need to tread lightly. On one hand, those who don't believe in reincarnation will shut us down. On the other, those who do believe—and if something fishy did happen that day on the bridge? Someone might not want us poking around. It's hard to know who believes what, though. Maybe best not to say anything at all.

But I still had so many questions for Karin. It makes no sense, biologically, that my brain could contain synapses from someone else's life. "That's where the spiritual comes in," Karin said with a shrug. "The divine."

I wish I were more spiritual. Sometimes I hear the divine in the music of the opera. Sometimes I thought I had felt it on the beach, or in writing. But it's hard for me to believe in something so miraculous as reincarnation.

Now, Jake is still looking at his phone. "So do we just confront Beau with some other angle?"

I close my eyes. It's odd that Beau is blocked from my memories of Becky entirely. I'm afraid it's for sinister reasons. I keep telling myself it was Will who abducted Becky the day of her wedding . . . but why was she so happy about it? And then I think about that strange sliver of . . . something . . . that had come to me when talking to Jake's mom. That flash out of the corner of Becky's eye. Something appearing suddenly from a side road. How she'd grabbed Will's arm. How she'd screamed.

I haven't shared that memory with Jake yet, though. I'm not sure if I'm seeing it because I want to see it, and that's all.

"Just in case Beau is someone we need to worry about, maybe talking to him is our last option," I say. "Who else might know something about Becky and Will—or that accident?"

Jake thinks. "What about that other person quoted in the news story about the crash? Wasn't there a woman?"

I nod. "Right! What was her name again?"

Jake is already looking up the story again. "Desiree Lofgren." He clicks some more. Then he grins excitedly. "Yes! She's on Facebook. At least I think it's her. It says she grew up in Avon Shores. Lives only a few beach towns over. How many Desirees can there be?"

I peer at the picture of the woman on Jake's screen. Desiree's small features and heart-shaped face mean nothing to me and don't conjure up any flashes, but that doesn't prove anything. She was quoted in the story about Will's and Becky's deaths. She must know something.

Jake looks at me. "You okay with riding in a car? We can't walk there."

I bite my lip. I'm not okay. I'll never be.

Jake takes my hand. "I'll help you through it again."

Our eyes meet. Jake softens. He leans toward me just a little, and I know what we both want to come next.

But I pull away. "Jake . . ."

"Sorry," he says quickly, lowering his eyes, fluttering his hands. "I didn't . . ."

"No, it's just . . ." I take a breath. "I want to. But I'm so scrambled. I mean, first I hate you, then I like you . . ." I laugh at my feeble attempt at a joke. "But seriously. Diving into something, I'm not sure I'm ready."

Jake nods. "I know."

I stare across the street at the blank construction site with the Uccello Construction placard. "Once I know who I am, maybe things will change. Who I really am."

Jake cups my face with his hands, his gaze tight on me. "I'll wait for you however long it takes. I'll wait for you forever."

●●●

I assumed that in small, sleepy beach towns, all the locals know each other. But when we get to Sea Frame, which is two towns over, and inquire about Desiree Lofgren in a series of establishments—a grocery store, the gas station, even a bar. No one has heard of her.

"Maybe that Facebook post is old?" I ask Jake. "Maybe she's moved?"

Jake studies the pictures on Facebook some more. "Wait," he says, pointing to a recent photo. "She's in front of a bowling lane—and she's wearing a name tag. I recognize the mural on the wall. It's the bowling alley nearby. I've been to it a hundred times. Maybe she works there."

It involves yet another car ride—and more white-knuckling on my end. There are few cars in the Sea Lanes bowling alley lot. The sky is a flat, dull gray, and the wind bites against our skin. As we walk across the parking lot, I feel my phone buzz in my pocket. I quickly pull it out and see Pippa's name on the screen.

Not to freak you out, but Fran texted me.

Pippa writes.

I said we were together. I said we were fine. But she's sniffing around, I think.

I clench my jaw. I should appreciate Fran looking out for me. But also—it's my life. If I want to go on a wild goose chase, if I want to buck my medical orders, then that's my right, isn't it? Why does she keep standing in the way?

I start to compose a text to Fran, saying that Pippa and I are fine and that I'm safe. But then I stop. Sending a text right now might tip Fran off that Pippa tipped me off. I should wait.

Something flutters in the distance. I glance around the parking lot, feeling a strange shiver. I swear someone just ducked behind a parked car.

The parking lot is dead. *This is all in your mind*, I tell myself.

Wilted Christmas decorations hang from the eaves of the front door. Inside the bowling alley, fluorescent lights hum. A country song echoes from an empty bar area. Arcade machines flash demo screens to the left. Not a single bowling lane is occupied.

Jake smiles. "Want to play a frame?"

"Sure, if someone actually worked here." I spin around and look toward the other end of the building. There's got to be someone who turned the lights on. Maybe that person at least knows about the crash.

"Wait." Jake has turned toward a doorway. A small, thin woman walks, head down, past a back office. "Is that her?"

He strides off before I can answer. When Jake calls out, "Desiree?" the woman stops and frowns.

She looks back and forth between us. For a moment, I'm struck with the fear that she knows. She can tell we're Becky and Will.

"Yeah?" She sounds annoyed. Tired. But in no way suspicious. "If you want shoes, you gotta talk to Luke."

Jake shifts. "We're not here to play. We actually have, um, a few questions for you."

Desiree squints. "For me?"

Jake and I glance at each other. I hadn't actually thought what we'd say if we found Desiree. We don't have a plan.

"We're journalism students," Jake blurts. "I'm Mike. This is Renee. And we're looking into old stories from these beach towns to do some projects on."

Desiree crosses her arms like she doesn't buy this for a second. "And you want to talk to me?"

"There's an interesting story from a while back that we're, um, looking at for our class," Jake says. "A car crashing over a causeway bridge? Two people dying? One of them in a wedding dress?"

Desiree freezes. A muscle in her cheek twitches.

"You were quoted," I add. "But it doesn't tell us much, and we thought you might know more about what happened?"

"I should never have talked," Desiree says quietly.

"What?" My heart starts to pound. "Why not?"

Her eyes narrow. "Sorry, what school do you go to again?"

"SUNY Stony Brook," Jake says. That rolled off his tongue fast. "Look, can you tell us anything about the two people who died? From what we gather, they weren't the couple getting married."

"No," Desiree says softly. Lights from the arcade machines flash against her face, turning it a sickly green, then neon pink. "They weren't."

"Their names were . . . Becky and Will?" Jake asks. "Were they friends? Why were they driving away when she was in her wedding dress?"

"Did you know them?" I ask, even though Desiree must, because she's quoted.

Desiree glances over her shoulder into the office building. She turns back to us, shaking her head. "I can't get into this."

"Why?" Jake asks. He walks after her. "Did you lie to the paper? Say you knew them when you didn't, just to get fifteen minutes of fame?"

Desiree whips around, indignant. "'Course I knew them. We all went to school together. They were good friends. Becky and Will . . . they were crazy about each other. One of those couples that made you sick. Everyone aspired to be them."

It's true, then. They were together. In love.

"So why weren't they the ones getting married?" I ask.

"Because," Desiree says matter-of-factly. "Will left town the year after he graduated."

"Why would he do that?" Jake pounces.

Desiree leans back. "Sorry, what does that have to do with how they died?"

"We just want, um, the full picture," I hedge.

Desiree shrugs. "It was something about Will not feeling good enough for Becky. He wanted to make a name for himself. So he went into the city."

My mouth drops open. "And then Becky turned around and got engaged to Beau Uccello? That's rude."

Desiree flinches. "Thought you knew nothing about what happened."

Jake shifts from foot to foot. "We know a little. We've done some research. But we've hit a dead end. Did you go to the wedding?"

The woman's limbs stiffen. "I was on my way there, yes."

"So you didn't see Becky leave?"

"Hadn't gotten there yet."

"Did anyone else see her leave?"

Desiree squares her shoulders. "Who are you really? Who sent you?"

I shiver.

Jake clears his throat. "We're journalism students. No one sent us." He pushes his hands in his pockets. "Is this uncomfortable to talk about?"

Desiree stares into the middle distance, her mouth a straight line, her jaw tense. "I don't know anything." Her gaze flicks down. "And I don't want trouble."

I can't help it. I have to ask. "Trouble? With whom?"

But Desiree's expression is hard now. Shut down. "Unless you want to bowl, I think it's time to leave."

She glances to her right, and suddenly, a burly guy appears from behind a desk. He wears a plaid shirt, has giant hands, and walks toward us calmly. The aggression is coiled up inside him, though. It vibrates through his shoulders, his massive thighs.

"Okay, okay. No problem." Jake raises his hands in surrender, nervously eyeing the man, too. "We'll totally go. But, um, is there anyone else we could talk to about this? Another wedding guest, maybe?"

Desiree's eyes narrow. Her expression is clear: No more questions.

The security dude walks toward the door. I follow, my heart pounding hard. But then I turn back. "Wait."

"Casey," Jake says, trying to grab my arm.

I shake him off and hurry back to Desiree. "Can you tell me more about what she was like?"

Desiree looks stricken. "Who?"

"Becky."

"Casey," Jake urges, rushing to my side. "Let's just go."

But Desiree gives the burly guy a quick look that I think means *hold up a sec*. She turns back to me. "Becky . . . She was a lot of fun. Everyone loved her."

"And what was she into?"

She doesn't have to think for long. "Reading. Writing. She had a huge imagination. Wrote a whole play for the drama club. They put it on her junior year."

A writer. Just like me. My heart pounds hard.

"She died too young," Desiree says stiffly as she turns away and busies herself with stacking the scorecards on the counter. "They both did."

"I know," I say softly. "Listen. If you change your mind . . ." I grab a scrap of paper from the bowling alley's shoe rental desk and scribble down an email address from my childhood. It's one I barely use anymore, but it doesn't include my real name or any identifying information.

"Here's where you can contact me," I say. "I'd love to hear from you."

I slide it across the counter. Desiree glances at it, then crumples it up and puts it in her pocket. There's something I can't read in her expression. It's not that she's closed-off or even angry. There's hesitation, too. Maybe even regret.

Outside, the air has turned colder. Jake and I walk halfway across the parking lot until we speak. "Mike and Renee from SUNY Stony Brook?" I blurt.

"Sorry. Just popped into my head. *Jesus*. That was weird."

"Do you think Desiree is hiding something?"

"Uh, yeah." Jake chews on his lip. "It almost sounds like someone threatened her about talking to the press."

"So maybe she knew more? Saw something? And . . . what . . . Someone thought she was going to tell?"

Above us, a flock of birds fly in a V across the miserable gray sky. Something glints to my right—in that same spot where I thought a figure had ducked behind a parked car. *Is* someone watching us? Another shiver zips down my spine.

Back in the car, I do my calming breathing technique to deal with the drive. Jake revs the engine. "Maybe this crash did involve someone else. These two didn't want to die that day; even Desiree seems to think so. Maybe someone forced them to go over the side. Maybe it was a car chase."

I'm quiet for a moment. Jake looks at me, sensing my hesitation. "What is it?"

"I might have had a vision," I admit. "But I wasn't sure it was true."

I explain to him the tiny snippet of something I remember—that unexpected something from the side road, Becky screaming.

"But I just didn't think it added up to anything," I explain.

"Maybe it does," Jake says. "Maybe someone was after them. It would make sense, wouldn't it? Girl flees her wedding? Of course someone would want her back. It's what we've been circling around all along."

"But who would it have been?" I whisper.

We exchange a look. We don't even have to say what we're thinking. One person makes the most sense. Beau Uccello. The jilted groom.

EIGHTEEN

It's lunchtime. We swing back by Woody's, the burger place, and get a seat by the window. I don't even mind the sawdust on the bottom of my shoes. To be honest, it's nice to be in a restaurant after spending so much time in the hospital.

But my time feels borrowed. *Someone* is going to figure out that I've left. How long will Pippa's lies hold? What if Fran decides to check on me at Chadwick Lake? What if the hospital calls Mr. Coleman, since he's paying the bills? I need to figure out what happened to Becky—and why I am the way I am, and that Jake isn't someone I should be afraid of—fast. But even if I do prove something, who's to say Fran and my father will believe me?

"You okay?" Jake asks me as he takes a sip of Dr Pepper.

I pretend to be interested in the newsprint wallpaper. I should tell him about Fran's warning that I should never see him again and let Becky go. But whenever I try, my mouth won't form the words.

"If you're worried about confronting Beau, don't be," Jake says when I don't answer. "We just need an angle. A way to get him to talk without revealing who we are or that we're onto him."

"Because that worked so well with Desiree." I dip a fry into ketchup. "Who's to say she hasn't already called Beau to warn him about us sniffing around?"

"Yeah, but he'll be looking for a Mike and Renee, not a Jake and Casey," Jake says with a wink. "But seriously, if that's the case? Then we have our proof that he is hiding something."

Suddenly, Jake's phone rings. He glances down at it—once again, I'm afraid it's Fran—and then his face lights up. "It's Mrs. Rao. From school."

He answers, and I listen to him talking to his old contact. He nods a few times, and then looks hopeful, and then looks disappointed. "Okay, thanks," he says, his voice low.

He hangs up, sighs, and looks at me. "The school did have Becky's address and family in the system, but it might be a dead end. There's no record of her dad. Her mom moved out of the area shortly after her death. They don't have a forwarding address."

I sigh. Maybe it's for the best. Like Karin said, speaking with family probably isn't our best angle. Still, I'd love to at least speak to Becky's mom, even if it's about something trivial. Maybe her voice will trigger another flashback.

"Maybe we could ask a neighbor about them," I say. "Or contact the post office?"

Jake looks at the address he'd scribbled down on the placemat. "I can have my mom check it out. It's close to the office."

As he texts his mom, my mind wanders. I wonder why Becky's mom left town. Maybe the accident was too traumatic for her to remain here.

Then I ask Jake, "Was there any more information about Becky in the school's system?"

"According to Mrs. Rao, Becky's grades were excellent. She was extremely intelligent." Jake pauses on me. "Just like you."

"What about that play she wrote for the drama club?" I ask, remembering what Desiree told us. "Does that check out?"

"She mentioned a play, yeah. She said Becky was a prolific writer. Head of the literary magazine."

It's so strange to hear that Becky was drawn to the same things I am. Again, it makes me wonder—am I less myself if I'm piggybacking off her experience? It's a strange conundrum. Having a past life makes me feel special and less special all at once.

"Is there any information about her going to college?" I ask.

"Mrs. Rao didn't say. Though she commented on it—she thought it was odd that Becky didn't have college plans. But again, this was before her time. She's seeing if she can wrangle a teacher we can speak to who might be able to shed light on that."

I stare out the window at the dead street. "Is it possible Becky didn't apply to college because, at that point, she knew she was getting married?"

"We're not talking 1950."

"Even so, maybe Beau didn't want her to go." I clear my throat. "Maybe he was controlling. It could be part of why she was so miserable about marrying him."

And wow, was she miserable. Standing out on that patio, trying to get some air, trying not to cry. I think again about the yearbook pictures of Will and Beau side by side. They were so different. I can't understand why Becky would have even agreed to date Beau after Will left. The idea of Will leaving is confusing, too.

"Do you think it's true that Will went off to the city to try to . . . I don't know, prove himself to Becky?" I ask.

Jake fiddles with his straw wrapper. "I wonder why he came on the day of her wedding instead of earlier. Was he just trying to be dramatic? Had he just found out?"

"Maybe he'd been traveling." I wish I had flashes that would explain all of this. All I see was how thrilled Becky was when Will appeared. Relieved, actually.

Had she been forced to marry Beau? Only, why? Or maybe it was all about Beau being successful, settled. Maybe Becky had a conversation with Will and he took it to heart—even overreacted, leaving for good. But then, what, had he cut Becky off? Cell phones were around then. People were traceable.

And why didn't she visit him in the city? It's only a train ride away. Did he break it off for good?

It could make sense. And maybe Becky was lonely. And maybe Beau swooped in and took advantage of her loneliness. She said yes because she figured Will would never return.

I voice this theory to Jake, and he admits it's plausible. "Guys can be pretty sensitive when girls tell them they're not successful enough. Maybe Will figured he'd go make his mark somewhere and then return worthy of her."

"But Becky either couldn't wait that long or didn't want to?" I'm just hypothesizing. "I don't know why she just didn't go with him. She'd graduated from school. She could have gotten an interesting job in the city. An internship." I stare at the printouts we'd made of what we'd found on Becky and Will. We had no information about what she planned to do after high school.

Jake's quiet a moment, drinking the dregs of his Dr Pepper until ice rattles in the glass. "It's kind of what's happening now, you know."

"What do you mean?"

"With us. And that dude you were dating. Rich guy, totally a step up . . ."

I stare at him. "You feel like you're not good enough for me?"

Jake shrugs. "It's sort of hard to compare to Marcus Coleman."

"But . . ." I sputter. "If anything, Becky's story parallels my feelings of why Marcus chose me. Not about me choosing you."

Jake waves his hand. "Please. Of course Marcus would want to date you. Anyone would. But you know, maybe that's why Becky said yes to Beau. She was so astonished someone like Beau—prominent, rich—would go for someone like her. Maybe that is how history is repeating itself."

"Are you saying that's why I'm dating Marcus?"

Jake crosses his arms. "I thought you weren't dating him anymore."

"I mean . . . I'm not. But . . ."

I trail off. Had I only dated Marcus because I'd felt flattered? Maybe Jake is right. All this time, I've walked around so grateful that Marcus has even given me a crumb of attention that I haven't thought about what I wanted—or what he did.

I'm struck with clarity. I shouldn't be walking on eggshells around Marcus just because of who he is. Nor should I think I owe him something for choosing me. The only thing I owe him, actually, is the truth.

Suddenly, I pick up my phone. Jake cocks his head. "Making a call?"

"Sending an email. Something I needed to do a long time ago."

I start a letter. *Dear Marcus.* The words flow out of me. Is it cowardly to break up with Marcus in an email? Of course. But writing is so much easier for me than saying it out loud. He'll want to talk about it, surely, but this is a first step.

I tell him I need to figure myself out first. I thank him for our time together, that me breaking up with him has nothing to do with what happened in Avon Shores, and that I wish him well. The Avon Shores part is a bit of a fudge of the truth. I'll always feel a little humiliated by that. But it's done now.

There's a *whoosh* as the I hit send. I think of Marcus, squirreled away in his family compound in Turks and Caicos, receiving this letter. Reading it. Feeling hurt, confused. It makes me cringe. I'm not one for confrontation.

Woody hobbles out from the kitchen and slams a check on our table. "Thanks, man," Jake says. "It was delicious as usual."

The old guy grunts. As he turns, Jake's eyes widen at the back of his shirt. He nudges me, and I look, too. It's a tee for a local baseball league team. The back lists the sponsors. One is this restaurant. The other is Uccello Construction.

"Woody," Jake calls out.

The man turns, looking astonished that someone is trying to make conversation.

"You know Beau Uccello?" Jake asks.

Woody's gummy mouth turns gummier. He gives one gruff nod.

"Know where his main office is?" Jake asks.

Now Woody's eyebrow arches. "Who wants to know?"

"Business proposal," I say smoothly. "A friend's parents from the city want to build a house out here. I heard he's the guy to do it."

Woody nods, taking this in. "Over on Marple, in Ryan Shoals. That's where he usually is, too. Unless he's on a job."

He turns around then, grumpily trudging back to the kitchen. Jake turns to smile at me. "Look at you, being the detective! And I love the little role-play."

"Guess I'm not the only actor here," I tease. And then I squeeze his hand under the table. It feels good that Jake squeezes back.

●●●

We're nervous on the drive over. I keep my head out the window like a dog, sucking in the cold air, trying to handle my anxiety for being in a car and confronting this person who seems more and more like someone troubling from Becky's past—maybe even the person who killed her. We still haven't come up with a plan of how we're going to talk to Beau, either. Jake seems to think that it's best if we just wing it, but I'm really not so sure.

I'm also nervous because I kind of can't believe I'd written Marcus a break-up email. He hasn't replied. What if it went to his spam? What if he read it but doesn't believe it? What if this sounds all kinds of alarms—he thinks I'm being Becky again?

Was writing him a mistake?

Jake's phone rings. His mom has information. "I sent her over to check out the house Becky lived in," Jake reports when he gets off the phone. "She spoke to some neighbors. This one lady has lived there since the seventies. She remembers Becky and her mom."

"Really?" I feel a bolt of excitement. "What did she say?"

"She didn't know Becky well, but she spoke with Becky's mom a lot. Said Becky's mom was so proud Becky was marrying that Uccello boy. He was so successful. The right kind of husband."

I sigh. "So maybe Becky felt pressure."

"Maybe. This neighbor also says Becky's mom was in total shock after the accident. Angry, too—she blamed it on Will. Well, she called him 'the old boyfriend.' She saw the whole thing as Will's fault."

"She didn't say anything about a car chase?"

"Nope. But get this—shortly after Becky and Will died, Becky's mom went over to Will's father's house with a baseball bat. She was angry. She tried to smash in all his windows, but Will's dad called the police. The neighbor said it was a big story for a while. Becky's mom was so humiliated, and she moved shortly after."

"Where did she go?"

"Florida. She and this neighbor exchanged Christmas cards. Not long ago, she died."

I shut my eyes. A trail gone cold. It saddens me that I'll never get to meet Becky's mom, not that she would have accepted me anyway.

"So in this neighbor's mind—and Becky's mom's—Beau Uccello was Mr. Perfect, and Will was the bad guy?" I ask.

"Sounds like it."

"Do you think Beau was paying them off, too?"

Jake hesitates. "We don't know if Beau's paying anyone off." Then he looks at me. "Do you have a memory of Becky's mom from the wedding?"

My mind drifts back to that first scene that had poked through—getting ready in that room off the patio, that view of the beach stretched out before me. The women in there with me felt like strangers. To be honest, I don't have any memories of Becky's mom at all. The only distinct person in Becky's memories, for the most part, is Will.

"I don't," I suggest. "Though it sounds like she wasn't supportive of her. And if she pushed Becky into this loveless marriage . . . maybe she didn't bother holding her in her memory." I knock my head back on the car's headrest. "This is all speculation. I wish we had something real. I wish we could talk to Desiree again. Find out more."

"Have a feeling Desiree isn't giving out any more quotes," Jake murmurs. Then he flicks the turn signal as a sign appears in the distance on the right: Uccello Construction, Main Office.

My heart jumps. We're already here.

We pull in. The building is redbrick and siding, and the parking lot is only half full. I spy a luxury SUV in one of the spaces and wonder if it's Beau's. He's the head of the company. The guy making all the money.

Jake cuts the engine, but for a while, neither of us move.

"Are we doing this?" I ask. "We don't even have a plan."

"I think we say we want to build something?"

I look at him crazily. "We're both eighteen. Like he's going to believe us?"

Jake stares down at his shirt. "Should we use the college student reporter angle? Or we could say we're business students. Looking to interview local entrepreneurs."

I rub my eyes. "I feel like he'd see right through us."

"Yeah, but he's not going to know who we are—or were," Jake argues. "I think the goal is to see if he's even aware of us," Jake says. "Like, if Desiree warned him, maybe he'd know someone was coming. I think we'd be able to sense that. But even so, we're just college students, right? We're not Becky and Will in Casey's and Jake's bodies."

I stare at the building again. We've come all this way. It feels like Beau is our answer, maybe the secret Becky and Jake want us to know. It would be silly to turn back now.

"Come on." I press the latch to open the door. "Let's go."

As we cross the parking lot, I feel my own cell phone buzz in my bag. When I pull it out, I'm greeted with the name I've been dreading: *Fran*.

I stare at the name for a beat, my heart leaping into my throat. Has Marcus already told her? Has he circumnavigated talking to me and gone straight to my stepmother?

I hit ignore. Talking to her is important—vital—but there's no way she could be in Avon Shores. As far as I know, she's still in Boston. Hours from here.

Her call will have to wait.

NINETEEN

The office is sleeker than I expected: clean lines of wood and glass, fancy furniture in the waiting area, fresh flowers. There's a blond receptionist behind a desk with a marble top. She glances up as we walk in.

"Can I help you?" she asks. She isn't that much older than I am. There's something familiar about her face, especially her smile. It's the same smirk I saw in Beau Uccello's senior picture. I wonder if this is a relation.

"We'd like to talk to Mr. Uccello," Jake says smoothly.

The receptionist's smirk deepens. "Do you have an appointment?"

Jake looks at me, and I want to stomp on his foot. Why do *I* have to answer?

The receptionist doesn't wait for either of us to reply, picking up the phone once more as though to make a call. "Mr. Uccello isn't in. And if you'd like to see him, you need to make an appointment." She folds her hands. "You realize this is a building development office, right?"

"Uh . . ." I trail off and spin around, grabbing Jake's sleeve. "Sorry. Let's go."

I pull him back into the sunshine. My cheeks blaze. "This was a bad idea," I tell Jake as I hurry away from the door. "There's no way we can just walk in there and expect them to take us seriously."

Jake runs his hand through his hair. "Right. But did you notice she didn't seem to have any idea who we were? She definitely hadn't been alerted about us."

"True," I say. "But that doesn't mean anything. Maybe Beau didn't tell her."

I peer toward the street. Beau isn't in the office now, but presumably he'll be coming back to the office at some point. Should we plant ourselves in the parking lot and ambush him the minute he pulls in? Jake's right—the first hurdle is to see if he's aware we exist. I'm guessing his expression will give it away—if Desiree warned him about us, likely she described Jake's fluffy hair and my small stature. If he does know who we are, we'll press the issue—either follow him inside or find some sort of backup to help us. Another adult, maybe. The police.

But as I'm mulling this over, I feel Jake's nails dig into my arms. Before I know what's happening, he's yanking me back through the double doors and into the office.

"What the—?" I sputter, but Jake shushes me, gesturing to the reception desk. To my surprise, it's unoccupied. The assistant is gone.

"She just ran to the bathroom," Jake whispers. "Now's our chance."

"Our chance to what?"

He starts down the hall. "His office."

Jake has truly lost his mind. I glance over my shoulder. This plan makes absolutely no sense. Someone is going to hear us.

"Here!" Jake whispers from a doorway.

He's at the end of the corridor. Outside the door is a placard that reads Beau Uccello, President.

Jake waves me to come in. Considering the alternative is standing in the middle of the hallway like a sitting duck, I hurry after him. Once I'm inside, Jake gently closes the door until it's almost shut.

I grab his forearms. "Have you lost your mind?"

He shrugs. "We look around quickly. Maybe we'll find some sort of evidence."

"And what about the receptionist? She won't be in the bathroom forever!"

"We'll figure that out. It's okay."

The air feels thin. My head feels disconnected from my body. "Jake, this feels really wrong."

"We won't get in trouble." He shrugs. "We've caught all kinds of crackpots in the back rooms of the vet's office. Most people are looking for animal medications to use on themselves. We've never reported any of them—just asked them to leave."

But this feels different than a vet's office. Someone in this office will take two kids snooping around far more seriously. Right?

Jake gestures around the room. "We're here already. We might as well look. Just be quiet. And this office is big enough—if we hear her coming, there are places to hide."

I lower my shoulders and look around. "But what are we looking for?"

Jake strides over to Beau's desk. "Aha. A message log. That receptionist writes down everyone who's called on a slip, and they're either here . . ." He ducks to the wastepaper basket. "Or here."

He starts to sift through them. It makes me squeamish how he does it without gloves. Isn't he worried about fingerprints?

A moment later, he drops all the messages to the desk. "No message from Desiree Lofgren. All of these look like business stuff."

"Great," I say. "Now let's get out of here."

"Wait!" Jake walks over to the bookcases, perusing the photos. "Guys fishing . . . more guys fishing . . . Beau posing with the mayor of New York City . . ."

"What are you looking for?"

"Kids. A significant other."

"A significant other doesn't mean he didn't hurt Becky," I whisper.

"True. But maybe we could ask her questions." Jake chews on his lip. I watch as he runs his fingertip against the spines of a few books with business-y titles. I wrench his finger away.

"You're touching everything," I whisper. "You're the worst criminal ever."

But then a small, narrow wooden box on the bookcase sidelines my attention. It's a paperweight, I think—and it's familiar. I don't know why. Have I seen it in Avon Shores? Or in the psychic's office. Or in Woody's?

I've seen it somewhere.

Something clicks down the hall. We freeze. Jake is on one side of the bookcase, and I'm on the other. I glance around for someplace to hide. Can I squash myself between the bookcase and the wall?

We stay still for ages, waiting for footsteps. A phone rings in the lobby. The receptionist answers it in a singing tone, "Uccello Construction!" She's back at her desk, then.

The door to Beau's office doesn't creak open. Maybe we're safe.

I let out a breath. "We need to get out of here."

"Okay," Jake says, defeated. "Sorry. I thought this would be more . . ." His gaze lands on something past me. "Wait. Is that . . . ?"

He turns to a shelf of books and grabs one of them off the shelf. As soon as I see the spine I realize why. It's the same yearbook he brought home from the high school yesterday. Avon Shores High, 2003.

The year Beau and Will graduated.

"Huh," I whisper. Do most thirtysomething men have their high school yearbooks in their offices?

Jake cracks the spine. The seniors' now-familiar faces greet us. Unlike the yearbook Jake borrowed, this one is filled with signatures and inscriptions—it's Beau's personal copy.

And clearly Beau was popular. There are notes over practically every senior's picture. I think of my own yearbook the last year I'd gone to school—when I was technically a sophomore. It was practically bare.

Then I realize something. "See if Becky wrote something!"

"On it," Jake murmurs, flipping the pages.

We get to Becky's junior picture—her smile is so bright, her hair a little longer than when she was a senior. But she hasn't signed that page. Jake leafs past more candid photos and club group shots and sports montages. Nothing, nothing, nothing.

The reception phone rings again. I glance nervously over my shoulder. How much longer should we be in here?

"Look," Jake says, pointing to a back page. Then his eyes widen. "Oh, shit."

His thumb stabs something at the bottom. *I hope you burn in hell, asshole,* someone has written. *Becky.* This is Becky's handwriting. It's the same as those hand-penned pages of the play she wrote.

I stare in horror. Then I read the rest. *Beau Uccello, You are the meanest, nastiest, grossest person ever, and I wouldn't touch you with a ten-foot pole! This year in school with you has been AWFUL and I hope to never see you again. Hope you burn in hell, asshole!*

"Jesus," Jake whispers. "This is bad. Really bad."

"Why would she marry a guy if she felt this way about him?" I can't wrap my head around it. "Did he force her?"

A slam breaks our concentration. A tall man stands in the doorway, a jacket slung over his arm. He blinks at us in disbelief. His gaze bounces from our faces to the yearbook we're holding. And though my vision is clouded with fear, it doesn't take me long to realize who it is.

"Who," Beau Uccello says, his voice tight and unkind, "the fuck are you?"

TWENTY

Beau Uccello is tall but not as broad as I expected, his build almost slim. His hair is cut as short as it was in high school, and his eyes are bright. He's wearing jeans and black Vans sneakers— the same pair I have in my dorm room closet, actually. I wouldn't have expected a serious businessman to be so unassuming or casual.

I hope you burn in hell, Becky wrote. A shudder shoots through me.

"What are you doing in here?" Beau doesn't even look angry—more like confused. His gaze darts to the yearbook Jake is still holding. "What are you doing with that?"

Jake steps in front of me. "This was all my idea. I should be the one who gets in trouble." He touches my hand. "Casey, run."

But I can't run—not that I would anyway. I'd never do that to Jake. If we're going down, I guess we're going down together.

The assistant appears behind Beau. "What the . . . ?" Her face a mask of both disgust and concern. "Mr. Uccello, these kids came in wanting to see you. I had no idea they snuck in."

Beau's gaze is still on the yearbook. "Can you put that down?"

"Yeah. Sorry." Jake sets it on the bookcase. Then he blurts out the same story we used before. "Sorry, Mr. Uccello. We're, um, college students. In journalism. Researching some old stories—and one of them is about an accident about eighteen years ago."

Beau cocks his head. "Accident?" He glances at the yearbook again. His expression is guarded. Does he remember that letter Becky wrote? Those seething sentences?

"Mr. Uccello, I am so sorry," the assistant interrupts. "Do you want me to call the cops? We should definitely search these two. They probably stole something."

Beau stares at us, still puzzled. There's something else in his eyes, too. Maybe understanding. Maybe he knows we're onto him. He looks at me in particular.

"Why do I know you?" he asks. "Why are you familiar?"

Words freeze in my throat. Desiree. She's told him. *He's onto us.*

Jake grabs my hand. "Listen, when we talked to Desiree, we were just looking for answers. Details. As journalists. That's all."

Beau's eyes narrow. "You talked to . . . who?"

"Desiree Lofgren." Jake squares his shoulders. "We know she called you."

"Desiree Lofgren . . . from high school?" Beau wrinkles his nose. "She was supposed to call me?"

I shift my weight. Should I believe him? Obviously he's been alerted somehow about us.

"Look, we're really sorry," I say, opting for the cowardly approach. "We'll go."

I try to skirt around him, but Beau holds out an arm like a security gate. "What accident are you talking about?"

"Nothing," I say quickly, my heart thudding. His arm is so close. He could grab me so fast. "Forget about it."

"Uh-uh." Beau's voice is stern. "You're in *my* office. The least you can do is tell me what the hell is going on."

I glance at Jake. We're trapped. So Jake says, quietly, "The accident with Will Woodson and Becky Kinkaid."

Beau crosses his arms and is silent for a while. His face gives nothing away. Finally, he glances over his shoulder. "Tracey, you can go."

The assistant scoffs. "You aren't going to call the police?"

"I'll handle this."

"But—"

"Tracey," Beau says in a warning tone.

Tracey storms out.

Beau turns back to us. His posture is stiffer now, his arms tight against his chest.

"I'm guessing you know by now that Becky and I were supposed to be getting married the day of that accident. If you're researching it."

We nod. I look at the guy again, trying to spark something from Becky's time—fear, worry, dread. It's got to be there. She hated this guy. That call to Will's father in his house—it was a cry for help.

"And let me guess," Beau adds, his voice thick. "You're in my office because you think I had something to do with it?"

Next to me, Jake pulls in a breath. "I mean . . ." he fumbles. "We just . . ."

"She was supposed to be with me, you're thinking," Beau interrupts. "And maybe I got angry and chased after her. Ran her off that road. *If I can't have her, no one can.*"

I bite my lip. He said it, not me.

I point to the yearbook. "We, um, saw her letter to you. It was . . . intense."

"She . . . hated you." Jake's voice cracks. "Didn't she?"

Beau stares at us for a moment, a furrow in his brow. Then, a strange sound escapes from his lips. It takes me a moment to realize—laughter.

His laugh is sad but also a little bitter. He grabs the yearbook from the shelf. "That's what the cops thought, too. But it's just the way Becky and I talked to each other. I'm guessing you didn't read the whole letter?"

Beau flips the pages of the yearbook to the back. He finds Becky's note, the one about him burning in hell. Then he turns to the next page and shows us. "It continues on the other side, if you'd bothered to look."

We stare at Becky's same bubbly handwriting. Sure enough, there's more to her letter. *Psych!* she's written. *Got ya! Love ya like a brother, doofus. I'd say have a great summer, but I'll probably be seeing your ugly ass every day.*

Jake and I blink, stunned. "Oh," I say stupidly. "Uh. No. We didn't see that part."

Beau slaps the book shut. "Becky and I were in study hall together starting her freshman year. We wrote notes back and forth ribbing each other, making fake insults. We found it funny. Neither of us were the sappy type. It was much more fun to bust each other's balls. So in our yearbook messages, that's what we did." He eyes us. "You're telling me neither of you had inside jokes like that when you were in high school?"

Then he reaches past me and picks up another book from the shelf. This one is more like a notebook. He flips through it, pulls out a wrinkled piece of paper from the back, and shoves it into our faces. Words swim in front of my eyes. *Police report*, it reads.

"Not that you deserve to see this, but I had nothing to do with that accident, and there's proof." His thumb jabs a paragraph halfway down the page. "I had an alibi. I was getting ready for my wedding. Most of the guests weren't there yet, but I had a few friends and family members who'd come early. A whole bunch of people vouched that I never left. I never chased after them in a car, or in a plane, or on a bicycle, or anything in between." His voice cracks. "I wouldn't do that to Becky. Not in a million years."

I skim the report. Witnesses corroborate that Beau never left that big, beautiful blue-gray home. That's all it says, though. It doesn't say that someone else didn't go after him. He could have paid someone, maybe. Ordered someone else to do it. *Get Becky back.*

But there's something about the tears in Beau's eyes and the way his voice has cracked that makes me wonder. He has regrets, and he wanted to marry Becky, but maybe he really didn't have anything to do with it. The guilt hits me hard. Here we are in this random guy's office, poking at a sore old wound.

"Mr. Uccello," Jake says quietly. "That must have been terrible."

"It *was* terrible," Beau breathes. "For a while, we didn't even know Becky was gone. There was this scramble to find her. Guests were arriving, everyone was asking questions—it was a mess. We were like, 'Did she go in the water? Did she walk to the pier?' But then I heard the sirens in the distance. Toward the bridge." He lowers his eyes. "That's when I knew. I just knew, somehow, that she was gone."

"I'm so sorry," I whisper.

He shakes his head. "I knew Becky didn't want to marry me. I was her second choice. But she was so sad after Will left, and I just thought—she wasn't with anyone, I wasn't with anyone, and we were best friends—why not?"

I bite down hard on my lip. This is more information than we've gotten about Becky so far, but the details are so different from what I expected. *We were best friends.* Why didn't any of Becky's memories show me those details?

"I loved her," Beau says. "But I also wanted her to be happy. I knew she didn't want to be with me, not really. She was settling. I wasn't Will. I'd never be Will."

"So . . . you knew about them?" Jake asks in a small voice.

Beau rolls his eyes. "Of course I knew about them. And was fine with them being a couple. I mean, did I want to be with Becky? Maybe. Kind of. But I'm not the asshole who's going to be jealous of her for finding real love. Our friendship went deeper than that. I knew we'd always be in each other's lives even if she was with someone else."

I run my tongue over my teeth. "But if Becky was so in love, why did Will leave her?"

Beau shrugs. "He got in his head that she deserved someone better. I think he was always comparing himself to me, my family—but he shouldn't have. Becky didn't care. I guess they had a fight shortly after she graduated. He moved away. Went to the city—to get some fancy job, I guess. He just . . . cut her off. Stopped calling her. Lost all contact. It was awful for her. We even went to the city a few times to look for him. But, I mean, it's Manhattan. Kinda like finding a needle in a haystack. Plus, social media wasn't around then. Google wasn't as useful."

"You both went to the city," I breathe. And suddenly, annoyingly, I get a glimmer of this:

You walk down the sidewalk, near 42nd Street. Neon lights flash on either side of you. Cabs whiz by. There's someone at your side. "This is like finding a needle in a haystack," the someone says. "Even if we knew where he worked—which we don't—it might be tough."

I blink, coming out of it. That was Beau with her.

"Why do you think he came back on your wedding day?" Jake asks. "Of all days?"

Beau shoves his hands in his pockets. "I'm guessing that was just when he found out. Terrible timing. Terrible end."

He clamps his lips together then, a pained look crossing his features. "Sorry," he says, pressing his hand over his eyes. "I don't think about this much anymore."

Jake and I exchange a heavy glance.

"I lost two people I cared about," Beau murmurs, his face still hidden by his hand. "It was the worst day of my life. And even worse, I was investigated after it. Like I wasn't suffering? And now you're here, dredging it up again."

"We're so sorry," I whisper.

But then something occurs to me: Should I tell him that I'm Becky? That's she's in me? Would that be a salve?

I think of Karin's warnings. He might not buy it. It might hurt even worse.

Beau sniffles. Jake shifts awkwardly. I make up my mind. Our time here is up

"We'll go. We shouldn't have bothered you, Mr. Uccello. Clearly we had this all wrong . . . We're very sorry," I say.

Beau wipes his eyes. It's incongruous to see this grown man, someone I'd so recently feared, looking so wrecked.

"To be honest," he says. "I don't think there is much of a story. An investigation, I mean. Two people crashed. The end."

"So you don't think there was anything suspicious about the accident?" Jake asks. "Nothing . . . no one . . . chasing them, anything like that?"

Beau trudges back to his desk. "We all wanted answers, some sort of reason. But they never found anything."

He sits down in his chair and suddenly looks authoritative again. Steady. "It's the thing everyone who knew them had to come to grips with, in the end. It was just an accident. Two people, deeply in love, died together." Then he smiles sadly. "Kind of poetic, I guess. Just wish *I* had been the one she loved. Maybe she'd still be here if I was."

TWENTY-ONE

"Do you want ice cream?" Jake asks me later.

I shake my head miserably. "Too cold for that."

"A soft pretzel? Salt water taffy?"

"Not hungry," I say, skirting around a parked bicycle.

Jake gives me a sidelong glance. "You need to eat something, Casey. We just narrowly avoided death."

"That's an exaggeration." I laugh. "And you know it."

"Okay, but for a minute there, maybe?" He blows out a breath. "I mean, that yearbook inscription . . . What were we supposed to think when Beau walked in?"

Jake and I are strolling along the boardwalk in the same town where we spoke with Beau. I wasn't ready to get back in a car, and this town is a little more built up than Avon Shores, some of the establishments on the boardwalk open even in winter.

The water is to our left, dark blue and cold. On a nearby pier, a Santa's workshop has been assembled. There is an impressive display of animatronic elves and reindeer. But no one is visiting. Christmas is over. No one cares.

Beau was decent about us leaving his office without pressing charges. I'm not sure he bought that we were college students working on a story, but he didn't press to know who we really were. I feel bad we didn't tell him. There was the small chance Beau would have believed that we were Becky and Will. I mean, if my mother came back in someone else's body, I'd want to meet them.

I think.

"I don't understand why you're so down," Jake says after a beat. "Isn't it a good thing that the guy Becky was going to marry wasn't a total jerk—and that he didn't try to kill her?"

"Yeah," I concede. "But I wanted everything I saw—or I thought I saw—to make sense and have some closure."

"And match up with your thinking that someone was after Becky and Will?"

I nod. Because based on what Beau said—and what it sounds like the investigation concluded—the accident was just that. Nothing more. No conspiracy. Not a murder.

Except if that's true, then that means the memory I saw— that flash to the right, that car coming from the side road, Becky screaming—isn't real. It's worrying. What else have I seen isn't real?

"I figured Will and Becky wanted us to find something." I move out of the way of an old lady on a motorized cart. "Something we needed to expose—for them. And that's why they're still here, in us."

"Maybe, but maybe not. Who knows why souls—if that's even what it is—hang around or find other bodies? Who knows why you and I have memories of Becky and Will?"

"I guess I just want it to have meaning." The sickly-sweet smell of cotton candy wafts into my nose. "I want it to explain things. Explain me."

Jake glances at me, and then looks away. Does he know what's going through my mind? Does he realize I'm right back at that day with my mom? It's what I've been chasing all this time. Ever since I was told that I'd been the one to crash my mom's car, killing her, I've been searching for answers to why I'd grabbed her steering wheel. I want to think it's because I was trying to steer her away from something. Something that wasn't there, maybe, but something that had been there right before Becky's accident. Like a second car suddenly trying to ram them from a side street. Like someone after them, something so scary that Becky had screamed.

Except maybe that never happened. Maybe Will really did take the turn too quickly and sent the car careening into the guard rail and into the water. And maybe I, in my current life, steered my mother into the water . . . for some other reason.

Or maybe there is no reason. Maybe I'll never know.

"Arcade's open." Jake points down the boardwalk. "Challenge you to some video games?"

I sigh. "Sure."

He turns to face me. The corners of his mouth turn down. "I know you want it all to mean something, Casey. But I think it does. Maybe Will and Becky remained behind because they wanted to find each other again. They wanted us to find each other."

Tears fill my eyes. He's right, of course. He's so right.

The wind kisses our cheeks. Jake's fingers entwine with mine. It's been a while since we've touched—really touched—and my heart pounds with the sensation. The last few days have been filled with tons of meaning. And who better to have gone through it with than Jake? It hasn't been for nothing. I feel like I know more about myself now than I ever have. I know who I am. I know what I'm capable of. I know what I want.

And that includes Jake. Forever.

I look up and meet his adoring gaze. "Jake," I say, my voice cracking. "I want—"

"Shh," Jake says, putting a finger to my lips. "I know."

He leans in and kisses me. Right in the middle of the board-walk, Santa and his bored elves in full view. It's the kiss I remember from before, but somehow even better. Because this time, I don't feel it's wrapped up in Becky and Will and the memories of how they were.

This time, this kiss is just ours.

●●●

The next few hours we spend at the back of the arcade making out. We kiss hungrily, without vulnerability—after what we've been through, a lot of that has gone out the window. My heart pounds when Jake touches me, but it's a safe sort of pounding—a warm, intense rush. Jake is my person. I've never felt so comfortable with anyone. And now he's here.

And yet, the afternoon feels like an ending of sorts. A Sunday evening. The last day of a vacation. We found out what we needed to find out. There's nowhere else to go. I don't want time to end for us, though. I don't think it has to. Why can't we just exist like this forever? Or better yet, I could stay out here for the winter semester and then Jake could come with me to the city to attend college next year. We could make it work. It doesn't even sound hard.

Over slices of pizza—Jake finally convinces me to eat, and suddenly, after all that kissing, I'm starving—we discuss a future. "You'd better not ghost me in the city like Will did with Becky, though," I warn him. "Don't go off and make your mark."

"I wonder why Will felt like that, anyway." Jake shakes his head, baffled. "I wish I had some sort of insight into it."

"Do you have any memories at all from him when he was in the city?"

Jake peers up into the wintery, late-afternoon sky, which is growing dim. "Like I said, I do have these glimmers of New York City that I don't think I've actually experienced. Like going to the old Yankee Stadium. Which was torn down in—what? 2009?"

I shrug. "I don't really follow baseball."

"So technically I could have gone. As a four- or five-year-old. But the memory is really sharp. Makes me wonder if it was Will's memory, not mine."

"So Will went to Yankee Stadium. I wonder what else?"

Jake pulls the cheese from his pizza with his teeth. "That's all I've got for now."

A shadow behind me catches my eye and I turn, heart suddenly in my throat. It's only a middle-aged woman in a dark wool coat, but for a moment, I'd thought it was Fran.

Jake frowns. "You okay? Look like you saw a ghost."

"No, just my stepmother."

He chews thoughtfully. "Are you really that afraid of her? It's your life, Casey. What can she do to you?"

I stare at my greasy paper plate. I have to admit it. The thing I'd promised. "I sort of said, when I went into that particular hospital instead of a more secure, serious one, that I'd never see you again. Or go down the Becky rabbit hole. Or any of it."

Jake's eyes widen. He lowers his slice.

"It was stupid. Just one of those things you say."

"Yeah . . ." He slowly picks up a napkin and blots his mouth. "Did she say the consequences of what would happen if you did see me?"

"Then she would check me into that other hospital. Because, clearly, I'm still dealing with my Becky issues. I'm not cured."

Jake's silent. The cheesy eighties radio on the stereo blares. I can't tell if he's just thinking or angry.

"I think you need to stand up for yourself, Casey," Jake decides. "You're not a kid anymore. And you know your own brain—and this whole story. Sure, it sounds delusional, but it isn't. It's your reality."

"But all I've put them through . . ."

"So what? And even if you did wrench that steering wheel and send your mom's car into the water—you were a kid! They should forgive you, not make you feel like a murderer for the rest of your life! Not hide things from you, and sneak around, whispering behind your back, and make other people check up on you, and threaten to commit you!" I start to protest, and he holds up a hand. "I'm not saying there wasn't some validity to doing those things, especially when you didn't remember the first time you'd visited Avon Shores. And I firmly believe you've been through trauma and benefited from therapy. It's just . . . maybe Fran needs therapy, too. And your dad. Maybe it isn't totally clear here who's right and who's wrong. And maybe they should let you figure yourself out. Because, to be honest? I've been around you for a few days, and you seem completely in control of who you are, and what you want, and what's best for you." He crosses his arms as if to say *so there*.

"Right," I say slowly. "Well. Thanks for the vote of confidence. But I still feel afraid."

He points to my bag. "Call her now. Explain exactly where you are."

"What? No!" I pull my bag from him as though I expect he's going to reach out and snatch it. "They'll come straight here!"

"So what? You're eighteen, Casey. They have no right to control your life." Then he cocks his head. "Unless you want them to come? Haul you away? Lock you up and throw away the key?"

Do I? Has it felt comforting to have Fran as a sort of safeguard? All my life, I have felt like I've had a sort of net to catch my

SARA SHEPARD

fall. Little did I know it was people tiptoeing behind the scenes, tidying up my mistakes, but it's certainly made my life easier.

I shake my head. "Every time she's made a decision for me, I've just sort of . . . gone with it. Even when I went behind her back and asked to have a roommate—that was after she left. I've never confronted her. I've just let her bulldoze over me, almost like I deserve it."

"Nobody deserves to be bulldozed."

"She was protecting me. But maybe that's not always the best thing."

"Exactly," Jake agrees. Then he smirks. "Says the guy you're supposed to stay away from." But then he leans forward and takes my hand. "I'll stick by you. Whatever you need."

I nod and take a deep breath. It is time to stand up to Fran. And to my father, too—because he's been hiding behind her all this time. It hurts that he might have been blaming me since the accident. Silently seething, maybe, or questioning at least, but too afraid to ask. They won't understand Becky. Maybe it's not even worth explaining her. But hopefully they'll understand that I'm okay. That I have clarity to continue on with my life. That I feel strong in my choices.

And, most importantly, that Jake isn't a bad guy. He's someone I want to be with. Forever.

My chest buzzes with nerves as I pull out my phone. It's only when I see the message alerts on my screen that I realize I haven't looked at the thing since before we went into Beau Uccello's office. I'd been too distracted—and then too caught up in kissing Jake. Fran's call in the parking lot rushes back to me. I'd completely forgotten she'd called. And I certainly haven't called her back.

Deep breath. If that's the case, stay strong. *You know who you are.*

But when I look closer at the alerts, Fran hasn't left a message. Nor, for that matter, has Marcus reacted to my break-up missive. I've received an email, though—at an old account.

My vision blurs at the name. *Desiree Lofgren.*

I gasp. Then I stab my screen to pull it up.

Dear Renee, it reads.

It takes me a minute to realize that *I* am Renee. The fake name Jake gave her at the bowling alley. I keep reading.

I shouldn't be telling you this. I could get into some real trouble. But Beau Uccello? He isn't the person you should be looking into.

That's all I can say. It's someone else.

Don't write back. Goodbye.

TWENTY-TWO

I have to endure another car ride because there's no way we both want to digest what Desiree has written in public. The ride back to Jake's place is tense and silent—and that's on top of the discomfort I already feel. I keep staring at Desiree's email. *It's someone else.*

Who? What does she mean? I compose email after email to her, but I don't send them. She asked me not to write back. I don't want to get her in trouble. Someone is watching her, then. Threatening her. Who?

It's only when we're safe in Jake's apartment that we feel we can talk—and that's only after Jake sweeps through the house making sure no one is hiding in a closet or under a bed, spying.

Someone else is culpable.

"Okay," Jake whispers when we finally sit down on his couch. I'm stuffed into the corner, my knees to my chest. He's rocked forward, his elbows on his knees. "So that memory you have of being pursued—maybe it is real?"

"I don't know. And why would Beau say it was an accident? Did he lie?"

Jake stares at the ceiling. "He seemed to care for Becky. I think he's telling the truth. Besides, Desiree said he isn't the one we should be looking at. Maybe he didn't know."

"True," I murmur. "But Beau would have looked into the facts with the cops. Made sure that if they said an accident, it really was."

"But he wasn't on the scene. It seems like no one saw what actually happened. Or if they did . . ."

"They were asked to keep quiet," I finish. "Desiree said she was on her way to the wedding, remember? I'm wondering if she saw something. Another car. A person."

"And maybe whoever was chasing them threatened Desiree after the fact, especially after she talked to the paper," Jake goes on. "Made her promise not to say anything else."

"But they're still threatening her?" I wrinkle my nose. "This happened years ago."

"They must be."

I pinch the bridge of my nose. "When I think cover-up, I think of a wealthy family who has a lot of income at their disposal. Which brings us right back to Beau's family. Could it be a Uccello? His father?"

"His father died when he was in high school, remember?"

Right. I'd forgotten. "His mother?"

"Do you really see a forty- or fiftysomething race after a couple on the run and have a car chase through Avon Shores?"

"If that's what happened. And don't underestimate the power of a pissed-off mom." But he sort of has a point.

"I bet there were other wealthy people at that wedding, too," Jake says. "The Uccellos seem pretty prominent."

I groan. "So now Beau needs to give us a guest list? How do we even go back to him without getting Desiree in trouble"

We sit like that for a little while. The sun slants through the windows, sinking lower into the trees.

"I wonder why Beau found you familiar," Jake asks after a while. I look at him curiously. "Remember? In his office? He was like, *Why do I know you?*"

I'd forgotten. "I initially thought it was because Desiree described us to him. He knew what I looked like."

"But Desiree didn't reach out to him, remember? You're sure you haven't met him before?"

"Where would I have met him?" Then again, Jake and I met at the house where he used to live. But it seems unlikely Beau would have been there. It was a party for younger people. Beau seems like the sort of guy who goes to fancy steakhouses, wood-paneled bars, even stuff in the city. He seems like a hobnobber. It's unlikely our circles ever would have crossed.

But then I catch myself. Or *had* our paths crossed? I think of the fancy event I'd attended the night this all started. That Christmas party. At the Met.

I blink hard. Beau hadn't been there, had he? That seems impossible. Implausible. The Uccellos are builders on Long Island, small potatoes to a media scion.

And yet something's nagging at me. Did I see him there? Did he see me? But that means Beau knows the Colemans.

And then it comes to me. I clap a hand over my mouth.

"That box," I whisper. "In Beau's office. It was wooden. Long. It had a logo on it. Did you see?"

Jake shakes his head. "No . . ."

I close my eyes, remembering sitting on Marcus's couch in his sun-drenched living room in the city, perusing various objects on his coffee table. He was a person with actual coffee table books, all published by Coleman media. I'd flipped through a few—*The Art of Motorcycles*, *Iceland*, *Great Record Covers of the 1960s*—before noticing a couple of wooden boxes on the coffee table's lower shelf. They were long and narrow, emblazoned with an old-fashioned *C*.

Marcus had noticed me looking at them. "Nothing interesting. Just letter openers."

"C for Coleman?" I'd asked.

"It's the old logo for the company. Changed in the mid-2000s, but Dad likes things retro. He told me he had them custom-made by these Japanese guys who normally made samurai swords."

"Wow, and *you* got some?" I teased.

Marcus made a sour face. "He gave me a few. Made it out like they were really special. Told me to give them only to people I cared about, people I wanted to impress." He stared at the floor. "Later, Dad noticed how I still had most of them. He laughed his ass off. He was like, 'You realize that samurai sword story was bullshit, right? Bought them at a wholesale store in New Jersey.' He thought it was so funny that I'd been duped. He was like, 'If you were an ice fisher, I bet I could sell you ice cubes.'"

It's got to be a coincidence. Beau knows the Colemans? Marcus knows Beau? They aren't remotely the same age. And again—why would the Coleman family know these small-time builders on Long Island?

I grab my phone. All this time, I'd been searching for Beau Uccello and what he'd been up to in 2005 in Avon Shores, but maybe I hadn't seen the whole picture.

Into Google, I type *Beau Uccello and Marcus Coleman*. I close my eyes when I hit the search icon. When I open them again, dozens of hits have appeared.

Beau Uccello and Marcus Coleman pictured at the Dream Big Gala, 2020.

Beau Uccello and Marcus Coleman share drinks at Soho House.

But it's an article halfway down the page that makes my heart really stop.

Beau Uccello and Marcus Coleman in attendance at the Whitney Holiday Party

I blink hard at the date. This party was only three weeks ago.

I'd been in the hospital then. Dealing with untangling Becky. A few days later, the Colemans went to Turks and Caicos.

My skin starts to prickle. Suddenly, I can't breathe.

The almost-fiancé of a past life inside me knows a guy I'd been dating in the present. It doesn't feel like a coincidence. Something has been manipulated. Only what? There's also the fact that Marcus came to Avon Shores to retrieve me and made no mention that he knew someone who lived here—someone, maybe, who was a key to Becky's past. Then again, should he have mentioned it?

Still, it feels like all of these worlds are dangerously intersecting. Marcus heard me talk about Becky when he and Fran ambushed me. And surely he—or at least his father—knew that Beau had been poised to marry his best friend Becky but then she died in a horrific car crash on the day of the wedding. Yes, a lot of people are named Becky, but how many Beckys lived in Avon Shores, and how many girlfriends had fugue states where they wandered off to said Avon Shores claiming they were someone named Becky in a past life?

"Casey." Jake is next to me now, looking at me with concern. "You're really pale. Tell me what's going on."

"I don't . . ." I whisper. I press the heels of my hands to my temples, desperate to make the pounding stop. "I can't . . ."

My head hurts so badly that I hear actual pounding between my ears. It's only when Jake jumps up and whirls around that I don't realize it's all in my brain but an actual pounding on the door.

We freeze. Stare at each other.

Three sharper knocks sound. I bite down hard on my cheek. Where can we go? Where can we hide?

Silence. I want to breathe out. Relax. Maybe it was just a coincidence. Maybe whoever it was has moved on, realized they got the wrong place. But then something sharp flies through the drywall next to the doorjamb. Pieces of the wall splinter to the floor in flakes. A cloud fills the air. I see a flash of metal as whatever it is disappears and then chops into the wall again, this time slightly lower. The blade is sharp. *An axe.*

Jake and I scream as the blade of an axe chops three more times until there's a ragged, fist-sized hole. And then an arm—an arm wearing a suit jacket and a very nice watch—reaches in and unlocks the apartment door.

I'd know that watch anywhere. A Rolex Submariner. Market value: $27,000. Marcus never leaves home without it.

The lock slowly clicks, and Marcus prepares to let himself in.

TWENTY-TWO

Jake's fingernails sink into my forearm. "Hurry!" he hisses.

We dart into his dark bedroom. He pulls me around the bed, and we wriggle beneath it. My nose tickles with dust, but I don't dare sneeze. With the dying sunlight, it's nearly pitch-black in here.

Footsteps sound in the hallway. Marcus doesn't call out, but it's obvious he knows we're here and is looking for us. I glance over my shoulder at the sliver of window I can see from under the bed. Do we dare try to climb out? It would be better than being in this place with this madman.

My heart breaks. My chest burns with hurt and fury. Beau had to have tipped him off that we visited—it's the only thing that makes sense. Beau must have realized why I looked familiar after we left and called up his old friend, his younger buddy Marcus, and . . . and *what*? This might have nothing to do with Becky and Will. This could be a matter of Beau and Marcus being friends, and Marcus losing his girl just like Beau lost Becky eighteen years before. I think about my breakup email going unanswered. Maybe

Marcus never replied because he was furious. And his good friend Beau doesn't want Marcus to lose me like he'd lost Becky.

The footsteps come closer. I picture the axe curled in Marcus's fingers. Swallowing hard, I tap Jake on the arm and point back to the window.

"*There*," I mouth.

I can just make out Jake shaking his head. "It won't work," he whispers.

"We have to try."

Jake squints, checking out the window. It feels like ages pass, but then he nods faintly. Go time.

We wriggle out from under the bed and dart for the window. Jake yanks at the bottom to open it, but the window is stuck. He pulls harder, the cords in his neck straining. The window gives, letting out an awful screech as it lifts up. I glance over my shoulder in trepidation. If Marcus didn't know where we were, he does now.

"Go," Jake grunts, gesturing for me to climb on his desk.

The window is narrow. It exits onto a little piece of the roof, so at least it's not a straight two-story drop down. I heft myself up to the sash, and Jake pushes against my feet to propel me through. My chin scrapes against the shingles. My palms grapple to hold onto something solid. The moment I'm out, Jake climbs through next. But he's only halfway when I see the figure in the doorway.

Marcus.

No.

"Jake," I wail, reaching for him.

Marcus's eyes blaze. He bounds into the room, shouting something—something I can't hear because of the droning sounds in my head. Jake tumbles out moments before Marcus gets to the window, but it's too late for us to shut it again. Marcus shoves his hands out to try to grab Jake's ankle. Jake scrambles away just in time. We scrabble down the roof, all the way to the gutter.

"Wait, damn it," Marcus growls as he tries to push the window up more. "You can't run, Casey."

"Marcus." I can feel the tears in my eyes, on my cheeks. My voice is tight and trembling. I think of the fears I'd had about this person, the visions that popped into my head at the end of the holiday party and then after—maybe they were all true after all. Maybe Becky was indeed warning me about him in the only way she could think of. She threw her scariest memory at me, the moments before she died, hoping it would get my attention.

"Marcus," I whimper as Jake jerks from him and jiggles the ladder to activate the fire escape. "Just let us go."

"You *can't*," he hisses. Now he's climbing out of the window himself—or at least trying to, hefting the window higher, angling his shoulders to fit through the narrow space.

Jake points over the side. "I think we hang onto the gutter and then drop."

But the gutter looks flimsy. The pavement seems miles away from up here. "The gutter won't be able to hold my weight," I moan.

"*Try.*"

Marcus is broader than Jake is, and his shoulders are wedged in the window. Squatting, I hold onto the gutter, shimmy until I'm almost over the side, and let it take my weight. The gutter groans in protest. I lower myself as best I can as the gutter screeches and begins to detach from the siding. Mustering up my courage, I let go. The drop to the pavement is long. My ankles protest when I land. I roll to the side sharply on my hipbone, and the pain shoots through me, white-hot.

I lie on the ground a moment, stunned. But I can still wiggle my toes. Nothing feels broken.

"Casey!" Marcus screams, still on the roof. I can only hear him. I glance over my shoulder toward the street. Why doesn't anyone hear us? Why isn't anyone coming?

Jake holds onto the gutter next. With his weight, it does detach from the house with a horrible scream. Jake's legs scissor. The gutter tilts down, rocketing for the ground, but Jake lets go, landing about as awkwardly as I have, tumbling backward onto his butt.

"Are you okay?" I cry.

He winces as he rolls an ankle. "Yeah. I think so. Let's go."

Then, a figure appears over the side of the roof. Marcus. He's gotten himself out. "Casey!" he screams. "Listen to me!"

"I'm sorry, Marcus," I call up. "I really am."

He looks at me with exasperation. "This isn't about being sorry. I'm trying to warn you. He's coming."

"Huh?" Marcus looks so desperate. It's a trick, probably. Something to freeze me up and buy him time so he can get down the ladder, too. I think of what Beau said in his office: *If I can't have her, no one can.*

"Look, I'm sorry I chopped your door. I'm . . . I'm sorry I'm here." Marcus goes on. Then he looks past us, and his eyes bulge. His expression is so startling that I follow his gaze.

An engine growls in the distance. Then, I spot a glint of chrome, a flash of black—something coming down the sleepy, empty road. A car. Driving way too fast. Heading straight for us.

With us distracted, Marcus has lowered himself from the roof, his fingers holding onto bare shingles and what remains of the broken gutter. He lands more gracefully than Jake and I did. Then he turns and looks at us. I scrabble backward on my butt.

"No," I whisper.

Jake throws himself in front of me. "Don't hurt her, man. Don't touch her."

"I'm here to help you." Marcus points at the car screeching toward the building. "You need to get away. We all do. *Now.* He's coming. He's going to kill you."

We blink. At the same time, the growling car is just a block away. Whoever it is, it seems pretty clear Marcus is afraid of him too.

Jake grabs my hand. I hear a jingle of keys. "Come on," he says, pulling me across the parking lot to his car. Again.

I stumble over my feet. Jake hits the unlock button, and we dive in. Then Marcus dives into the back seat. Jake lunges toward him and tries to shove him back out.

"What the hell?" Jake screams. "No way, man."

"I'm trying to help you!" Marcus screeches once more, his eyes wild. "I need to get away from him, too! We all do!"

I glance at the advancing car in the rearview mirror. It's mere feet from the parking lot. Who's in there? "Just go," I tell Jake. "We'll sort him out later."

Jake guns the engine of his rusty station wagon and peels out of the parking lot—well, as best as his car can peel out. He looks at Marcus suspiciously. "What the hell is going on?"

Marcus glances in the back window and grimaces. "He's following us. He knows."

"Who?" Jake explodes.

"My father."

I frown. "Your . . . *Roland*?"

Marcus looks at me repentantly. "Casey. If I knew, I never would have come for you with your stepmom. Hell, I would have never agreed to meet you in the first place."

"Knew what?"

Buildings whiz past. Houses. All of Avon Shores is a blur. Jake wrenches the wheel. "Where am I going? Why is this guy after us? Someone tell me something."

Marcus looks at me again. "He only told me a little while ago. I swear. I thought he was making all of it up. I honestly, honestly had no idea."

"No idea about what? Why are you here? Why is he here? Did Beau send you?"

"This has nothing to do with Beau—though my dad found out you'd talked to him. It's what's triggered this . . . escalation. But you've been circling around the truth for years, Casey."

"The truth about what?"

Marcus checks the back window again. That black car is still there. "About Becky. About the accident." He pauses. "The accident that wasn't an accident."

"Wait," Jake says slowly, glancing at Marcus in the rearview mirror. He blinks hard.

It takes me a second to catch up, too. "Was . . . was it your father?" I whisper. "Your father caused that crash?"

I don't wait for Marcus to answer, instead clambering to the back seat to look at the advancing vehicle myself. A figure hunches over the steering wheel in deep concentration. In a snap, I'm tethered between two worlds—mine and Becky's.

Something flashes to your right. It's something coming up fast from a side road. You grab Will's arm and scream. But it's too late.

"I don't understand." Jake's voice trembles. "Why?"

"My dad and Beau inherited their responsibilities at their respective companies almost at the same time," Marcus says. "Their fathers knew each other, so they got to know each other, too, even though they weren't the same age. I guess Beau did a better job at taking over his business than my dad did. Dad ran into money problems from the start. He was more interested in showing off than he was in actually running the company—the guy burned through cash. But he figured his dad's pal's kid from Long Island would be good for a loan. Don't know what made Beau give it to him. It was a lot of money." He looks at me. "Remember how I said Dad was in a lot of financial trouble in the early 2000s? This was that."

"Uh, where am I going?" Jake cries, whipping through a stop sign. "Where am I driving? I don't know what to do."

"Back roads," Marcus instructs. "Confuse him. You know Avon Shores better than he does."

"We can't drive all night! I'll run out of gas!" Jake screams. "We should go to the police! This man is unhinged!"

"Drive to the police, then," Marcus says. "Good idea."

Jake glances around almost like he has no idea what street he's on. When he gets his bearings, he nods. "Nearest one's on the mainland."

He makes a sharp left, sending a bunch of other cars honking wildly and skidding out of his way. I hold on to the door, praying we don't crash. The car bumps over a curb, and I swear I hear something pop. But we keep going. Yet when Marcus glances out the window, Roland is still with us. Gaining. He's in a much better vehicle than we are. Jake's car barely can get over sixty miles an hour. One of his tires feels flat.

I look at Marcus. "So Beau gave your father a loan. So?"

"Well, my father couldn't pay it back. Beau was starting to pressure him. Then comes this wedding. Beau and Becky. My dad shows up. Says Beau was being a real dick—which he probably deserved if he was cheating him out of the loan. The guy probably didn't even want him there. But I guess my dad witnessed someone come in and steal Becky away." He glances at me shiftily. "Will."

"He saw?" I whisper.

"He thought Becky was being kidnapped . . . but who knows. But I guess he took off in his car. He thought this would fix everything. He intended to get Becky back, return as the hero, and then Beau would let the loan money he owed him slide. But that's not what ended up happening."

I close my eyes, Becky's last moments pounding against my lids. That car coming out of nowhere from a side road. Roland was trying to cut them off, maybe. But he didn't slam on his brakes. That's why Becky screamed.

> The car ran straight into the side of yours. Metal slams against metal. You scream, feeling your body lift. Everything lifts. The world tumbles.

Was it really Roland?

"But what does this have to do with Casey?" Jake cries.

"And how long has your father known that I'm Becky—and that I might know something about what he did?" I add. "Since you and Casey's stepmother found us at the motel? Did you tell him?"

"I didn't know I wasn't supposed to tell him about you and Becky," Marcus pleads. "But I was worried about you, Casey, after we found you in Avon Shores. I wanted you to get better. So I asked my dad for help. He said yes right away—even had a treatment center in mind. I guess he knows all the doctors. He's in with all the doctors. It should have pinged me. I should have wondered, *Why is this man being so generous with a woman he barely knows?* He wasn't this way about any of my other girlfriends . . ."

Marcus's mouth twitches like he doesn't know how to say what he plans to say next. But I've already figured it out. *He's in with all the doctors.* I thought Beau Uccello was a man with deep pockets. Roland Coleman has the biggest pockets in the world.

"Your dad chose that hospital because he knew he could convince the doctors to talk me out of believing in Becky," I say. "They'd turn it into a dissociative personality disorder issue. Except . . ." I frown. "He must have actually believed that I was Becky in a past life to be that afraid. Why did he buy into it so quickly? No one else has . . ."

But then I think about something Marcus said. *You've been circling around the truth for years.*

"Wait," I murmur, my nerves crackling anew. "He didn't just find out about Becky and me, did he?"

Marcus swallows hard. He shakes his head.

"How long?" My heart starts to pound. "Did . . . did he know before we got together?" I don't want for him to answer. "Did he tell you to talk to me in that bar where we met? Was he pushing you to date me?"

"No," Marcus says quickly. "I mean, yes . . . but also no. He was interested in you. Said I should go check you out—and that you hung out a lot at that bar. But Casey, he was interested in lots of people. He'd see a woman on the street wearing an interesting hat and be like, 'Go see what she's about.' I figured he wanted to hire you for a job. He knew a lot about you—said you'd graduated early, he'd even spoken to some of your professors, talked about your writing. I went into that bar, Casey, just figuring I'd check you out for him. I had no idea he was keeping tabs on you—or why."

"He wanted to keep me close? In case I . . . what, spilled his secret?" I feel disgusted. "You really didn't know about this?"

"No!" he pleads. "Look. I went into that bar—he did ask me to do that. But then I fell for you. For real."

Jake screeches through another stoplight. Drivers lay on their horns. Behind us, Marcus's father runs the light, too, narrowing avoiding a collision with an oncoming sedan.

"I wondered why he seemed so interested," Marcus says, and then stops himself, starts over. "I mean, obviously you're impressive. Smart, beautiful, poised. But again, he'd never shown anyone I dated this much interest. Never wanted to know so much about anyone. He asked questions about you, Casey—all kinds of questions. But I was flattered. I was like, *Finally, someone my father likes!*"

"What kind of questions?" I ask.

"About . . ." He raises his hands, then drops them again. "I don't know. What you were studying. What you wanted to do. What you liked to do. Your family. Your parents. I told him your mom died. Actually . . ."

My hackles go up at the mention of my mom. "Actually what?"

"Actually . . ." Marcus takes a breath. "I got this weird feeling he knew your mom had been in a car accident before I said anything. At the time, I almost wondered if he'd googled you. There was a point, actually, where I thought he might be interested in you—like, in a dirty old man sort of way. Like a stalker."

Jake makes a disgusted grunt. But I barely hear it, my ears are ringing so loudly. *He knew your mom had been in a car accident before I said anything.*

I think of what my father told me about how Becky had always been with me. How I'd talked about her before my mother died. How my mother sometimes encouraged me to talk about her, even bought into the idea that she was a past life.

How much had I told her? What if I'd told her about Becky's accident—what if I remembered way more than I remembered now? Maybe I'd even seen that Roland Coleman had been the one who'd caused the accident. Maybe I'd even known his name.

My accident flashes in my mind. Listening to that aria with my mom. And then . . . and then something. Something that scared me. Something that made me grab the wheel.

And then, I see it. I can see my eleven-year-old self turning to my right and seeing a car shooting out from a side road just as Becky saw before her accident.

I see myself lunging forward to turn the steering wheel into the oncoming lane because I could tell, somehow knew, the car was going to hit us. I feel the wheel on my little hands. My mother tries to slap me away. There's confusion as we turn sharply into that other lane—too sharply, the positioning of the car suddenly perpendicular, facing the water.

I see myself looking to my right, relieved there's no one coming in the oncoming lane. But we're sailing too fast. My mother's too disoriented to slam on the brakes—or maybe the brakes have locked up. Before I know what was happening, we hit the guard rail. Her airbag explodes, but mine doesn't, and I go hurtling through the windshield, out of the car. I hit the ground. And for a split second, before I pass out, I glance to my right again and get another look at the only other car with us. The one that came from out of nowhere. The one that intended to hit us before I tried to stop it from happening.

The car is an expensive sedan. Its windows are tinted. There's a personalized license plate on the front. New York plates. The Statue of Liberty against a white background. Three letters: the first a *C*, the second an *M*, and the third . . .

I glance at the personalized plate on the grille of the car that's now on our tail. Three letters here too—and this time, I see all of them. The last letter is a *C*. Coleman Media Company.

That's when I know for sure.

"I didn't kill my mother," I whisper. "Roland Coleman did."

TWENTY-THREE

There's a thin sheen of sweat on my forehead. My heart is pounding with fear, but I also want to celebrate. I didn't kill my mother. That isn't my burden. I didn't do it. I was trying to protect her.

But I'm also plunged into despair. I didn't protect her. I'd led her straight to her death.

We're on the main road that runs parallel to the marshlands. Jake is heading toward the bridge, but the old car is sputtering. Roland's vehicle—faster, meatier, heavier—is right on our bumper, metal grinding metal. Even though I know what he's capable of, I'm surprised when he actually runs into us, sending the car jostling.

"Maybe being in the car isn't a good idea," I tell Jake and Marcus. "He might not just kill us—he could kill some random bystander." I look around. A few houses are lit up, but a lot are dark. Hopefully, only summer residents own them—summer residents who aren't here right now. "Could we pull over? Reason with him?"

"There's no reasoning," Marcus says. "He's snapped. I mean, he knows even I'm in the car. His son. And he doesn't care."

"So he has a death wish?" Jake's voice cracks. "He's going to stop at nothing until we're all flattened?"

"Wait," I say, grabbing my phone, which somehow survived the drop off the roof. It barely has any battery left, but I have to try. With shaking fingers, I dial 911. The dispatcher answers quickly, and I try to keep my voice steady.

"There's a man following us on . . ." I look around. "Where are we, Jake?"

"Coast Road and Heron," Jake says. "Hurry!" He sounds like he's going to cry.

I repeat this to the dispatcher. "He's in a car, and we're in a car. He's trying to kill us. His name is Roland Coleman. And . . . and also, he killed two people years before, in 2005. Becky Kinkaid and Will Woodson. They were in a crash on the Route 2 Causeway Bridge." I want to put this out there. This feels like the right opportunity. "And then, in 2016, he ran a woman and her child off the Gowanus Canal. The child lived. The woman didn't. Her name was Portia Rhodes."

The back of our car jolts violently again; Roland has rammed us a second time. Marcus screams, his chin hitting the back of Jake's seat. Jake struggles to keep control of the wheel. I go flying against the door, knocking my head hard against the window. The phone nearly slips from my fingers. I fumble for it and place it back at my ear. "Please!" I scream to the emergency dispatcher. "We need help!"

"We'll send backup. And an ambulance. Which way are you headed?"

"To the causeway bridge," Jake says, overhearing the conversation.

I stare at him, stunned. Really? That's where Becky and Will crashed.

Jake glances at me, sensing that I'm spooked. "There's nowhere else to go to get off this island. Otherwise I'm going to hit a dead end and he'll have us cornered. It's the only way to keep driving to the mainland."

Crash. Roland rear-ends us again. Jake's car coughs. It feels like the bumper is dragging, slowing us down. Ominous black smoke curls from the muffler.

"Please," I say to the dispatcher. "We're afraid to get out of the vehicle. We're afraid to stop moving."

"We'll set up a barricade at the bridge," the dispatcher says. "Police are heading there now. We're on it."

She asks if I'd like her to stay on the phone until we see the police presence. I say yes. Jake has his foot pressed on the accelerator, but it feels like the car is barely moving. Roland keeps smashing into us like he wants to crumple the car like a can of sardines. I glance behind us, but I can't see his face through his vehicle's tinted windows.

Then I look at Marcus. Tears are running down his cheeks.

"I'm sorry, Casey," he whispers. "I'm so, so sorry."

"It's not your fault," I tell him. "You didn't know."

"But if I hadn't dated you, if I hadn't brought you around him . . ."

"He would done this anyway. He was keeping tabs on me. He knew I knew something . . . and he knew it might come out. That I'd remember."

"I love you," Marcus says through tears. "And to have this happen . . ." He shuts his eyes, broken.

I press my lips together. I want to tell Marcus I love him, too. But I don't. Not like that.

I love Jake.

It hits me powerfully—I love Jake. Of course I do. It's like whooshing down a mountain, I'm so taken by the thought. I love him. I always will.

When I turn back to Marcus, he shrugs. "I know," he says, as if he can read my mind. "I know you don't feel that way about me. And I know . . ." He glances at Jake. "It's okay. Seriously. It's why I warned you. Both of you. Above everything else, I want you to live."

A stench of burning oil wafts into my nostrils. History is repeating itself in strange, eerie ways. Beau and Becky and Will. Marcus and me and Jake. Platonic love, romantic love, loving someone so much that you understand you need to let them go.

"Bridge," Jake says tightly as the car groans around the turn. And suddenly, here it is: past overlaying present, the long, narrow bridge with the barely there guard rails and the dark water beneath. In the distance, I see a flicker of blue neon. Siren lights.

"We see the police!" I tell the dispatcher. "We're almost there!"

Ram. This hit from behind is bone rattling. It feels like Roland's car comes into ours, metal slicing metal, the force greater than the other two collisions. I jolt forward so hard that my head cracks into the front window. Everything goes dark for a moment. My head rings, my brain feels stuffed with old newspaper. My vision tunnels, and when I look to my left, I don't understand what I see.

Jake is slumped against the steering wheel, his arms limp. But the car is still moving forward. Spinning, actually, out of control, with forces worse than an amusement park ride.

Then the sound rushes back fast. Marcus is screaming from the back. Jake opens one eye slowly. "Jake!" I scream, too. Our eyes lock. But in the next second, there's a horrible metal-on-metal *smash*. We've hit something. Hard, nose-first. So hard, in fact, that the impact launches the car skyward. And once again, I'm in a flying car, flying and sinking, a doomed metal can, flipping and diving. For a split second, I see the dark water below me.

Did Becky see this, too?

I feel a hand touch mine. Jake stares at me from the driver's seat, his face a mask of fear. *I don't want to die*, his eyes scream. I squeeze his hand back. I stare into his beautiful face, a face I know so well, regardless of our limited time together. A face I want to know more. This is how Becky felt when she and Will were in exactly this predicament—I just know it. I can feel it. I can feel her.

Don't be scared, a voice says.

A millisecond, airborne. I tilt my head toward the voice. *Don't be scared, Casey,* says a second voice. *It's okay. We've got you.*

The first voice is Becky. The second . . . it's my mother.

I swallow a scream in my throat. I choke down the taste of blood in my mouth. I look at Jake again and hold his hand hard. *Don't be scared.*

"I love you," I tell him.

He blinks at me. "I love you."

And then we hit.

And then there's nothing.

TWENTY-FOUR

Everything around me is white. White walls. White sheets. White lights. I'm on a cloud.

The metallic beeps are soft, far away. I'm annoyed as they grow louder and higher in pitch. Every so often, there's a deeper sound—a *bong, bong, bong*—that startles me into greater and greater wakefulness.

I remember that I have eyes and I'm able to open them. This seems like a revelation, having eyes. I stare around me at the blurry shapes. A bed. Walls. Machines. And a familiar face. It takes me a moment to place her.

"Pippa?" I say with a rasp. I've remembered I have a mouth. A voice. These revelations are coming slowly, almost like the nerve synapses are creaky from disuse.

Pippa's face lights up. "Casey! Oh my God. Oh my God. You're here. Hi."

Tears spill down her cheeks. She scoots closer to me—but not so close that I can't see all the machines behind her. I am hooked up to them. I slowly put all of this together.

"A-Am I in a hospital?"

She wipes her eyes. "You were in a car crash. Remember?"

I frown. *A car crash.* Am I a child? That was my car crash. But I didn't know Pippa then. I've only known Pippa for a little while.

"No . . ." I admit.

Pippa's smile dims. She glances over her shoulder. "Maybe . . . your dad's here. Or your stepmother?" But just seeing the grimace on my face, she quickly says, "Forget it. Though she's been worried about you. All of us have been." She grins at me. "Casey. You solved a years-old mystery."

I swipe around in my memory for what she could be talking about. "I did?"

She looks at me uncertainly. "About Becky. And Will. They arrested Roland Coleman on that bridge, just after you crashed. The cops witnessed it—him running into you and Jake and Marcus, sending you over that bridge? Thank God EMTs were there—they got you guys out really fast. It was all over the news! Though not the reincarnation part. I decided to keep that quiet. It would bring the more sensational news outlets out of the woodwork. We figured that's something you might not want."

I open my mouth, then shut it again. It's like Pippa is talking about the plot of a movie she's forgotten I haven't seen yet. I look at the IVs in my arm, a cast around my wrist—I must have been in some sort of accident. But I have no recollection.

Roland Coleman. That name does ring a bell. "The . . . the media guy? I was in a crash with him?"

"Yeah." Pippa shifts awkwardly. "You don't remember? Him slamming into you guys?"

"He was after me?" Have I met this man?

Pippa edges closer. "He knew you were close to figuring out the truth. He wanted to kill you. But you told the emergency dispatcher everything ahead of time. Even about your mom." Her eyes go wide. "It's all kind of incredible."

I stare at my lumps of legs under the sheets. I can move them, but they feel heavy. I get the sense I'm not seriously injured—I don't even feel that bad. I'm just tired, mostly. But it bothers me that I have absolutely no memory of what she's telling me.

"Where did this happen?" I ask, imagining tied-up New York City traffic. Or hadn't she said something about a bridge? Good Lord, had we plummeted into the East River?

"Avon Shores, of course," Pippa says, as if I'm supposed to know.

I frown. "Where?"

She leans back. Studies me for a beat. "Avon Shores. It's where Becky was supposed to get married. Where Becky led you? And then you met Jake? And you guys untangled it together?"

I'm still blank. Utter dead air. I'm walking on a moon of nothingness.

Pippa sits back. She seems shaken. "Surely you remember Becky . . ."

"Becky is gone," says a voice.

I crane my neck, and a woman with shoulder-length hair and wide-legged pants walks in. I'm pretty sure I've never seen her, and I don't think she's a doctor. Still, she looks at me with authority.

"Hi?" I say.

"Casey, this is Karin," Pippa presses. "Remember? You talked to her in Avon Shores?"

I'm starting to feel uneasy. I'm supposed to know this woman? And where is Avon Shores? Why does Pippa keep talking about it?

"We met a few times," Karin says. "But it's okay if you don't remember. You hit your head. You likely have some amnesia. Those memories might not ever come back."

"What did you mean Becky is gone, Karin?" Pippa asks her, looking frightened.

"And I'm sorry, who is Becky?" I add.

Karin smiles sadly. "Becky was someone who was with you, Casey. Someone who died tragically, and who was searching for answers. You found them for her."

"I did?"

"You did." Then her eyes lower. "But you were in that terrible accident. We weren't sure if you were going to make it. And it's possible that now that you've done what Becky wanted you to do—you found out what really happened that day, and you got justice—she's moved on. Left you." She glances at Pippa. "I would suspect Will is gone as well."

"Will?" I repeat, trying to place the name.

"Will, Casey." Pippa seems desperate. "Will!"

I search my mind. Still nothing.

"It may never come back," Karin says to Pippa. "All Casey's been through, all she's searched for with Becky . . . it may be all gone."

Pippa looks stricken. "Do you think she'll be okay—like, otherwise?"

"I'm not a doctor. But I've had a few other clients this has happened to. And they're fine. The souls found what they needed, and they moved on." She turns to me curiously. "How are you feeling, emotionally?"

"Besides very confused?" I ask, trying to make my voice light. But then I think about her question. Despite just having woken up and having no idea why I'm in a hospital, despite Pippa firing facts at me that I have no knowledge of, I don't feel panicked or uneasy or scared.

In fact, I feel sort of . . . settled. The edgy feeling I'm so used to experiencing most moments of my life isn't here. The knee-jerk sensation of hiding—behind a mask, in a disguise, or literally under the covers—isn't there, either.

I feel . . . reset, somehow. Like I went through a reboot. This calm thrums through me, a deep, leveling sense that everything's going to be okay.

"I feel okay," I admit. I take my hand and twist it from side to side. *Comme ci, comme ça.* Not so bad.

"Really!" Pippa says. She seems surprised.

Karin looks at Pippa. "That's to be expected. There's no longer someone with her who desperately wants answers. Casey's free to live her life now. Do what she wants to do. Go where she wants to go. Even love who she wants to love."

"But—" Pippa turns to me. "Casey. Maybe this part is important. There were two guys in the car with you in the accident. One of them was someone you dated. One of them was someone you loved. Well. Becky loved."

"Now, now," Karin says suddenly. "I would watch it. It's Casey's life now. No longer Becky's. She needs to be her own guide. That soul has moved on."

"But that love," Pippa argues. "They were magnetic. Instant. And also, what's the harm in—"

Karin cuts her off again. "But that was likely because of Becky . . . and Will. I wouldn't tell her too much. You don't want to force things. You don't want to create connections that are no longer there. Give it a little time, at least, before telling her. Let her get her footing again." Her phone buzzes in her bag, and she rummages for it. A mysterious smile appears on her lips. "I'm glad you're okay, Casey. Feel free to consult me if you need anything."

She walks out of the room. I look at Pippa a little helplessly. Pippa sniffs. "You know, for a psychic, she's awfully unromantic."

"It's okay," I say, that strange calm enveloping me. Again, I have no idea why Pippa's so upset, but it doesn't matter. "Whatever happened, I guess it was meant to be. Honestly, I just want to get back to school. How much have I missed, even? And oh my God. Is Jeremy totally mad that I've blown my shifts at Pet Planet?"

The look Pippa gives me is so befuddled and bemused that even I burst out laughing—even though I don't know what I'm laughing at.

"Only you would worry about Pet Planet," she groans. "Maybe that does mean you're going to be okay."

●●●

More guests trickle in over the course of the next two days. Fran, looking cowed, profusely apologizing to me—but again, about details I no longer remember. Becky is mentioned again and again. I'm slowly putting together the pieces of who Becky was to me, and that I helped her.

My father enters the room, too, looking healthier than I've seen him in a while. Apparently, he was in a clinical trial in Boston, and the treatment is helping. He leans close to my bed, his eyes gleaming with tears.

"What you found out about your mom," he whispers. "Roland Coleman confessed everything. He was there, that day. He forced you two off the road into the canal."

So much of this, however, I still don't understand. "What would Roland Coleman want with Mom?"

"You knew about him—as Becky. He saw both of you as a threat. He's the one responsible for this."

"Why would he see us as a threat?"

"Rob," Fran warns. "Let her rest."

But my father can't stop. "Your mother embraced Becky. Always did. She bought into the past life thing even when I didn't. I thought Becky was just an imaginary friend, but she believed you had these memories of a life you once lived. But then you started saying really scary stuff about someone having killed you in a car chase on your wedding day. Your mother was alarmed. She became focused on this crime she thought had happened. I told her to stop, and she said she would, but I don't think she did. I think she took it to another level. Asked you even more questions. Never told me the answers . . . or how she took care of it."

"What do you mean?" I ask groggily, trying to remember telling my mom these things—or, for that matter, for her being impassioned about something beyond opera, or her work, or me.

"I think she spoke to Roland," my father whispers. "It's the only thing that makes sense. I always wondered, but I had only a few details. I didn't want to know."

"Give her time before you inundate her with this," Fran warns.

My father squeezes my shoulder. "Sorry. I just thought . . . I was afraid. I thought it would be better if you suppressed Becky, afterward. Her past life . . . what happened with her . . . what happened to your mom. I was afraid people would judge you. I thought they'd misinterpret what happened, in the accident—so I thought it would be better if you just forgot. But I'm so sorry, Casey. I should have never kept this from you. I don't know if I'll ever be able to forgive myself."

"It's okay." I take his hand. The new Casey is serene and steady. "We'll work it out. I know you had my best interests at heart."

A few other friends from NYU appear. Then, an ash-blond woman in her late forties hesitates in my doorway. Her eyes are red. As she sits, her fingers twitch in her lap.

"Casey," she says softly. "It's Miranda. From the party at the Met?"

I smile faintly. I have no idea what she's talking about, and I find it hard to believe I'd been to a party at the Met. But it's easier to pretend.

"I'm so sorry about what happened." She shakes her head ruefully. "I'm just devastated. It's my job to know everything about that family. And I completely missed this. I feel awful."

Her face contorts like she's going to cry. "No worries," I say, even though I'm not sure what I'm absolving her of.

That just makes her squeeze her eyes closed even tighter. "I've always thought of Marcus as a son," she whispers. "I should have protected him." Then, abruptly, she squeezes my hand and stands. "Anyway. I won't bother you anymore. Just know I'm thinking about you. And if you need anything, please let me know."

I thank her, but I'm left puzzled. *Marcus.* Was he one of the people in the car crash with me? Did something terrible happen to him? I swallow a lump in my throat and look at the nurse who remained in my room during Miranda's visit.

"Marcus," I say. She nods. "He was in the accident with me? Is he . . . okay?"

The nurse lowers her eyes. "I probably shouldn't say because of privacy issues," she says softly, "but it's touch and go. We'll have a better sense tomorrow."

I feel a whoosh of dread. "And there was someone else in the car, too, right? Another guy? What about him?"

The nurse gets a strange look and opens her mouth to speak. But just then, a doctor marches in, clipboard in hand. He gives me a tight smile. "Hello, Casey. How are we feeling?"

And that ends that.

Reporters want to speak with me, too, but Fran is dogged about keeping them at bay. "She's not ready to talk, and she might never be ready to talk, and that's final," I hear her say to someone on the phone. Fran is brisk with me after her profuse apologizing, more like the old Fran, but there's more of a softness to her, a pliability. She fills me in on my father's treatment and prognosis. She also says I can come back to stay with them in Brooklyn—going straight back to the dorms seems a little overwhelming. I tell her that I'll think about it. It might be nice to spend some time with my father. All this stuff he said about my mom—I want to know more.

But at the same time, I feel eager to be with Pippa again, too. Resume my normal life. Karin's words echo in my brain. *Casey's free to live her life now. Do what she wants to do. Go where she wants to go. Even love who she wants to love.*

Love. Huh. The notion is like a balloon floating just out of my reach. A flash of something out of the corner of my eye. *Love.* Something about it feels close to my surface, still pulsing with life. Leftover glitter on my skin from a past party. But I don't know why.

•••

After another day and more monitoring, the doctors want me to stay in the hospital for one more night, and if I don't have any setbacks, I can leave tomorrow. It's strange to be entering the world with some missing memories—to be honest, the last thing I truly remember is deciding to room with Pippa. After that . . . there's very little. But as I mine my intellect, most things are intact. I remember the subjects I should have been studying for finals. I recall which subway lines take me to different places. I conjure up book characters and quiz myself on SAT vocabulary words and make myself mentally solve random geometry equations.

My brain is working. And my emotions are holding, too, though I promise the doctors and social worker, who sees me because of the amnesia, that if I start to feel uneasy, I'll reach out to someone. She gives me names of therapists in conjunction with NYU's health services, and I promise to reach out to them. The idea of a therapist jogs something deep in my brain, too—but it's only a little ripple, and then it's gone.

I feel good. I do. Though something seems to be missing. I mean, I know: my memories. But there's something else. It's like I'm a puzzle with a missing piece. I keep whisking the thought away, though. I'm just disoriented. I've been in an accident. And despite everyone being hush-hush, someone I was close to has died. I'm probably traumatized.

I try to let it go.

Visiting hours end for the evening. Pippa, Fran, and my father ask me what seems like a thousand times if I'm really going to be okay being alone once again, and

I promise them that I'm just going to veg out and watch more bad TV. I don't seem to have a cell phone anymore—I guess it got swallowed up in the water I crashed into, never to be recovered. Fran says she'll bring me a new one tomorrow.

For a while, I flip through TV channels, finding old sitcoms that I remember watching the first time. It's reassuring that the old memories aren't gone. Even a lot of the commercials are familiar, which makes me think that I maybe didn't lose much time at all.

But after an hour or so of watching, I feel restless. I don't know if I'm allowed to walk down the halls, but I don't see why I can't. I'm no longer hooked up to IVs or even a blood pressure monitor. The only injury I have is the cast on my wrist from the car accident I don't remember.

My legs are wobbly as I start to pace. I feel a little silly walking in a thin gown and the giant fuzzy socks someone put on me while I was sleeping. And it's odd: While consciously I'm walking with no purpose, it's like something is leading me . . . somewhere. A vending machine, maybe? I'd love some junk food. One of the nurses mentioned a smoothie machine on the floor. Maybe I'm trying to find it.

The halls are empty. No one notices me. First, my feet carry me toward a room across the hall a few doors down. A marker board bears the name of the patient: *Coleman, M.*

There's a flickering in my brain. M. For *Marcus*.

I peer inside. A young man lies in a bed. His head is bandaged. There are a lot of tubes running into his body and machines binging and bonging. But his eyes are open, and he looks around groggily, maybe like he's just woken up. There's a small, puzzled smile on his face.

I step back from the door, trying to assess my feelings. I'm happy, I realize. Relieved that he's okay. I still don't quite know what this guy meant to me, but I do know that I would have been upset if he hadn't pulled through.

Then I hear a second voice inside the room. I peek in once more. The ash-blond woman who came into my room yesterday sits in a plastic chair next to Marcus's bed. She's crying, this time freely, a balled-up piece of Kleenex in her hand. It takes me a moment to access her name: Miranda.

The guy, Marcus, reaches over, sloth-slow, and touches her. "Gonna be okay," he says in a raspy voice. "Thanks for coming, Miranda."

"Of course, my sweet boy," Miranda says, and then she bursts into a fresh round of tears. "I'll do anything for you."

I'm touched. I feel like this is . . . *right*.

Then, Marcus's gaze moves off her, straight to me. I freeze as our eyes meet. He blinks once, twice. I try, desperately, to remember what he means to me—I know there's something, but I can't access it.

I hold up a palm in a wave. He gives me a small, peaceful nod. We get each other. I'm sure of that, deep inside myself. We understand each other, and we always will.

Marcus's eyes lower. His gaze moves back to Miranda. It's my cue to go.

But I'm not ready to go back to my room quite yet. Luckily, there are still no nurses roaming the halls, questioning what I'm doing up. So I continue on. I round a corner and come to a T—I can go right or left.

Right, a voice inside me says.

Right I go. I glance into each nook and doorway, maybe looking for a vending machine. Halfway down the hall, I realize how ridiculous that is. Even if I did find a vending machine, I don't have any money.

A door at the end of the hall is also ajar. My feet carry me there. There is no patient name written on the marker board, but there's definitely someone inside. I poke my head in to see. There's the usual array of machines, one of them beeping that steady heart rhythm; another making that annoying *bong*.

Then I look at the person in the bed. It's also someone my age. He's covered with a thin white sheet. Like I'd been doing a few minutes before, he's flipping through the same TV channels, pausing on the same commercials I had.

I look at his face. He's got floppy dark curls, big eyes, a bow-shaped mouth. He looks too tall for the bed, and his Adam's apple juts prominently. When he comes to a commercial about a local plumbing company that features a bunch of talking dogs, he chuckles. I'd laughed at that commercial, too.

Then he looks over.

"Oh." He straightens. Looks me up and down, seemingly tracking my hospital gown and stupid socks. Then, smiling, he wriggles his foot out from under the sheet, show-ing me his own pair of fuzzy socks. "We match!"

"Yeah," I say, and then I feel heat rush to my cheeks. It's not normal to stand in a patient's doorway. He probably thinks I'm a weirdo.

But he keeps staring. And I keep staring. And something tells me—I have no idea why—that I should ask him about books. Library books.

I shake my head. Just because I'm a bookworm doesn't mean everyone is.

Finally, he clears his throat. "You want to watch? I can't find anything great on except these terrible sitcoms, but . . ."

"Oh. Um . . . sure."

Tentatively, I walk into the room. There's no way I'm going to sit on the bed with him—I also notice he's got a pretty sizeable cast on his leg, and I wouldn't dare want to bump it. Instead, I pull a chair over. I notice it has a cardigan draped over the arm. I glance at it a moment. Black with silver threads.

"That's my mom's," he says. "She went home. She'll be back tomorrow." Then he smiles at me. "It was impossible to get her out of this place. She was so worried I wouldn't be okay. Moms, am I right?" But then a little furrow comes over his brow—almost like he thinks he's said something he shouldn't. It doesn't even occur to me that he has—not at first. But right. I don't have a mom. Some-times I flinch when moms are mentioned.

There's no way he'd know that.

I settle into the chair as he turns up the volume a few clicks. "I'm Casey, by the way."

He smiles warmly. "Jake."

"Nice to meet you, Jake."

We smile at each other. Part of me wants to laugh, but I don't know why. The sitcom isn't funny. But I feel that sense of serenity again, settling over me like a warm blanket. I shift in the chair, curling my legs to my chest, funny socks and all. "Nice to meet you, Jake," I say again.

"Nice to meet you, Casey."

And then the show comes back on, and we start to watch.

ACKNOWLEDGMENTS

In 2018, I was fortunate enough to attend a book festival in Los Angeles where I was on a panel with Matt Wise, who was then an agent. We connected, and Matt mentioned he was in touch with Kevin Williamson and Julie Plec, and that they had a film treatment pitch they'd put together years before that they thought would make a great book—they just needed a good writer. As a huge fan of Kevin and Julie, I felt intimidated to work with them, but as it turned out, they are amazing, encouraging partners. It also didn't hurt that the idea for *Wait for Me* was a tantalizing one that I fell for right away. As a writer, ideas are sometimes hard to come by, and it's sometimes difficult to find a starting point. So thank you, Kevin and Julie, for not only giving me a great starting point for this story but also a rich world to play in. And thank you, Matt, for making the connection and remaining a steadfast friend and partner ever since.

Thank you, also, to everyone at Union Square & Co. for taking a chance on this story: Emily Meehan, Tracey Keevan, my editor Suzy Capozzi, Stefanie Chin, Jenny Lu, the amazing art dept including Marcie Lawrence, Whitney Manger and the cover designer, Erin Fitzsimmons, as well as project editor, Grace House, Lori Paximadis in copy editing and Hayley Jozwiak in proofreading. And thank you to Richard Abate for believing in this book and working hard to get it out into the world.

It was a strange journey, writing *Wait for Me*. I began it in 2018, trying it out as first a YA novel, then an adult novel, then back to YA again—so in a way, this story has lived past lives, too. Looking back on the 2018 world now, so much has changed, most of it unpredictable. I'm grateful that my family is still here and still as supportive and loving as ever—especially my husband Michael and sons Kristian and Henry. If reincarnation is real, maybe we'll all come back as a family of butterflies, or dogs, or birds—just as long as we're together. Thanks for the wild ride

WAIT FOR ME

SARA SHEPARD

Discussion Questions

DISCUSSION QUESTIONS

1. Why does Casey feel like she has to use different disguises in everyday situations? Have you ever pretended to be someone you weren't? Why?

2. Why might Casey have been so reluctant to tell anyone—even a close friend like Pippa—about her flashbacks and the voices she was hearing?

3. When Casey becomes stressed, she copes by taking time to be by herself. What are your go-to self-care methods for when you feel overwhelmed?

4. Do you believe that past lives and reincarnation are possible? Why or why not?

5. Worried about Casey, Pippa betrays Casey's confidence by telling Fran where she was hiding. Do you think Pippa was being a good friend, even though she broke her promise?

6. On the drive away from Chadwick Pond, Jake tells Casey he regrets not mentioning his own connection with Will to Fran and Marcus. Have you ever regretted not speaking up when you think you should have?

7. How do Casey's feelings about Fran and about her behavior towards Casey change throughout the story? How do yours?

8. What causes Casey to stop being frightened by her visions? Now that you know the backstory, how does your experience reading the visions and voices change?

9. How much of Casey and Jake's connection do you think is because of Becky and Will's past love?

10. In their search for the truth, Casey and Jake resort to lying about who they are to find answers. Do you think their actions are justified? Why or why not?

11. Several characters grapple with loss, whether it's the deaths of Jake's dad, Casey's mom, or Will and Becky. Does having a reason or explanation for how someone died make it easier or harder to process grief? Does it have an impact at all?

12. Why might Casey's father have so readily believed that the death of her mother was Casey's fault? Can you think of other instances where scapegoats have been used to make sense of something tragic or inexplicable?

DISCUSSION QUESTIONS

13. The actions of Casey's dad and stepmom hurt Casey deeply. Casey sees them as being controlling, but they believe they're just being overprotective and acting out of love. Who is right, and who is wrong? Can you understand both sides or just one? Why?

ABOUT THE AUTHOR

Sara Shepard is the #1 *New York Times* bestselling author of the sixteen-book Pretty Little Liars series, which has sold millions of copies worldwide, has been translated into more than twenty languages, and became a popular TV show on Freeform. She has also written other young adult series and novels including *The Lying Game*, *The Heiresses*, and *The Perfectionists*. Sara lives outside of Pittsburgh with her husband, sons, and dogs. Sara is also active in the screenwriting and podcasting spaces.